BAD VIBRATIONS

THE SEDONA FILES: BOOK 1

CHRISTINE POPE

DARK VALENTINE PRESS

BAD VIBRATIONS

ISBN: 978-0-9836841-2-1

Copyright © 2011 by Christine Pope.

Revised version copyright © 2019

Published by Dark Valentine Press

Cover design by Lou Harper

Book formatting by Indie Author Services

CHAPTER ONE

IF IT HADN'T BEEN FOR HIS AIR OF EXTREME AGITATION, I could have ordered my first client of the day from Central Casting. Perfectly tousled hair, abnormally white teeth, clothing meant to look loose and casual but which he probably overpaid for at Fred Segal or any number of the high-priced shops along Melrose Avenue.

Alex Hathaway. He'd called for an appointment the day before and had seemed quite frustrated that I hadn't been able to see him sooner than this. But I couldn't see more than four or five clients a day, and it was only because Olivia D'Ambrosio had canceled that I'd been able to squeeze him in at all. Too many clients, and I'd be so overloaded I wouldn't be able to read the information off their driver's licenses, let alone interpret their auras or a tarot layout.

Another West Hollywood pretty boy, I thought automatically, then gave myself a mental shake. Of all people, I shouldn't be prejudging anyone else. Lord knows I'd been on the receiving end of some serious side-eye more than once in my life.

I let my hand rest lightly on the Tarot deck. I never knew when I met with a client what sort of reading would speak to me. I didn't bother with a crystal ball—they'd always been mostly for show, as far as I was concerned—but I found the Tarot useful…some days. At other times, I might as well be consulting a poker deck for advice.

"What seems to be troubling you?" I asked, and waited for the telltale tingle from the deck to let me know it was receptive to my client's vibrations. Nothing. Just a stack of coated cardboard. With a sigh, I folded my hands on the tabletop and hoped Otto at least would be on the line for this one. I hated flying solo, as my own sixth sense tended to be about as reliable as my spirit guide.

Alex Hathaway shot a nervous glance over his shoulder. At what, I wasn't quite sure, since my small office didn't even have a waiting area. It was simply a cramped little space I'd tried to make more welcoming by painting the walls a serene sage green color and lining the tops of my bookcases with a variety of plants in painted ceramic pots. The peace lilies and pothos and philodendron seemed to thrive in the fluorescent light, even though I hated it. I'd always meant to replace the office-standard fixtures with something a little more friendly but somehow had never gotten around to it.

"It's my girlfriend," Alex said, after one last look at the door.

That particular confession was a little surprising. Considering his outward perfection and the area of L.A. where my office was located, I'd just sort of assumed he must be gay.

Sooner or later I'd get past the assumption stage. I hoped.

"What about your girlfriend?" I asked, thinking, *All right, Otto...any time you want to drop in would be fine by me....*

Another one of those shifty looks. "No one can hear us in here, right?"

"Of course not," I replied in soothing tones. I wondered whether Alex had smoked a bowl before coming over to his appointment. True, the twitchiness indicated something a little stronger than marijuana, but I knew people sometimes got paranoid when coming down off a pot high. I couldn't comment from personal experience—I'd had enough mind-expanding experiences on my own without messing around with drugs.

I went on, "We're the only ones here, and I always schedule my clients at least fifteen minutes apart so no one can see you coming or going."

These words didn't appear to have reassured him. "But they could still be listening."

The DSM-V strongly advised against labeling

anyone as crazy, but either he was exhibiting sure signs of paranoia, or at the very least had been watching way too many spy movies. "I'd know if someone were spying on me," I said. "Trust me."

That was only half a lie. Sometimes I really could sense when other consciousnesses were trying to impinge on my space. Not always, of course—like the rest of my powers, that extra sense wasn't one hundred-percent reliable. But even eighty percent was pretty good odds, and that tended to be the percentage of times I turned out to be right.

Right then, the only consciousness I wanted focusing on my office was Otto's, and he remained conspicuously absent. Sometime soon we were going to have a talk about that. After all, what good's a spirit guide who's never around when you need him?

Alex stared at me through long-lashed baby-blue eyes that were narrowed with suspicion. But after a few more seconds, he gave a slight lift of the shoulders which seemed to indicate he'd decided to confide in me after all. "I think my girlfriend is possessed by an alien."

Oh, great. It was times like these that I really wished I'd gone into something a little less wacky, like selling insurance or used cars. I was pretty sure most people in those fields didn't have to deal with clients who claimed their family members were possessed, or that their dead relatives had come back and taken up residence in the cookie jar, or any of the other questionable tales I'd heard over the years.

Still, rolling my eyes or letting out a put-upon sigh wasn't exactly the professional way to handle this. Besides, Alex was obviously upset by something, so I owed it to him to at least say something comforting.

"Actually, there really isn't anything such as possession—not the way books and movies show it," I told him. "Spirits do speak through some people, but their intentions are always benign. And ghosts can't possess people."

"I'm not talking about ghosts," he said stubbornly, arms crossed. "I'm talking about aliens."

This time, I didn't bother to keep the skepticism out of my voice. "As in little green men from Mars?"

"They're not from Mars—and they're not green. I mean, I don't think they are. I've never seen one in its true form."

"But you think one has taken over your girlfriend."

"Yeah." He rocked back in his chair and then hunched forward, fixing me with an intense stare. "Don't you think I know how crazy that sounds? Why else do you think I'd come see someone like you instead of the cops or something?"

"'Someone like me,'" I repeated. I knew exactly what he meant, but that didn't mean I had to like the sound of it.

He waved a hand. "Well, you know—you have to

believe all sorts of stuff to do what you do…don't you?"

Like six impossible things before breakfast? I figured it was best for me to keep that thought to myself, though. I took a calming breath, drawing in the air through my nose the way I'd been taught, and said, "I consider myself a professional, Mr. Hathaway. Just because I deal in things that not everyone can believe in or can tap into doesn't make them any less important to me, or any less real. I assure you, I only believe in phenomena I've experienced myself. It's just that my experiences tend to be a little different from those of people who don't have any psychic abilities."

"Hmm."

I could tell Alex was both angry and disappointed. I hated it when a client went away from a session feeling he hadn't learned anything or gained new insight, so I knew I had to keep trying, even though I really didn't know exactly how I could help him. "What led you to believe your girlfriend was possessed? Has her behavior changed?"

"Yeah—I suppose."

"How?"

"She's just sort of distant, I guess."

Oh, well, that's an indicator of alien possession, no doubt about it, I thought wryly, but again I stepped on my tongue and assumed what I hoped was an expression of concerned interest. "Anything else?"

"She started reading *Variety*."

I suppressed the urge to burst into laughter. If reading *Variety* was a sign that space aliens had taken over your body, then about two-thirds of Los Angeles had to be possessed. "I take it that's not something she was in the habit of doing?" I inquired. Somehow I managed to maintain a neutral tone.

"No. I mean, she wants to be an actress, but I don't remember her ever reading much of anything before. Now she's got *Variety* all over the place—she got an actual physical subscription—and is always on the *Hollywood Reporter* site, along with a few others I can't remember now. TMZ, maybe." He clenched his hands on top of his knees and added, "She never used to read anything except some online gossip sites. And she keeps making comments about how 'I wouldn't understand' if I try to ask her questions about the stuff she's reading. Which is kind of ironic, since she used to miss at least four out of five of those 'are you smarter than a fifth-grader?' questions."

While this all did sound a little unusual, it wouldn't be the first time someone woke up and decided they needed to be more proactive about their career. I couldn't exactly figure out how Alex had made the jump from a simple attempt on his girlfriend's part to improve her marketability to concluding the brain in question had been possessed by aliens. Maybe that was easier to handle psychologically than realizing your significant other was about to leave you behind in the dust.

"When did you first notice the change in her behavior?" I asked. I wasn't sure how this particular piece of information was actually going to help me, but I thought I might as well try to go about this interview in an orderly fashion.

"Right after she got back from a trip to the tanning salon," Alex replied promptly.

That response came from so far out in left field, I could feel my eyes widen for a second before I forced a noncommittal expression on my face. "Excuse me?"

"She went to one of those places where they spray them on. She claimed being pale made her look flabby." He scowled and added, "I told her that spray tans were stupid and that they just made people look orange, but she didn't want to listen to me. She said it looked perfectly natural and I didn't know what I was talking about, and she wasn't going to lie out in the sun and get wrinkly. Like she needs to worry about that."

Maybe not now, I reflected, *but in fifteen years....* Although my mother was Greek, I hadn't inherited her olive skin, unfortunately. No, I got my complexion from my Irish father, and so I tended to flash-fry the second I stepped outside. Not exactly the best survival trait for living in Southern California. I cleared my throat, "Actually, that's just being smart. Sun damage is cumulative."

Alex made another off-hand gesture. "Whatever. So off she goes, and she comes back all orange—and I tell her so, and she just give me this flat stare and tells me I need to get my eyes looked at. She had a stack of newspapers and magazines with her, and she sat down and started to read them and barely talked to me for the next two hours. And she's been like that ever since."

"How long has this been going on?"

"About a week." He frowned. "It's getting pretty old, Ms. O'Brien. 'Cause not only is she barely talking to me, but she's not—I mean, we haven't—"

From the flush I saw under his tan—natural, I assumed, since he was definitely brownish and not orange—I guessed Alex was trying to say he and his girlfriend hadn't been intimate. Well, I supposed if an alien had taken over a human's body but wasn't really into the more down-and-dirty aspects of being an Earthling, it might try to avoid the horizontal mambo for as long as possible.

I didn't really know what to say next. Obviously, something was going on between him and his girlfriend, but it sounded like the natural growing apart of a relationship, not anything extraterrestrial. I could tell him that, of course, even though I had an idea it probably wasn't what he wanted to hear. Too bad I couldn't talk to the girlfriend as well, but I figured my chances of getting her in to talk to me were approximately the same as my getting a hot date that night.

In other words, about zero.

If Otto had decided to drop in on this cozy little session, maybe I would have been able to come up with something a bit more useful. I wasn't getting much from Alex, except the frustration and anger and worry that seemed to pour off him in waves. Not that reading his emotions really helped me that much —I'd gleaned just as much from talking to him. But I wasn't getting any answers from the astral plane, and my Tarot deck had dummied up on me as well. I hated this feeling; it rarely happened, but on the few occasions when it did, I was always left feeling impotent and a little foolish after a session, as if I weren't any better than the sham psychics who gathered all their tells from people's behavior and speech patterns and who didn't have any more psychic ability than a footstool.

"Well," I said after a pause, knowing what I needed to say and hating to have to say it, "I'm very sorry, Alex, but I'm not getting any clear vibrations from you regarding this situation. My advice would be for you to talk things over with your girlfriend." I added, as I saw his jaw clench, "Of course there's no fee for this reading."

"That's it?" he demanded. "This is bullshit!"

It wasn't the first time a client had sworn at me, and it probably wouldn't be the last, but that didn't mean I had to like it. "No, it would have been bullshit for me to feed you an easy line and take your money. I'm sorry, but sometimes even I draw a blank. This just happens to be one of those times."

"So what am I supposed to do now?"

"I'm not a relationship counselor—I just relay

what the spirit world tells me." This wasn't the strictest truth; I actually did have a master's degree in marriage and family counseling, although once I'd gone to work as a psychic full-time, I'd quietly put away my diplomas and certificates. For whatever reason, people didn't seem to like a psychic who was also a psychologist—it made them nervous, maybe because they didn't know exactly how to regard me.

"You think I'm nuts."

Well, that wasn't how I would have put it, although I was starting to get the distinct impression that Alex Hathaway was just a wee bit unbalanced. It would have taken a few more sessions to get to the bottom of his current fixation, of course, but I knew that wasn't going to happen. He hadn't come to me for psychological counseling—he'd just wanted outside confirmation that his girlfriend wasn't, strictly speaking, his girlfriend anymore, and I wasn't prepared to make that kind of determination.

I said, "Of course I don't, Alex. I believe something has gone wrong between you and your girlfriend—it's just that I don't feel confident enough to offer you any corroborating evidence."

"Great," he said, looking as gloomy as someone as sunnily Southern Californian in appearance could. "Well…thanks for not charging me, I guess."

"Don't mention it," I said. "I would be a fraud if I took your money when I couldn't even give you a true reading." I stood then, hoping he'd get the hint that the session was over.

He hesitated, but after a few seconds, he got up out of his chair. I crossed to the door and opened it for him. As he passed me, his shoulder brushed against mine, and for a second, a shiver of freezing cold ran down my spine. I'd experienced that sensation before…from clients who were about to leave this plane of existence, usually in unexpected and often nasty ways. I opened my mouth to warn him, but then again, I hadn't received any visions of how he was going to die—if he were even going to die at all. Maybe I'd just been hit by a stray draft.

Oh, yeah, a sub-zero draft when it's eighty degrees outside, my brain mocked me, and by then it was too late—Alex Hathaway was out the door and gone.

Somehow I knew I'd never see him again.

About a half-hour after Alex had left the office, Otto finally decided to make an appearance. By then I was safely home, ensconced in my apartment with my feet up on an ottoman and a cup of mint tea on the table next to me. I'd considered pouring myself a glass of chardonnay instead, but decided it was probably better to avoid the whole concept of solitary drinking as long as I could. Maybe my neighbor Ginger would be back soon, and we could share a bottle while I tried to justify my self-medicating.

Anyhow, I'd just picked up the remote for the TV and was about to turn it on when Otto wavered into existence a few feet away, floating three feet off the living room floor as he sat in a modified lotus position. He couldn't manage a true lotus—his legs were too chunky for that.

"Nice of you to drop in," I remarked. "I could have used a little help earlier this afternoon."

He gave me a heavy-lidded half-smile. "The world of the spirit does not work on demand."

This statement might have sounded impressive— if I hadn't heard the same thing about a hundred times before. "Well, unfortunately, I do. I drew a perfect blank. The client was annoyed, and I looked like an idiot."

The Mona Lisa smile never left Otto's lips. "You are not here to be concerned with how others see you."

"Then boy, did I pick the wrong town to live in." To hide my irritation, I picked up my tea and took a swallow. It tasted good. The chardonnay could wait. "So what, did you have an urgent pedicure appointment in the otherworld or something?"

His mouth thinned a little. I knew he hated it when I made comments like that about the spirit world. It wasn't respectful. Actually, I had a lot of respect for the alternate plane of existence we mortals thought of as the afterlife or heaven or nirvana, depending on our beliefs. If nothing else, knowing it was out there had given me a certain perspective on my day-to-day troubles. On the other hand, it didn't make me feel much better about the wasteland otherwise known as my social life.

"I am your guide," Otto said, and now his tone was distinctly testy. "Not your errand boy."

"Too bad, because this guy today was a live one. Thought his girlfriend was possessed by an alien or something."

Usually Otto wasn't above finding amusement in the foibles of mere mortals. Of course, he purported to be impartial, but I knew he also enjoyed a joke at our expense. I tended to forgive him this quirk, considering he'd been a eunuch in sixteenth-century Turkey and probably had a good deal of resentment toward mankind stored up. Now, however, he looked a little strained—which was my tipoff that what I'd just said had disturbed him.

"Do you know something?" I asked suddenly. "Because if we actually are getting overrun by aliens or something, I'd sort of like to know about it."

"I cannot speak of matters that impact you personally."

I didn't like the sound of that at all. "What, am I next I line for alien possession or something?"

A flash of irritation crossed his normally cherubic features. "Which part of 'I cannot speak of matters that impact you personally' did you not understand?"

"Fine," I said. It wasn't the first time we'd had this sort of discussion. Otto was there to help facilitate my contact with the spirit world, but he was either unable or simply unwilling to tell me anything about my own future. Just as well—half the time I wasn't sure I really wanted to know. But when he threw out cryptic comments like that and refused to elaborate, I had a tendency to get a little pissy. "So was there a reason for you dropping in tonight...like maybe apologizing for going AWOL this afternoon?"

His sparse eyebrows drew together, and for a second he looked distinctly transparent. Usually he appeared just as solid as any other human being—except you could walk right through him. Not that I recommended doing any such a thing. I did once, and got a lecture about showing respect for beings from other planes and how I wouldn't appreciate it if he decided the shortest path between two points was right through me. At the time, I had thought his comparison was a little faulty. After all, I was corporeal, and he, well, wasn't. But I'd also learned fairly early on that a disgruntled spirit guide was of no use to anyone, so I'd apologized and said it would never happen again. Ever since then, I'd noticed that Otto had an odd tendency to discorporate partway if something disturbed him. Maybe it was the spirit equivalent of blushing.

So I knew now something was up, but I could also tell from the firm set of his chubby chin that if I pressed too hard, he'd just evaporate, and it might be several days before he deigned to speak to me again. I couldn't have that—I depended on him too much for my readings. Sure, I could whip out the tarot deck and hope for the best, but Otto's guidance tended to be a lot more reliable.

"I wasn't AWOL," he said primly. "You're not my only psychic, you know."

As a matter of fact, I did know that, and I had never been overly thrilled with the fact. To be fair, from what I could tell, his other...clients, for lack of a better term...seemed to be located in different time zones from mine, and since a spirit didn't need to sleep, he could flit from one to the other of us without too many conflicts. But if one of his other psychics had a crisis in the dead hours of the night, it would of course impact my afternoon readings. It hadn't happened too often, but it did add a certain element of uncertainty to my practice.

So was it coincidence that he was called away the same day Alex Hathaway came to my office, or was there more going on here than met the eye?

My personal experience told me there was almost always something more going on than the most logical explanation. Now, however, was probably not the time to confront Otto about his bouts of unreliability. If he wanted to tell me something, he would. If not, threats, cajoling, and bribes simply wouldn't work. I'd found that out the hard way.

"Well, I hope it was important," I grumbled, and set my mug back down on the side table. After that, I picked up the remote and said, "Was there some reason you popped in? Because the latest season of

The Santa Clarita Diet just dropped, and I feel like a binge."

He shook his head. "Really, Persephone. Why you waste your time with such petty diversions—"

"It relaxes me," I retorted. "No one likes a stressed psychic."

"Hmph." Otto crossed his arms. "As a matter of fact, I did have something I wanted to tell you."

"I'm waiting breathlessly."

His expression was as sour as a Turkish eunuch's round face could manage "Just this—if Ginger asks you to go with her for drinks tonight, you should."

"Isn't that crossing the line?" I inquired innocently. "What about all that palaver about not letting me know anything about my future?"

"I'm not giving you any concrete facts—I'm just offering a piece of advice."

If a spirit guide offers you advice, it's usually wise to take it. Never mind that I was tired and more than a little cranky, and the effort it would require to get myself presentable enough to face a bar or club didn't seem worth the amount of time it would take. On the other hand, what else did I have to do? Netflix would still be waiting for me when I got home. Actually, it tended to be one of the few constants in my life.

"All right," I said, and tossed the remote onto the table, missing my mug by about an inch. "Any spiritual advice as to what I should wear?"

Otto looked a little pained. "I hope one of these days you'll realize such things are immaterial."

Tell that to the producer of every makeover show ever made, I thought. But getting into an argument with Otto over my preoccupation with what he considered earthly frivolities would just be silly. So maybe I was the world's most earthbound psychic. Sue me.

"Maybe I will," I replied, and pushed myself up out of my chair. "Until then, I've got some spackling to do."

I'd never been able to figure out how a being who had no actual lungs was capable of producing such prodigious sighs, but somehow Otto managed to do it. He dredged one up now, then said in sepulchral tones, "As you wish." After that, he sort of melted away in his usual fashion, disappearing like mist evaporating in sunlight. Even now, after being visited by him for almost twenty years, I found the sight a little unnerving.

Once he was gone, though, I had to turn my mind to more important matters. Although I knew there wasn't a snowball's chance in hell that I'd get a date out of tonight's bar hopping, I was damned if I was going to hit the clubs without making an attempt at bringing my best game. After that, well, we'd just have to see. There had to be one guy in this town who wasn't freaked out by the prospect of dating a psychic, right?

Right.

CHAPTER TWO

GINGER CAME SAILING INTO THE APARTMENT BUILDING'S courtyard a little before six. Since I'd been lurking on my balcony, waiting for her to come home, I wasn't exactly inconspicuous.

She paused directly below the balcony, then removed her sunglasses. At that hour on an early March evening, they were mostly affectation, but then again, a lot about Ginger was for show. "You up for drinks tonight?" she asked.

"Sure—I'm sort of getting cabin fever," I replied.

A frown barely etched itself into her brow. "Bad day?"

I figured this probably wasn't the best time to go into a discussion of Alex Hathaway and his alien obsession. "No, but the usual TV offerings have sort of palled."

"All right. Just let me change. Meet you at your

place in twenty." With that, she disappeared under my feet; her apartment was directly below mine.

Luckily, it was a Thursday, and so she didn't have any evening classes to teach. A former professional dancer, she ran a ballroom dance studio in Hollywood, a studio she'd bought with cash when her first husband, a producer, dropped dead of a sudden heart attack and left her a tidy sum. That tidy sum came into dispute when her second husband, another dancer, tried to get her to pay spousal support even though they'd only been married for two years. The lawsuit fell apart when she was able to prove he'd been cheating on her with a male student from her own studio, but the experience had left her more than a little wary about the male half of the species. On more than one occasion, I'd seen her crowned with three gold rings, sort of like a weird triple halo, which indicated husband number three was somewhere in her future, but I knew better than to tell her that. She'd sworn off men—besides letting them buy her drinks—so I figured it was best to let her be surprised by her third foray into matrimony.

I, on the other hand, hadn't even gotten close to one trip down the aisle, let alone three. Why I continued to torture myself by venturing out into the singles world instead of just giving up and turning into the crazy cat lady, I wasn't sure. Probably the same streak of stubbornness that had led me and my mother to continually butt heads over the years. Besides, I was only thirty. The biological clock had gotten a little louder these past couple of years, but it hadn't swung over into "countdown to detonation" mode yet, so I kept telling myself I had plenty of time and that the situation would work itself out eventually.

That's sort of the sad thing, though. You live your life, and you have your work and your small circle of friends, and you think everything is going just fine. And then your mother asks a few pointed questions about your dateless state, and you realize it's been months, with no prospects of anything better to come. So you make excuses, and you joke and look away, and hope that you're better at blocking your own emotions than you are at reading those of others. And so it goes.

So far, the men I'd met had fallen into one of two categories. The first type were the guys who, once they found out I was a psychic, were convinced I'd know everything about them, down to every single impure thought they'd ever had, and headed for the hills at the earliest opportunity. Now, that was just ridiculous—I didn't read minds, although I could sense people's emotions if they were strong enough. But who would want to go tromping through every corner of another person's mind, even if they were able to? No, thanks.

The other type were even worse in a way. They seemed to think that dating a psychic entitled them to tips on the stock market and the results of every World Series and boxing bout for the next five years.

I couldn't do that any more than I could directly read someone's mind, but they always seemed to think my refusal to supply them with that information was purely personal. Those relationships usually didn't end very well, either.

Despite this wretched track record, I took my usual care in fixing my makeup and selecting something to wear. Now, my closet had its fair share of what the style mavens might disparagingly refer to as "loosy-goosy, airy-fairy" clothes, but that was just sort of how people expected a psychic to dress. But I also had some nice pieces I'd picked up at local boutiques, and it was one of these I selected now, a sapphire blue silk top just low-cut enough to be interesting but not too extreme. I discarded my baggy cotton drawstring trousers and Börn flats in favor of dark jeans and kitten-heeled boots.

It'll do, I thought, giving my reflection one last critical look. Not much could be done about my hair at this late notice—if I wanted to beat my unruly curls into submission, I had to give myself at least an hour to blow-dry my hair and then flat-iron the waves that remained. Still, it wasn't as if I was going out to a speed-dating session or something. It was just drinks with Ginger.

I heard a knock at the door and headed over to let her in. She'd changed as well, but her crossover top and clingy skirt didn't look all that different from the dance garb she wore while teaching. Ginger had a good fifteen years on me, but she'd kept herself in great shape. And although I knew she had to have had some work done, she hadn't gone overboard with it the way so many other women in this town who were approaching fifty had. No frozen foreheads or freakishly lifted eyebrows for Ginger—she just looked fresh and at least ten years younger than her real age. I hadn't worked up the guts to ask her who her plastic surgeon was—not that I needed one...yet—but when the evil day came, I was definitely going to swallow my pride and get a recommendation.

"So where do you want to go?" she asked, after giving me a quick once-over and an approving nod.

"I don't want to drive," I said. Even on a Thursday night, navigating around West Hollywood could be a nightmare, and I wasn't sure my nerves could handle it. But luckily, we had several candidates within walking distance.

"El Churro? We can make the tail end of happy hour and get four-dollar mojitos."

Personally, I thought El Churro's mojitos were pretty weak, but the purpose of going out wasn't to get blotto. I just wanted to do something normal so I wouldn't be seeing space aliens around every corner.

"Sure," I replied, and gathered up my purse. Besides, El Churro was only two blocks away, easy to navigate even in heels.

As we walked over to the restaurant, I kept getting distracted when people with fake-looking tans walked by. But none of them seemed to be showing evidence of alien possession—no flat stares, no antennas sprouting out of their heads.

"Something wrong?" Ginger asked as we paused at a corner and waited for the light to change so we could cross the street to the restaurant. "You seem a little jumpy."

Automatically, I replied, "I'm fine," even though I felt far from fine. Maybe going out had been a bad idea after all. Who knew that one random client could set me so much on edge? Especially since I'd never been the type to believe in UFOs and alien abductions. Oh, sure, I'd enjoyed watching *The X-Files* back in high school, but that was probably more because I thought David Duchovny was hot than because of the show's actual subject matter. I'd always had a thing for the brainy types, starting with a crush on the Professor from *Gilligan's Island* and working my way on from there. Too bad the science-minded guys tended to bolt at the first mention of psychic abilities.

Ginger shot me a dubious look from under her expertly applied false eyelashes but said nothing. Thankful for that small bit of grace, I followed her across the street with the rest of the pedestrians and on into El Churro's waiting area.

It was packed, but as we had already decided that we were just going into the bar, I knew I didn't have to resign myself to a forty-five-minute wait. Even so, there weren't any seats available, and we had to grab a precarious spot at the end of the bar and hope that someone would leave soon. At least there it was easy enough for the bartender to see us, and we had mojitos in our hands before I had a chance to complain about the crowd.

Maybe the bartender had taken pity on us and our unfortunate perch, because the drinks were definitely stronger than the norm. I sipped and let the cool flavors of mint and rum run over my tongue. A tension I hadn't even realized was there began to leave my neck and shoulders, and I let out a little sigh.

"Better?" Ginger asked, and I nodded.

"Much."

"I never thought I'd be telling a psychic she works too hard, but you do work too hard, 'Seph."

I lifted my shoulders. "Not really."

"Yeah, really." She opened her mouth as if she meant to say more, but then her eyes narrowed, even as she raised her brows. "Mmmm...what have we here?"

"Huh?"

"Look...but don't look like you're looking."

Right. Easy for her to say, since she was facing the entrance to the bar and my back was squarely to it. Still, I'd spent enough time in bars and clubs that I wasn't completely unpracticed at the surreptitious glance over my shoulder. So I shifted my position a fraction and then took a sneak peek in the direction she'd indicated.

El Churro had its usual crowd, which generally

consisted of a mixture of well-dressed gay couples, singles stopping by after work, some industry executives in suits, and a sprinkling of tourists. I could tell at once the man I was looking at didn't fit into any of those groups.

He might have been my age, or maybe a few years older, and he wore a rumpled sports jacket over a white shirt and some khakis. I couldn't tell what color his eyes were, because he was a few yards away and the lighting in the bar wasn't that good, and he carried an honest-to-God hard-sided briefcase in one hand. I didn't think anyone used briefcases like that anymore. Despite all that—or maybe because of it—I thought he was definitely worth the crick I was getting in my neck. Tanned, but not the fake kind, and his hair was an indeterminate light brown and in need of a trim. In short, he stuck out in El Churro the way I, with my pale skin and curly dark hair, would have stood out at a Miss Sweden competition.

All of which was great...until his eyes locked on mine and he headed straight for me.

"Shit, he saw me staring," I hissed at Ginger.

She grinned. "Good."

Then I heard him say, "Excuse me."

I'd never been very good at the whole sophisticated and blasé thing, but I did my best. *Cool, be cool,* I told myself. Turning slowly, not lifting my eyes from my drink, I replied, "Yes?"

"Do you know the way to the Sheraton Universal hotel? The GPS in my rental car is malfunctioning, and my cell phone is acting up so I can't use it to navigate."

Oh, boy. I should have known. No one was going to approach me in a bar on purpose. I really needed to stop kidding myself.

Still, he looked more than a little stressed-out, and it wasn't his fault my dating life was in the crapper. I managed a smile and said, "Sheraton Universal? Your GPS must really have died. That's all the way across the city from here."

He glanced at his watch, one of those big black jobs that hikers and other outdoorsy types tended to sport. It clashed terribly with his tweedy jacket and wrinkled khakis. "I have to be at the Sheraton no later than seven."

That didn't give him much time, but luckily, I knew my way around L.A. as well as I knew my way around my apartment. "It'll be tight, but you should make it. Just head east on Santa Monica Boulevard until you get to Highland. Hang a left and take Highland until it merges with the 101. Get off at Lankershim and follow the signs. Ignore the stuff for Universal Studios—the hotel backs up to the lot, but you can't get to the hotel parking structure from Barham unless you go the long way around."

The stranger nodded, brow furrowed. Most people would have asked me to repeat at least part of the directions, but he seemed to have absorbed them immediately. "Thank you…?" And then he hesitated, as if expecting me to provide my name.

I didn't bother to sigh anymore. It wasn't usually until the second date that I explained my Greek mother and my father's minor in Classics. Until then, people could think whatever they wanted of my name. "Persephone," I told him.

He didn't even blink. "Thank you very much, Persephone." And then he turned and headed out back through the foyer, and presumably to the parking lot. I found myself hoping he hadn't popped for the valet.

"You just let him go?" Ginger demanded. She drank down the last of her mojito and signaled the bartender for another one.

"What was I supposed to do—tie him to the bar? All he needed was directions."

"And yet he asked you, out of everyone in the bar."

"I'm closest to the door," I pointed out.

Since that was the simple truth, she didn't have much of a rejoinder. "Still…."

"Still nothing. Yeah, he was good-looking. I got my quota of eye candy for the night." I couldn't help smiling to myself. There was something about the way the stranger talked, and the way he dressed, that told me he'd probably be horrified to be referred to as "eye candy." I guessed he didn't move in the kind of circles that used those sorts of terms. I took a long pull on my straw, thus finishing my own mojito just in time for the bartender to come over and take our order for another round.

Ginger waited until the bartender had gone, then said, "Think he might have been a college professor?"

"What makes you say that?"

"Mmm...not sure. Just something about him. He definitely wasn't the West Hollywood type."

I chuckled. "That's for sure!"

Afterward, Ginger seemed to abandon the topic, thank God. I really didn't see the point in discussing the stranger anymore.

After all, it wasn't as if I was ever going to see him again.

I said my goodnights to Ginger and climbed the stairs to my apartment. After two mojitos and just enough bar snacks to dilute them a little, I was ready to kick off my heels and call it a night. Maybe I'd finally get that delayed binge session with Netflix.

When I stepped into my living room, however, I found myself confronted by Otto, who was floating a yard off the floor in the center of my Persian rug. His eyes were shut, but they snapped open immediately as I entered.

Staring straight at me, he intoned, "You must go to the Sheraton Universal hotel."

"What?" I shot him an irritated look. "You channeling Obi-Wan Kenobi or something?"

"I do not know this Obi-Wan. I do know that you must go to the Sheraton Universal hotel. Immediately."

Of all the—"What happened to not interfering in my life?"

"I never said I wouldn't interfere. I have merely stated that I could not give you direct information pertaining to your future."

Talk about splitting semantic hairs. "And what precisely am I supposed to do at the Sheraton Universal hotel?"

"That I cannot say. Only that the consequences will be dire if you do not."

It didn't take a genius to make the connection. Mystery Man had been going to the Sheraton Universal; therefore, it must be that my business with him wasn't quite as finished as I had thought. "Any other hints? Like a name?"

"You'll know when you get there."

By that point, I was fairly used to Otto's penchant for cryptic remarks, but that didn't make me any less crabby about the situation. Never mind that I was tired and tipsy and also a bit crabby, and I just wanted to call it a day. How bad would it look for me to show up at the hotel in pursuit of this man whose name I didn't even know? I'd come off as a crazy stalker.

"Tick-tock, Persephone."

"I just had two mojitos," I pointed out. "I shouldn't be driving anywhere."

"Take some bottled water with you."

I knew it was pointless to argue when Otto got like this. Despite his fondness for making himself scarce when I needed him, he also could hang around interminably when I wanted him to be gone. As spirit guides went, actually, he was sort of a pain in the ass. I supposed I should be glad he was my one and only guide; some psychics tended to boast of being visited by numerous entities from different planes, and I could never quite figure out why that was supposed to be a good thing.

Arms crossed, I demanded, "Are you going to bail me out if I get a DUI?"

"You will not get a DUI."

That response didn't reassure me quite as much as it probably should have. His predictions, when he finally got around to making them, were almost always correct. But since I also knew he would hang around like the ghost of that one annoying relative who would never leave a family party at the end of the evening unless I did as he said, I shrugged and went to retrieve my black leather jacket and throw it on over my silk top. Despite the warmth of the day, it had started to get fairly chilly as soon as the sun went down.

"Anything else?" I inquired as I dug around in my purse for my car keys. "Do I need to know a secret word or something?"

"Just go."

This time, I didn't bother to repress the sigh. I just let it out, complete with raised eyebrow, but Otto appeared supremely unimpressed. He continued to float in the middle of my living room, doing a fairly good Buddha impression. Well, a Turkish Buddha, anyway.

"If you're going to hang around, you could water my plants. The African violets are looking a little droopy."

Otto didn't deign to reply, but only shut his eyes. Since there was no point in putting off the inevitable, I let myself out and headed down the stairs to the carport.

By that time, the sky was lit by only the haziest remains of sunset. The fluorescent glare overhead in the carport more than made up for the lack of light, though. I squinted and pushed the button on my remote to disengage the alarm and unlock the car. After depositing my purse on the passenger seat, I slid behind the wheel and fastened the seatbelt in grim silence. The satellite radio blared the second I turned the key; I'd forgotten to turn it off the last time I'd driven the car, which had been during a run out to my parents' house in Claremont the previous weekend.

I wanted silence now, though. Music sometimes helped to soothe my jangled nerves, but I knew this wasn't one of those times. I maneuvered out of the carport, waited at the light, and then headed east on Sunset.

Even though rush hour had technically been over for almost an hour at that point, the streets in West Hollywood were still clogged. I tried to ignore the traffic, since I knew I couldn't do anything to change it. That strategy was only partly successful—some of Otto's urgency seemed to have rubbed off on me. I found myself drumming my fingers on the steering wheel every time I missed a light, muttering curses at the drivers who swung into my lane at the very last minute for reasons that seemed to be obvious only to them. Not very mature behavior, I'd admit. Mentally, I berated myself for letting Otto bully me into this fool's errand. Why couldn't I have just stood up for myself for once?

That wasn't completely true. There had been or two instances in the past when I had put my foot down over one of Otto's more, shall we say, inspired suggestions, but annoying as he could be, he'd been part of my life for the greater part of twenty years. He hadn't been fooling around. For whatever reason, he truly did believe that it was of the utmost importance that I go haring off to the Sheraton Universal hotel.

At least it wasn't raining. Earlier in the week, a late-season rainstorm had scrubbed L.A. all clean and shiny. I appreciated what the weather had done for the city's aesthetics, but I hated driving in the rain. Especially when I was tired and—if we were going to be completely truthful about the situation—not entirely sober. Oh, I knew I wasn't horrendously impaired, or anything close to it, or I would have told Otto to stuff it, no matter what the stakes. However, I could tell I wasn't at the top of my game.

As I'd told Mystery Man, I knew most of Los

Angeles like the back of my hand, so I didn't have any trouble negotiating the sometimes tricky entrance onto the Hollywood Freeway from High-land Avenue, and I pointed my Volvo toward the Lankershim off-ramp as if I took that route every day. Actually, I hadn't been there for at least five years. My college roommate Jess had held her wedding reception at the hotel. Now her marriage was on the rocks. I hoped that wasn't an omen of what I might encounter at the Sheraton myself.

I pulled into the parking garage, winced a little at the prices listed at the entrance, then grimly pulled the ticket from the machine and headed into the structure. Something had to be going on at the hotel, because the garage was packed. I had to wind all the way down to the lowest level before I found a spot at the far end near one of the utility elevators. Lovely. Just the perfect spot to get mugged.

Clutching my purse a little more closely to myself, I speed-walked over to the elevator—thank God I'd worn boots with kitten heels instead of the ankle-breaking stilettos Ginger had talked me into at one of last summer's end-of-season sales. On my way to the elevator, I couldn't help noticing that there seemed to be a good number of somewhat shabby-looking vehicles in the structure, some of them emblazoned with bumper stickers that read "I want to believe" or "MUFON"...whatever that meant.

Maybe the hotel was hosting an *X-Files* convention. But weren't they about twenty years too late for that?

I was the only person in the elevator, and was profoundly grateful for that. I took advantage of the solitude to adjust my hair as best I could, using the polished steel of the elevator doors as a makeshift mirror. My lipstick was mostly gone; I scrounged a tube out of my purse and did a hasty reapplication just before the doors opened and deposited me in the lobby.

Okay, time for some recon. I guessed that Mystery Man must be here for some sort of conference or convention—he certainly didn't have the air of a casual tourist. So most likely my best chance of finding him would be to go to the meeting room and conference section of the hotel. If, of course, he was even the reason Otto had sent me on this fool's errand.

A quick scan of the floor plan map by the elevators told me that the meeting room spaces were all downstairs, on the Terrace Level. I followed the signs to the escalator and headed down, all the while telling myself this really wasn't as crazy as it seemed, that there had to be a perfectly logical explanation as to why I was here.

When I got off the escalator, I found myself facing a large banner that said, *Mutual UFO Network Symposium—Welcome!*

UFOs? Seriously?

And then I remembered Space Boy, and how he

believed his girlfriend was possessed by an alien. A sick feeling rose in my stomach that had very little to do with the two mojitos I had downed earlier.

I was beginning to understand just why Otto might have sent me here.

CHAPTER THREE

A PASTY INDIVIDUAL ROSE FROM THE TABLE SITUATED directly beneath the banner. "Help you?" he inquired.

Oh, you can help me, all right...help me right into a straitjacket. I cleared my throat, "Um...actually, I'm looking for someone."

"Are you attending the conference?"

"No." The last thing I needed was to have to pay even more to find out where Mystery Man might be hiding. Then inspiration struck. "That is—I think one of your guests left his cell phone at the bar where he stopped for directions." I fished my iPhone out of my purse and flashed it at the conference worker, glad that I'd opted for a plain silver model this time rather than rose gold. Somehow, I doubted the man with the briefcase would have gone for a pink phone. "I couldn't call him, though, because he has the phone locked down. Tall guy, mid-thirties…tweed jacket and khakis?"

"That sounds like Dr. Oliver." The other man at the table, who could have been anything between thirty-five and forty-five, pushed his glasses up his nose and frowned. "He's giving the keynote address right now." Another frown, as if my bad timing were a personal affront. "It's almost over, but there's a cocktail reception afterward—"

"It'll only take a minute," I said. "Really, all I have to do is slip in and give him the phone."

"You could give it to me."

Crap. As I flailed mentally for a reply to the man's remark, I heard a wave of applause through the doors to the ballroom immediately to the left of us. A few seconds later, people began to stream out through those same doors.

"Looks like it's over!" I chirped, flashing a smile that I hoped appeared friendly and not at all stalker-ish. "I'll just pop in there and give the phone to Mr. Oliver myself."

"That's *Doctor* Oliver—and—wait!"

But I didn't wait. I turned at once and began pushing my way through the crowd, feeling a definite affinity with all those salmon who had to spend their lives swimming upstream. Luckily, there was such a crush that if anyone had been checking for membership badges at the door, there was no way they could have seen me clearly enough to know whether or not I was wearing one.

After a breathless minute, I found myself in a mostly empty ballroom. What if this Dr. Oliver had left, too? But the few conferences I had attended generally had the speakers and other guests leaving by way of the backstage area, not going out with the rest of the general attendees. I had to hope that was the case here as well.

Then I spotted him, standing at the far end of the stage and chatting with an older woman with improbably platinum blonde hair. His back was toward me. Thank God. That way I could take a second or two to catch my breath and steel myself to move forward. I just knew I didn't dare wait too long in case the guy from the information table was in hot pursuit.

I dodged a couple of stragglers and paused a few feet away from the stage. "Dr. Oliver?"

He turned and stared down at me in incomprehension, and then an expression of astonishment flitted over his features. "Persephone?"

I didn't know whether to be impressed he'd remembered my name or worried that I'd made a little too indelible of an impression. "That's right. Look, I—that is, I really need to talk to you."

"Talk to me? About what?" He sounded more than a little impatient, and I guessed I couldn't blame him too much. After all, I'd interrupted what could have been an important conversation. And he had to be wondering just what the hell I was doing there.

"About—" I hesitated, aware of the older

woman's slightly irritated gaze. "Um…could I talk to you in private?"

"Ms.…" He trailed off; I hadn't given him my last name.

"O'Brien," I supplied. It couldn't be a good sign if he was falling back on addressing me by my last name.

"Ms. O'Brien, I'm here as a guest of the conference. I'm expected at a reception—"

"Five minutes. Just give me five minutes, and if you don't want to hear any more, I won't ask anything else."

For a few agonizing seconds, he didn't say anything, but only scanned me with a pair of hazel eyes that were a little too penetrating. He certainly didn't look like your standard-issue UFO crackpot. I found myself wondering what he was a doctor of.

Then, "All right. Five minutes." He turned back to the woman with the platinum beehive and said, "Let everyone know I'll be a little late."

She nodded but apparently couldn't resist sending me another annoyed glance. "Of course, Paul."

So his name was Paul. I filed that tidbit away, then waited while she disappeared somewhere backstage and he came down the risers they were using as steps to the platform. As he approached, he seemed a lot taller than he had back at El Churro. Maybe the difference had something to do with the half-frown that creased his forehead, making him look almost forbidding.

"Where's the bar?" I asked.

"Why on earth do you want to go to the bar?"

"Because I have a feeling you're going to want a drink after you hear this."

The hotel's lobby lounge featured moody neon lighting and sleek black furniture. Appropriate—I almost felt as if I were aboard a UFO. Paul Oliver sat down across from me at a small two-seat table but waved off the waitress when she approached. Obviously he didn't think he was going to be giving me anything more than the agreed-upon five minutes.

I resisted the urge to order a drink, but I did ask for some Perrier just so we wouldn't seem like complete freeloaders.

The waitress left, and he leveled a very direct gaze at me. "So precisely what is so important, Ms. O'Brien?"

There wasn't any way to phrase it without sounding like a complete idiot. "Do you believe aliens can possess human beings, Dr. Oliver?"

That question threw him a little, I could tell. He sat back in his chair and tilted his head slightly, as if considering. "What makes you ask?"

"This morning, I had a client come to me who was convinced that his girlfriend had been taken over by some sort of alien intelligence. He was quite adamant about it."

"Client?"

I didn't bother to lie. What would be the point? He'd only find out sooner or later. You didn't get a lot of different hits when you Googled "Persephone O'Brien."

"I'm a psychic."

Almost at once, a shuttered expression took over his face.

"Don't you dare get all judgey," I snapped, a familiar irritation stirring in me. "Not when you're the guy who just gave the keynote speech at a UFO convention."

"Symposium," he said absently, and then almost smiled. The softening of his expression did all sorts of wonderful things to his features...and a few interesting things to my stomach as well. This might have been easier if he wasn't so damn good-looking. "What kind of psychic?"

Somehow, I managed to gather my wits. "Clairsentience and precognition mostly, although I've done some psychometry as well if the wind is coming from the right direction." That comment prompted an actual smile, and I continued, hoping I wasn't blushing and, if I was, that the lounge's dim lighting hid most of it. "I get a good deal of input from Otto, my spirit guide. He said I had to come here tonight but wouldn't tell me why. I've learned to follow Otto's directions or risk the consequences.

So I came here, and saw that the hotel was hosting a UFO con—symposium, and the pieces came together. He must have sent me here so I could get your advice."

"Shouldn't your spirit guide be the one providing you with advice?" Paul's tone was amused, but not so much that I could construe it as mocking me.

"Not always. Not if it's something that affects me directly."

"And how does this affect you directly? I thought you said it was a client who had come to you with the problem."

Good question. With a lift of my shoulders, I said, "Otto wouldn't tell me. But he looked...worried. So tell me, Dr. Oliver, was my client crazy? Or is alien possession something that can actually occur?"

For a long moment, he didn't say anything. During that silence, the waitress arrived with my Perrier. She set it down in front of me, then asked, "Anything else?"

Paul spoke up then. "Vodka martini, two olives."

I blinked at him. "Thought you weren't ordering a drink."

He smiled again, but it looked a little strained. "I have a feeling I'm going to need one."

"What about the five minutes?"

"I'm considering an extension." And he pulled out his own phone and began to enter a text— begging off from the cocktail reception, I guessed.

Well, in that case.... "I'll have a glass of pinot

noir," I told her. "And an order of the Thai spring rolls."

She nodded and wrote down our orders, then made herself scarce again.

"As to your question," Paul said, apparently unfazed by the assumption that this might take a while, considering I'd order an appetizer along with my drink, "there are accounts where individuals state their bodies have been taken over by entities not of this world, or that they have felt the presence of some 'other' within their thoughts. It's far less common than abduction, but it isn't unknown."

The image of Alex Hathaway's haunted eyes rose in my mind, and I shivered. Not that I believed in possession—as I'd told Alex, ghosts couldn't possess people, and in all my time working with troubled people, I'd never seen any evidence to suggest that demons or devils even existed. But Paul Oliver seemed to believe, or at least be open to the idea.

"So you believe in alien abduction?"

He crossed his arms and watched me over the flickering little tea light in its blue glass holder at the center of our table. "Of course I do. Wouldn't make much sense to have me as the keynote speaker here if I didn't, would it?"

I had to admit to myself that he had a point. "Have you ever been abducted?"

"No."

"But you believe it happens?"

"Absolutely."

It was my turn to settle back in my seat and give him a narrow glance. "Exactly what are you a doctor of, Dr. Oliver?"

"I have Ph.Ds in astronomy and astrophysics," he replied imperturbably. There might have been the slightest glint in his hazel eyes as he watched me...or maybe it was just a reflection from the candle flame. "From Stanford."

Oh. While I knew it was entirely possible for a university as prestigious as Stanford to churn out its share of crackpots, I was becoming less and less convinced that Paul Oliver was one. After all, there were plenty of people in the world who didn't believe in psychics, and yet here I was.

"So, my client," I went on doggedly. "He was absolutely convinced that his girlfriend had been taken over by some alien intelligence. He noted changes in her behavior and personality...none of which seemed all that strange to me, but of course, I didn't have a chance to meet her."

At that moment, the waitress showed up with our drinks and the appetizer. I made myself take several bites of a spring roll before I had any of the pinot. Best to lay down a base. At least it seemed as if the ghosts of mojitos past had pretty much disappeared by that time.

Paul didn't bother with the appetizers, and lifted his martini right away. He had long, strong fingers, but not pale and smooth the way I might imagine a scientist's would be. No, they were tanned and even callused, as if he did some kind of physical labor as well. Maybe setting up telescopes took more work than I had thought.

"What were these personality changes?" he inquired.

"Well, primarily reading *Variety*, from what I can recall."

He choked, then helped himself to a medicinal application of martini before replying, "Reading what?"

"*Variety*. And the *Hollywood Reporter*, apparently, along with some other entertainment industry websites. And the two of them hadn't—" I felt myself flush but persevered. "That is, Alex claimed they hadn't been intimate for some time."

"That actually follows with a good deal of what I've read on the topic. But the reading material...."

"I know." It hadn't made any sense to me, either. "What use would aliens have for Hollywood trade rags and gossip sites?"

"I'm not sure." Paul rubbed his chin absently, as if considering. Then he seemed to notice the spring rolls, and bent down and picked one up. "What's the young woman's profession?" he asked before taking a bite.

"Out-of-work actress, from what I gathered. Not exactly someone in a position to assist much in world domination, as far as I can tell."

"No, I wouldn't think so. Anything else?"

"My client believed the change had come over her after a visit to a tanning salon."

"'A tanning salon,'" Paul repeated, obviously nonplussed by that particular piece of information.

All along, I'd been hoping maybe the story wouldn't sound so crazy on repetition, but I reflected that it actually sounded worse. My companion's expression didn't change, but it didn't need to. He gave the distinct impression of someone who was struggling to be polite.

"The sort of place where they spray it on," I said, my voice sounding strained even to myself. "Look, don't you think I know how ridiculous all this sounds? Normally, I would have brushed it all off as just one of the left-field things that happens to me from time to time, but this can't all be a coincidence, can it? You coming into El Churro for directions, Otto telling me I had to come to this one hotel out of all the hundreds in L.A.?"

"How do I know this Otto even exists?"

"You tell him I most certainly do exist," came Otto's voice at my ear.

I started, spilling some of my pinot. Luckily, I had just picked it up from where it sat on the table, so most of the wine splashed on my hand and on the little cocktail napkin, and not on my clothes.

"What are you doing here?" I whispered fiercely.

"Checking in."

"Well, don't. This is hard enough as—"

"Is he here now?" Paul leaned forward over the

table that separated us, his eyes eagerly scanning the space above my head.

"Yes," I said. "But he's actually behind me, on the left side."

"Fascinating."

"You see?" Otto demanded. "At least someone appreciates me."

"That's because he doesn't know you the way I do. Anyway, don't you have better things you could be doing?"

"Yes, but I thought I should warn you that you were followed here."

"Followed?" I squeaked.

"Do keep your voice down. Yes, followed. If you look out toward the main lobby area, you'll see a suspicious individual loitering near the elevators."

I did as Otto suggested, and stared over Paul's shoulder and in the direction of the bank of elevators that led to the tower rooms. People milled about, going this way and that, but I saw at once that one man wearing a dark suit and an entirely unnecessary black overcoat never moved, but only stood in one spot, apparently engrossed in some sort of brochure. I say "apparently" because his gaze kept flickering in the direction of the lobby lounge...straight at me.

Immediately, I looked down.

"What's he saying?" Paul asked. "Did I hear you say you were followed? By whom?"

"How the hell would I know? I've never seen the guy before."

"What does he look like?"

I sneaked a quick peek and then lifted my glass of pinot and took a sip with what I hoped was an air of complete unconcern. "I can't really see his face too clearly. Tallish. Dark suit and a black overcoat."

"A black overcoat," Paul repeated in flat tones.

"Yes." A sudden thought hit me, and I said, "You're not telling me that this guy is a—a man in black, are you? Come on!"

"What else? Maybe there's more to this client of yours and his possessed girlfriend than you realized. At any rate, I think it's a good idea if we can find a discreet way to get out of here."

Otto said, "Very sensible. I think you should listen to him."

"What, and not your sterling advice?"

"Go!"

There were very few times in my life when Otto had outright commanded me—one being the time his shout of warning had kept me from getting hit by a car just as I stepped out into an intersection during my senior year of high school.

I stood and wrestled a couple of twenties out of my wallet. "Otto thinks we'd better leave."

Paul rose as well, and began reaching for his own wallet.

"Never mind that," I said. "We can settle up later."

"He's moving!" Otto hissed.

Sure enough, when I looked over toward the

elevators, I saw the black-coated individual coming in our direction, not running, not moving so quickly that he would attract any undue attention, but it was clear to me we were his intended destination.

Paul didn't miss a beat. "Not that way. Let's go out through the service entrance."

And he began to move as well, striding purposefully toward the bar. As I trotted along behind him, I realized he was actually headed toward a door to the right and a few yards behind the bar itself, which must lead to the kitchens. My suspicions were confirmed when I saw a waiter emerge through the door carrying a plate of sliders and one of the biggest orders of nachos I'd ever seen.

I risked a quick glance over my shoulder. "He's following us!"

Sure enough, the man in black had increased his stride and had now entered the lounge area.

"Excuse us," said Paul, and pushed past the waiter and on through the swinging door.

"Hey!" the waiter shouted. "You're not supposed to go in there!"

"So sorry," I mumbled as I slipped by. Then I had to pick up the pace, because Paul had begun to run as soon as we were out of the public eye.

The scent of hot grease and grilling meat hit my nostrils. It appeared that the lounge and the café shared the same kitchen space—at the end of a short hallway, we entered the kitchen proper.

Someone else shouted at us, but since they were

yelling in Spanish, I had no idea what they were saying. However, I guessed they weren't exactly welcoming us to the hotel.

"You have a car?" Paul asked, after glancing backward to make sure I was still behind him.

"Yes. What about yours?"

"Valet parking. It'd take too long to get the keys."

I nodded. "How do we get there?"

He pointed toward a glowing green "Exit" sign in the far wall of the kitchen. Just as well, because a group of kitchen workers was converging on us. None of them looked too thrilled to see us there. Well, I was less than thrilled to be there myself.

At least we had a lead on the mob, and so we hit the door running and came out in a dark alley that smelled as if they'd dumped about two months' worth of rotten broccoli back there. I wrinkled my nose. "Now what?"

He looked around, then pointed off to the left. "There's the parking structure. We'll have to see if there's a way in from this side."

And he took off running. I cursed my heeled boots under my breath and pounded after him, thinking that if Otto had had the prescience to tell me I needed to come to the Sheraton Universal, he at least could have told me to switch into some athletic shoes. After that, I didn't have much time to think about anything at all, because I heard the door bang against the wall behind us, followed by the sound of running feet.

"Stop!" an unknown voice bellowed at me. "Federal agent!"

Oh, shit. I didn't want to think what the penalties might be for resisting arrest or fleeing a government agent. Then again, it wasn't as if I'd been charged with anything. Hell, I didn't even know what I'd done wrong. Besides, Otto had told me to go.

So I was going.

The parking structure loomed ahead of us, its interior dimly glowing with the strange pinkish light that sodium vapor bulbs gave off. I didn't see any entrance, but the structure wasn't really enclosed—it had concrete pillars separated by stretches with dual rows of metal railings. As I watched, Paul reached out and grasped the top railing, and hauled himself up and over as gracefully as an Olympic gymnast propelling himself over a sawhorse. Easy for him— he had almost a foot on me and a much longer reach. Still, it was kind of amazing what you could do with fear motivating you.

I wrapped my hands around the cold metal and pulled myself upward. As I dangled there, Paul grabbed me by the biceps and yanked me the rest of the way. I stumbled against him but didn't have much time to think about how nicely solid he felt.

"Which level?" he demanded.

"The bottom."

"Figures."

The stairs were a few yards away. We rushed to the door and began hustling down the steps, which clattered so loudly under our footfalls that I thought the occupants of the entire hotel should be able to know where we were. Sure enough, less than a minute later, I heard the door above us clang open, and then footsteps began pounding down after Paul and me.

"Here," I said, as we reached the door at the lowest level.

He yanked it open and then waited for me to move ahead of him—made sense, since obviously he had no idea what my car looked like.

Somehow, it seemed much farther away than it had been when I parked it here less than a half hour earlier. But there it was, my shiny red Volvo sedan. I pushed the button on the remote to unlock the car.

"Inconspicuous," he commented.

"Well, I didn't know I was going to be using it to evade federal agents."

"Better give me the keys."

"Like hell!"

A door banged open, and feet began tramping their way toward us.

"Have you taken a course in defensive driving from ex-Secret Service agents?"

"Well, no."

"Then give me the keys."

Delaying any longer would get us caught. I bit back a retort and tossed him the keys. He caught them neatly in midair, and then opened the driver-side door and slid into the seat. I jumped into the passenger side and fastened the seatbelt.

I looked up from the seatbelt to see the man in black bearing down on us. I couldn't help letting out a frightened little squeak.

"Hold on," Paul said.

His foot went down on the accelerator, and the Volvo bolted out of the parking stall as if it had been goosed. The agent swerved to follow us. His hand reached for my door handle.

A clunk, and Paul engaged the door locks. I heard a muffled shout and saw the agent wince as he dropped back behind us. Maybe he'd just lost a few fingernails.

That wasn't enough to stop him, apparently, because I saw him reaching toward his shoulder. Reaching, and pulling out a deadly-looking firearm.

"He's got a gun!"

No response from Paul, except that the car surged forward, and then whipped around the turn up to the next level with a scream of brakes and a cloud of smoke worthy of any Hollywood street chase. I looked into the rearview mirror and saw the agent dropping back before he disappeared from sight.

"Taking the stairs," Paul said as he piloted the Volvo through another one of those rubber-burning turns. "Probably hopes he can head us off at one of the upper levels."

"Can he?"

A flicker of a smile. "He can try."

We hurtled upward as I prayed all the while that we wouldn't run into anyone else coming down the ramps, since Paul was taking the turns pretty wide in order to maintain our headlong momentum. On the last one, he swung out a little too far, and I heard a slight crunch and a tinkle of glass as the left rear bumper made contact with an Escalade that was sticking too far out of its parking space. Ouch. There went my good driver discount.

"Shouldn't we leave a note?"

Paul didn't bother to dignify the question with a response. Instead, he pointed the car toward the exit, which of course was blocked by one of those remote-controlled gates and watched over by an attendant in a kiosk. I didn't even have time to wonder where my ticket had gone—a blur of black came out of the stair-well, blocking our way. Jesus, had that agent *flown* up the damn stairs?

I thought I heard Paul mutter a curse under his breath, but he didn't slow down. Not even as the agent raised his gun and pointed it straight at us.

How the hell had I managed to fall in with the UFO community's answer to Dirty Harry?

Fear paralyzed me, kept me silent as we barreled down on the man. I clenched my jaw, waiting for the inevitable bullet to shatter the windshield. At the last second, though, he jumped out of the way, and we crashed through the slender arm of the gate as if it were made of Popsicle sticks. A few flying bits of debris hit the roof of the car and bounced off as Paul shot down the driveway, then onto the street. Luckily, the only real traffic there was either headed to the Sheraton or the Hilton a little farther up the hill, so it wasn't much work for him to maneuver around a few tour buses and SUVs.

"Which street is that?" he asked, as we barreled down on an intersection.

"Lankershim," I replied immediately.

"Is there an airport close to here?"

What, were we about to run off to South America together? But I didn't have my passport. "Burbank," I told him. "A couple of miles away. Turn right."

The light turned green just as we got to the intersection, and Paul swung the car around and began heading east. "What now?"

"Don't stay on Lankershim. After this next curve, it'll split off onto Cahuenga. Take that."

He nodded and did as instructed. I turned and looked behind us, but I couldn't see any signs of pursuit.

"Why the airport?" I asked.

"He knows what the car looks like. We'll leave it in long-term parking and get a rental."

These words were delivered so calmly and matter-of-factly that it took a second or two for them to sink in. What with the adrenaline-laced rush of pursuit and escape, I hadn't really stopped to think about what was happening. But now Paul Oliver, a man I barely knew, was talking as if this was just the beginning, as if from now on our fates were linked.

"I'm just supposed to leave my car there?"

"Yes."

"You run from the law much?"

A grim smile, although he never took his eyes off the traffic around us. "First time. But I know a few people who are pretty good at hiding themselves."

"Great," I said with a notable lack of enthusiasm. "Turn right on Verdugo, then left on Hollywood Way. That'll take us straight to the airport."

"Got it."

I slumped back in my seat and watched the businesses outside the window slide by. Whether it was circumstance, or fate, or just plain old rotten luck, it appeared I was now a fugitive.

CHAPTER FOUR

WE PULLED INTO THE ENTRANCE TO THE AIRPORT—
affectionately named after the late Bob Hope—
without further incident. I remained silent as Paul
guided the car around the perimeter of the parking
lots and brought us into one of the long-term areas.
No baggage to unload, of course. We simply got out,
and he came around and handed me the keys.

"Good car," he said.

I nodded. For some reason, my throat was a little
tight. It was dark outside, but not so dark that I
couldn't see the ding in the rear bumper from my
Volvo's encounter with the Escalade. I didn't even
want to walk around the front to see what breaking
through that security gate had done to the bumper
and the headlights.

Possibly sensing my mood, Paul didn't say
anything as we walked over to the terminal and then

followed the signs to the area where the car rental agencies were located. Otto was conspicuously absent, although I could have used some of his advice right about then. Maybe that frenzied dash out of the parking structure back at the Sheraton Universal had scared my spirit guide right out of this dimension. Whatever the reason, he obviously had decamped, and I was left to follow my own instincts, muddled as they were at the moment.

Some part of me thought the smart thing to do would be to walk away from Paul and call the police to turn myself in. How bad could the penalties be? No one had been hurt, after all. Yes, there had been some property damage, but I was ready to pay for that. Chalk it up to temporary insanity or something. Besides, all I'd really done was run when some random guy yelled at me that he was a federal agent. He hadn't even flashed a badge. How was I supposed to know he was legit?

However, my gut told me that going to the police would be a spectacularly bad idea. True, being a fugitive from the law was not something I'd envisioned when I left my house earlier this evening, but the pricking of my thumbs or my spider sense or whatever else you wanted to call it told me I needed to stick with Paul, that we really had stumbled onto something I couldn't walk away from.

So I nodded when he told me to hang back as he headed to the Alamo counter. It made sense; rental car places tended to get twitchy when unmarried couples tried to rent cars together. At least, that was what I'd heard. None of my relationships had ever lasted long enough for us to get to the "renting a car together" stage.

I loitered by a kiosk of brochures and pretended to be interested in horseback riding in Griffith Park. Actually, that sounded as if it could be a lot of fun, but I somehow doubted I'd be riding a horse any time soon—unless Paul couldn't manage to rent a car, and we'd have to try getting away from the feds on horseback.

He went out the door with the car rental agent, and I stiffened. Was he ditching me? Then I told myself to relax. They had probably just gone out to perform the inspection of the car, the one where they walk you around the vehicle and then try to up-sell you on the insurance. No doubt, he'd be back inside as soon as he could.

A few yards away, there was a small newsstand cum snack shop, and I spotted a refrigerated case with sodas and bottled water. I'd never been much of a soda drinker, but the water looked awfully good. Running away from federal agents was a good way to work up a thirst. Besides, getting something to drink would kill some time.

I'd just paid for two bottles of water when Paul returned. "Here," I said, and thrust one at him.

He appeared somewhat surprised that I'd thought of him, but he took the bottle and replied,

"Thanks. Well, we're set. I got a beige Camry—I thought that would be inconspicuous enough."

"I'll say." It was the type of car that every other person in Southern California seemed to drive. Something struck me, though. "What about the credit card?"

"What credit card?"

"The one you had to use to rent the car. Can't they —I don't know, trace you through that or something?"

A somewhat surprised smile. "Yes, 'they' probably could...except that I used a prepaid Visa card. It's not directly linked to my bank account, so it's much more difficult to trace."

"You in the habit of carrying those sorts of things around?"

He shrugged, then pointed at a door farther down the hall, out of line of sight for the rental car counter. "We can go out that way. As to your question, well, an acquaintance once told me those sorts of things could be invaluable in certain situations, so I've taken to carrying one for emergencies."

"An acquaintance."

"Yes. One I'll need to contact soon. But first things first."

I followed Paul through the door and out into the parking lot, where a beige Camry did in fact await us. Whatever was going on, I hoped it wouldn't involve my poor Volvo being left in that parking lot for more than a day or so. Yes, it was a long-term lot, so the car wouldn't attract any attention for awhile, but....

This would have been a lot easier if I'd known Paul better. Or at all, actually. With someone else, I might have been comfortable enough to express some of my misgivings, but as he was being almost preternaturally calm, cool, and collected in the face of adversity, I thought I should do the same. Even if I did feel like a bowl of Jell-O inside.

"How well do you know this area?" he asked as he clicked the remote to unlock the doors.

I waited until we were both inside and fastening our seat belts before I replied, "Well enough. One of my college roommates lives in Burbank, so I come out to visit every once in awhile when our schedules mesh." Those meet-ups depended more on Jess's schedule than mine, since she worked in merchandising for Disney and had a lifestyle that was a lot more high-powered than mine, but I guessed Paul didn't really need to know that.

"Good. Where's the closest electronics store? And would it be open?"

The clock on the radio told me it was 8:45. Scary to think that I'd met up with Paul Oliver only a little over an hour earlier. "There's a Best Buy up on Burbank Boulevard that we might make before it closes."

He didn't say anything, but merely guided the car out of the parking lot and in the direction I'd indicated. From there, it was only a mile or so to the shopping center where the store was located, but we still cut it close because of some extremely bad luck at a couple of lights. Despite that, we made it with five minutes to spare. I waited in the car while Paul carried out whatever transaction he'd planned. A few minutes later, he came back carrying a shopping bag, out of which he pulled a plastic clamshell case that contained one of those prepaid cell phones, the kind where you didn't need a contract.

"Let me guess," I said, as he pulled a Swiss Army knife off his keychain and began to slice the packaging open. "Not traceable."

"Precisely." And he extricated the phone, then set it on the console between the front seats and proceeded to open a second package, this one holding a car charger. "I'm not entirely certain that they're surveilling my phone, but it never hurts to be safe."

I probably didn't want to know, but decided to go ahead and ask anyway. "And exactly who are 'they'?"

He didn't answer immediately, instead plugging the charger into the cigarette lighter and connecting it to the phone. After a long pause, he said, "People you really don't want after you...or finding you."

Wonderful. "So what next?"

"How much cash do you have on hand?"

Ha. He was in for a bit of a surprise. "About fourteen hundred dollars, give or take."

That reply did seem to flap the imperturbable Dr.

Oliver. His head swiveled in my direction, and he said, "What?"

"My clients prefer to pay me in cash, for reasons that should be obvious enough. Although Mr. Jimenez does keep trying to persuade the IRS that my services should be a tax deduction, so he pays me by check." I grinned; that particular stratagem hadn't been working so well. At least, the last few times I'd finally gone on record and informed Mr. Jimenez that his creative bookkeeping would result in a terse letter from the Internal Revenue Service, which of course only proved to him that I really was able to see the future. Then again, it didn't take a psychic to know that playing fast and loose with the tax code the way he did was a surefire recipe for an audit. "Anyway, I'd meant to go to the bank, but what with everything going on, I just didn't. Good for us, though, right?"

"Very good for us," he agreed, and started up the car. "I have some cash, but nothing like that."

"And what do we need the cash for?"

"That should be obvious enough."

I waited for him to enlighten me.

He pulled back onto Burbank Boulevard, heading toward the freeway. "You can't go home, of course. I'm sure someone will be waiting for you. So the best solution is to find an inexpensive hotel or motel where we can regroup and I can attempt to make contact."

"Contact with whom?" Under other circumstances, I might have been a bit more anxious about spending a night in a hotel room with a man I'd just met, especially since I'd never been much of one for one-night stands. However, I knew Paul Oliver wasn't doing this as a convoluted way of trying to get me in the sack. If that was all he'd wanted, I was pretty sure he had a much nicer room back at the Sheraton Universal than wherever we were going to end up.

"An...acquaintance. Someone who might be able to help."

I didn't see how this mysterious acquaintance could get us out of the mess in which we were currently embroiled, but since I didn't have any better options to offer, I figured I might as well let Paul try.

"I know a place out in Pomona. They take cash and don't ask questions—at least, they didn't used to," I told him. "We need to head east."

Even though he was maneuvering us onto the on-ramp, he still managed to shoot a startled glance in my direction. I guess I didn't really give the impression of someone who knew all the cash-only, pay-by-the-hour dives.

I grinned. "Not what you're thinking, Dr. Oliver. I'm from Claremont—Pomona is the town next door. When I was in high school, the kids used to rent rooms at a couple of these motels when they wanted to party without anyone asking too many questions. Besides, I'm guessing Pomona is probably the last place anyone's going to be looking for us."

"Good strategy," he said. "I will admit to being something at a loss here in Southern California."

"Oh?" After all, I knew next to nothing about him, except that he was a double Ph.D., chased UFOs, and drove a mean getaway car. "So where are you from?"

"New Mexico."

If he was unfamiliar with Southern California, ditto for me and New Mexico. I'd always had a vague impression of the place as being overrun with New Age types and UFO hunters. Well, I supposed I'd been right on one count, anyway. Despite my profession, I didn't really buy into a lot of the whole New Age philosophy. I knew Otto existed because he'd shown up in an extremely inconvenient way the day I turned twelve, but as for the crystals and the Reiki and all the rest of it went, well, I could definitely leave it.

"Right," I said. "Roswell and all that."

"Actually, my parents owned a ranch about fifty miles outside of Santa Fe."

Paul hadn't struck me as the ranching type. Then again, a ranch might explain the calluses on his hands. But he had said "owned"—past tense.

As smoothly as if he'd done it a hundred times, he maneuvered the Camry over to the right and onto the long curving ramp to the 134 freeway, taking us east toward Pasadena and points beyond. After a brief silence, he went on, "We sold most of the land when my father died. I kept the house, but my mother moved into a retirement community in Santa Fe. Said she wanted to live someplace where someone would do for her for once." A corner of his mouth quirked, just a little. If I hadn't shifted in my seat so I was turned more toward him, I would have missed it altogether.

I didn't know exactly what to say. "I'm sorry about your father."

"It's all right. It was eight years ago. He was out driving fence posts, and he just went. Heart attack. At least he was outside, doing something he loved."

True enough, I supposed. Even though I didn't have any earthly idea of exactly what driving a fence post entailed, I thought it would be better to go that way, in the wind and the sun, and not in some hospital bed. Death didn't frighten me at all; I knew too much about what waited on the other side, knew that death was a transition and nothing more.

Pain, on the other hand....

"So is that how you got into astronomy?" I asked. The question probably sounded like what it was, an obvious attempt to change the subject, but I didn't see any point in dwelling on painful memories. "Big sky country and all that?"

"Technically, I think Montana is the real big sky country, but yes. Not much light interference out where we were. Where I am, that is."

I pictured him then, in some lonely farmhouse

stuck out in the middle of nowhere, surrounded by telescopes and star charts and whatever else it was that astronomers used. No wonder he wasn't used to Los Angeles.

"You said you were from Claremont," he commented. "Good colleges there."

His turn to change the subject, but I knew I was fair game as well. Maybe I should have been pleased that he wanted to learn a little more about me. Or maybe he just wanted to talk about me so we wouldn't have to talk about him.

"Actually, my father's a professor at Harvey Mudd," I replied. "Mechanical engineering."

"Really?" He sounded almost surprised, as if he couldn't believe a psychic could be connected to someone so...scientific. "We had a few graduate students come to the university from HMC."

"Is that where you teach?" I asked. "At the University of New Mexico?"

At once, his face went still, as if I had touched a nerve. "I used to teach there."

From his tone, I gathered that he really didn't want to discuss it. If I'd had Otto around, I might have been able to pick his brain—spiritually speaking, of course—but since Otto was still MIA, I decided to let it go. If we spent enough time together, maybe Paul would feel more comfortable discussing his past. In the meantime....

I glanced at the dashboard clock. Nine-twenty. We might be able to make it.

"When you get to La Verne, pull off at Fruit Street," I told him. "If we're going to be on the lam and hiding from the bad guys, I at least want to be able to do it with a change of clothes."

Paul watched in some bemusement as I met him at the cash register at the Kohl's in La Verne. "How did you even know this place would be open?"

"My mother never met a sale she didn't like. I've been dragged here more often than I'd like to say." And thank God for the store's late hours, and their perpetual discounts. I'd picked up a couple of pairs of jeans and a few tops, as well as a week's worth of underwear and a pair of flats. No more running from the feds in heels, that was for sure.

I noticed that Paul had done the same—that is, I spied some Levi's and shirts and a couple of packages of underwear and socks in the pile he was carrying. No shoes, but as he was already wearing some sturdy-looking lace-ups, he probably didn't need new ones.

He smiled then. "You are proving to be a valuable resource, Persephone O'Brien."

Valuable at getting you into trouble, I thought, but I only returned his smile. "And after this a stop at the drugstore for some toothbrushes and some other odds and ends, and then we should be set."

A nod, but he didn't say anything else, because it

was his turn to go up to the register. I watched him count his money carefully as he pulled it out of his wallet, and wondered how much cash on hand he really had. The prepaid Visa was probably tied up with the deposit for the rental car, so I guessed he didn't have enough money to be throwing it around. I hoped he wouldn't put up too much argument when I tried to pay for the motel. It was the least I could do, considering he wouldn't even be in this mess if it weren't for me. That is, I assumed it was because of me, and my connection with Alex Hathaway, the guy with the alien-possessed girlfriend. If the feds really had been after Paul and not me, they could have grabbed him at the Sheraton Universal any time they wanted

Luckily, he didn't protest when I paid for two days in advance. The motel was pretty much as I had remembered it, even though more than fifteen years had passed since the last time I'd set foot in the place. Maybe they'd swapped out the ugly brown and orange bedspreads for marginally better-looking blue and green ones, but the muddy close-pile carpet appeared to be the same, as was the lingering ghost-scent of old cigarettes, even though the room was supposed to be nonsmoking. I'd also made a half-hearted attempt to get us separate rooms, but Paul had only said tersely, "It's better if we don't separate," and I'd sighed and laid down the money for the one room.

When the clerk asked for our names, I'd briefly

considered putting us down as Mulder and Scully, then decided that was a bit too obvious. So Harry and LeAnne Smith occupied Room 52, which was luckily at the back of the building and not facing out on Foothill Boulevard, which could get pretty noisy.

I set down my Kohl's bag and the bag from the drugstore, which held toothbrushes and toothpaste and deodorant and all the other things I knew I couldn't live without. My beloved Clinique facial products were out of the question, but I knew I could get by with Olay in a pinch. At least the room had two double beds. I didn't think I was quite up to lying down next to Paul.

He immediately sat at the table by the window, and, after taking a quick peek outside and then drawing the curtains as tightly as he could, brought out the cell phone he'd bought. It must have been charged enough by then, because I saw him pull out the manual, enter a few codes, and then wait.

"Is it working?" I asked.

"Looks like it. I'm going to try texting my contact now."

"Can't you just call?"

"He doesn't believe in phone calls."

Lacking any kind of reply to that, I watched as Paul began tapping out a message with the kind of speed I'd previously only witnessed in preteens at bus stops. Those kids could text. I sidled up behind him and looked over his shoulder so I could see what he was typing.

Lunch tomorrow? What about Pad Thai—I know you liked #2.

What the hell?

"You're making a lunch date?" I demanded. "That's what all the secrecy is about?"

"No," he replied, his tone brusque. "We've set up a series of codes. This message lets him know which key to use to decrypt any future ones."

"Oh," I said. What was this, the *Bourne Identity*?

Then again, Paul obviously knew a thing or two about flying under the radar, and if he and his "contact" wanted to play spy with their decoder rings, then God bless 'em. "I thought you said this phone couldn't be traced."

"Yes, but we don't know anything about what kind if surveillance might be happening on his end."

Once again, I couldn't come up with a coherent response to that sort of comment, so I just shrugged and went on into the bathroom, taking the bag of drugstore goodies with me. I wasn't exactly thrilled about retiring for the night in front of Paul with no makeup on, but I knew my skin would give me grief if I didn't properly moisturize, so that was that. Reassuring myself that a man who spent his time chasing after little green men probably wouldn't notice whether I had mascara on or not helped a little.

By the time I emerged from the bathroom, he'd apparently gotten another message. Since he didn't even bother to look up at me, I felt a little more comfortable about leaning over his shoulder to read the text.

I shouldn't have bothered. Yes, the letters were familiar, but that was about it. They certainly didn't form any recognizable words. I saw a few numbers interspersed with the letters, again, in no discernible order.

"You know what that says," I said, my tone flat.

"Yes, of course."

"But how are you decrypting it without the key?"

"I do have the key." Paul closed the phone and slipped it into his jacket pocket, then rose from his chair. His gaze didn't flicker as he looked down at me, shiny face and all. I'd bought an oversized T-shirt off the clearance rack to sleep in, guessing that lingerie wasn't really the order of the day.

At least he didn't appear dismayed by my complete lack of cosmetics. "So where is it?" I asked, glancing down at the table. Its surface was noticeably clear of notebooks, cocktail napkins, or anything else that could have held such a code key.

"Here." He tapped his temple.

I realized my mouth was hanging open and quickly shut it. Sure, my toothbrushing had made me minty fresh, but that was no reason for me to stand there and look like a fish dangling from a hook. "You memorized it?"

"Yes. Memorized them, actually. We have five different systems set up, just in case."

Now, I had never thought of myself as anything

less than intelligent. My entire school career had consisted of honors courses, and I'd finished my master's in eighteen months instead of the standard two years. At the moment, however, I couldn't help feeling more like one of the kids who always sat in the back of class and ended up taking summer school in order to graduate on time.

However, since making a comment about his intellect seemed as if it would be grossly inappropriate, I settled for remarking, "You two must have a lot of spare time on your hands."

Another one of those half-smiles. "Enough." He shrugged out of his jacket and draped it on the back of the chair he'd been sitting in. "Are you done with the bathroom?"

"Yes." Maybe it was just my mind playing with me, but I got the distinct impression that he'd been a little dismayed by the length of time I'd spent attending to my nightly ablutions. That was nothing. He'd be in for a real shock if I decided to straighten my hair during any of our tenure together. "So what did it say? Your contact's message, that is."

"He's agreed to meet us tomorrow at eleven. I got the impression that's early for him."

"Where?" I had visions of going to some hermit's basement apartment, but somehow I doubted he'd be all that keen to have us over if he was as paranoid as all his actions so far seemed to suggest.

"Griffith Observatory."

"Huh?" I crossed my arms and frowned, trying to see the logic in the plan. "Isn't that awfully public?"

"Precisely."

Common wisdom did seem to dictate that people were less likely to start shooting up public places. Then again, you'd think with all the cloak-and-dagger behavior, there wouldn't be much chance of anyone even knowing we were meeting at Griffith Observatory in the first place.

"You do know how to get there, don't you?" Paul asked, for the first time looking a little worried.

"Oh, sure," I responded. Thank God his suspicious friend had set our meeting time for eleven; that way we might be able to avoid the worst of the inbound L.A. traffic. "Piece of cake."

"Good."

And he went off to the bathroom, while I decided it was probably a good idea to climb into bed. I took the one farthest away from the window. If anyone did try to invade our room in the middle of the night, I figured Paul was better equipped to fend them off than I.

I laid my head on the pillow and shut my eyes, trying very hard not to think about what one of those television investigative report ultraviolet cameras would probably reveal if it were run over the bed. Actually, the sheets did feel and smell clean. It could have been worse.

How, I wasn't exactly sure. After all, here I was, on the run from some mysterious government agent, on the trail of what might or might not be an alien conspiracy, shacked up with a man I had just met... only not in a good way. No, we might as well have been Ricky and Lucy with our nicely separated double beds. No hanky-panky going on there, that was for sure.

I heard Paul emerge from the bathroom and cracked an eyelid. Not that I'd really expected him to come waltzing out in his skivvies and nothing else, but you never know. He was wearing a plain white T-shirt and a pair of sweatpants that I hadn't noticed in the pile of clothing he'd purchased from Kohl's. Still, even though he was perfectly covered up, the clothes showed what the sport coat and khakis had hidden—a flat stomach, arms with a decent amount of muscle, although not the artificial, hyper-attenuated type you saw on guys who spent their entire waking lives at the gym. No, those arms had most likely come from driving fence posts and whatever else the family ranch had demanded of him.

A certain warmth started in my stomach and began to spread lower, and I closed my eyes. Ridiculous. He hadn't shown the slightest bit of interest in me, and here I was getting all worked up because of the way his arms looked. And his stomach. And his ass, to be perfectly honest.

Oy.

A creak of bedsprings, and then he said, "All right if I turn off the lights?"

"Fine," I mumbled.

He seemed to hesitate, but then a few seconds later, the room went dark. From a few feet away, I heard the sound of sheets rustling as he apparently attempted to find a comfortable spot in the well-used bed. "Good night, Persephone."

"Good night, Paul," I answered, and hoped I sounded reasonably normal.

A silence fell, only occasionally broken by the sound of the traffic from Foothill Boulevard. I wondered if he was listening closely, trying to gauge whether I was asleep or not. If only. As tired as I was, sleep seemed very far away at that moment. After all, what if he snored?

What if *I* snored?

His voice came to me, calm and reassuring in the darkness. "We're perfectly safe here. The best thing we can do is get a good night's sleep. After all, we don't know what we're going to face tomorrow."

As comments went, it wasn't the sort to exactly inspire restful sleep, but somehow I found I didn't mind so much. I made a mumbled sound of affirmation and rolled over on my side. If the aliens or feds or whomever somehow did manage to find us, I had a feeling Paul could handle the situation.

All I had to do was keep my libido in check and not blow it. So far, he seemed almost impressed by me. I wanted to keep it that way. The best thing to do now would be to follow his advice and fall asleep.

So I did.

CHAPTER FIVE

TO MY SURPRISE, I ACTUALLY OVERSLEPT. PAUL WAS already up and showered by the time I staggered out of bed. I supposed the excitement of the previous day had taken more out of me than I'd thought. But we still had plenty of time to make our rendezvous, even with having to get breakfast before we set out for Griffith Park.

The day promised to be cooler than it had been earlier in the week, with lowering clouds and spotty drizzle, so I was glad I'd picked up a lightweight blazer from one of the sales racks at Kohl's. I pulled it a little more tightly around me as we locked the motel room and headed down to the car. We'd already agreed to grab a bite at the Carrow's down the street from the motel, and there didn't seem to be much for either of us to say as Paul drove the half-mile to the restaurant.

He ordered coffee and I ordered tea, and an uneasy little silence fell. I pretended to be absorbed in reading my menu, but I noticed him glancing at his watch and frowning.

"It's all right," I said then. "We'll make it there in plenty of time. It's actually better if we wait a bit so traffic has time to clear."

"That's not it," he replied, and glanced out the window before focusing back on me. "I was supposed to be giving a lecture right now."

Oh, damn. I'd almost forgotten that he was here in Southern California in an official capacity, that he'd essentially bailed out on what had to have been an important gig. "I'm sure if you explained—"

"I already did. I sent the symposium chairman a text while you were in the shower, apologizing but saying that some important personal business had come up. Still, I don't like reneging on my obligations."

"Sorry," I murmured. Probably he hadn't meant to make me feel guilty, but I couldn't help the wave of self-reproach that went over me just then. I should have left well enough alone, told Otto to go stuff himself. And just where the hell was Otto, anyway? Nice of him to get me into this mess and then take himself off to another plane of existence. I wished there were some Bureau of Spirit Guides where I could make a complaint and ask for a replacement case worker or something, but I knew that wasn't going to happen.

"Don't beat yourself up." Paul's tone had gentled a little, as if he'd just realized he might have sounded a bit too harsh. "I wanted to know about this. It's the timing that's unfortunate."

"That's for sure." And then I sat up a little straighter, as I suddenly remembered I had my own obligations to deal with. Not as pressing as Paul's, but I did have two clients coming to see me this afternoon. Thank God it was only two. Fridays were always the lightest days for me.

The waitress showed up then with our drinks, and we placed our orders—steak and eggs for him, a vegetarian omelette for me. Not that I was a vegetarian, but I'd never been big on eating meat in the morning. Obviously Paul, raised on a ranch as he'd been, didn't have the same scruples.

After she'd left, I asked, "Can I borrow your phone?"

"Why?"

I explained about my clients. He listened and nodded, but said, "It's probably better if you don't use this phone to contact them. We have no idea whether they're under surveillance."

"You don't think *all* of my clients are under surveillance, do you? That's a bit much."

For a second or two, he didn't say anything, but only worked away at customizing his coffee—two little containers of half and half, no sugar. He swirled the resulting toffee-colored liquid with a spoon and replied, "Persephone, I'm afraid you don't have a very good idea of what 'they're' capable of."

I didn't much like the sound of that...but I also didn't like his insinuation that I was some innocent who didn't know what was going on in the world. "Hey, I've seen Oliver Stone movies, you know."

He laughed then, and shook his head. "Not quite the same thing, but point taken. Anyway, I think it's a better idea if you use a pay phone. They'll still be able to trace the call back here if they really are tracking your clients, but we should be all right if we keep on the move."

Oh, that was really reassuring. And a great idea, except in Southern California pay phones were about as rare as the El Segundo Blue butterfly, what with everyone's defection to cell phones pretty much complete. But then the waitress came by again, ostensibly to refresh Paul's coffee, although I got the impression she just wanted to ogle him a bit more. He hadn't seemed to notice her giving him some serious sidelong glances under her heavily mascaraed lashes, but I sure had. Some territorial instinct made me want to slap the coffee pot right out of her hands, which was just silly. I didn't have any claim on Paul.

But I managed to keep my voice level as I inquired whether there was a payphone, and it turned out there actually was one, down the hall by the bathrooms. So I excused myself—after the waitress was safely away—and made my calls.

Normally, I would have been worried about getting an actual person on the line, but my Friday clients were skittish entertainment industry types who let everything go to voicemail. In the past, that behavior had irritated me to no end, although I was certainly glad of it now. At any rate, it was simple enough to leave a message saying I'd had a family emergency come up and that I'd let them know about rescheduling when I could. Not that I expected them to take me up on the offer. Michael Horowitz had his entire life set by clockwork, and if he couldn't see me at 3:45 sharp on Friday afternoon, well, then, he'd just wait until the next week. And Lindsay MacIlvey probably was so embroiled in meetings that she'd barely notice not being able to come in and see me. Knowing her, she'd simply schedule a few more meetings to fill the gap.

Hollywood types could be exhausting, but they did pay well.

The waitress was loitering at the table when I returned. I practically had to push past her so I could slide into the booth, so I sent her a sideways glare. She pretended not to notice and went on, "Oh, New Mexico? Like, where they have the Grand Canyon and everything?"

I saw Paul wince and guessed I didn't have to worry about too much competition from the waitress. Not that I could claim to know him all that well, but what little I did know told me he probably didn't have much patience for ignorance.

"Actually, that's Arizona," he said. He looked over at me and asked, "Were you able to make your calls?"

"Yes, thanks." Some devilish impulse prompted me to add, "You really need to be more careful with your cell phone, dear. We're not always lucky enough to be someplace where there's a payphone."

Both Paul and the waitress caught the "dear," but whereas she scowled and then mumbled, "I'll check on your order," before stalking away, he only grinned and shook his head.

A little glint I hadn't seen before flickered in his hazel eyes before he said, "Yes, dear," and picked up his coffee.

I fought back a grin of my own as I reached for a packet of sugar. For some inexplicable reason, I suddenly didn't feel quite so nervous about the day ahead.

Griffith Park, the site where the Observatory was located, already had cars and people swarming the place when we got there, even though we were a little early and the place wouldn't officially open for ten more minutes. Still, we managed to snag one of the last parking spaces in the lot at the top of the hill, which made me breathe a secret sigh of relief. You could park farther away on one of the roads leading up to the Observatory, but from any of them it was quite a hike, and my feet were still tired from all the chasing around in heels I'd done the night before.

"So what does this guy look like?" I asked after we'd locked the car and joined the throngs massing outside the front entrance in anticipation of the doors opening. I'd forgotten how busy the place could be, even on a weekday; schools regularly brought up busloads of students, and today was no exception. I winced a little at the noise emanating from one particularly boisterous group of fifth-graders and tried to remind myself that I'd been that young once.

"I have no idea," Paul replied.

"What?"

His gaze swept the area briefly before returning to me. "We've only communicated through texts and a couple of forums online. I've never met him in person."

"So how do you know he's who he says he is?" I crossed my arms and made my own quick scan of the crowds around us. No one looked suspicious, or even like a government agent in disguise, but that didn't mean much...although I guessed the man who had chased us through the parking structure at the Sheraton Universal probably hadn't disguised himself as a harried elementary-school teacher.

"I suppose I don't," Paul said, but he didn't appear all that worried. "If this has all been an elaborate ruse to gain my confidence, however, I'll be surprised."

"What makes you say that?"

"Up until now, my movements have been very easy to track." That glint was back in his eyes. "I don't do much to conceal my activities. I speak at symposiums and conferences. I do book signings. Anyone who wanted to find me or communicate with me really wouldn't have to go to the elaborate lengths my contact has gone."

"You wrote a book?" I inquired, a little impressed despite myself.

"You've never heard of *Investigating the Unknowable*?"

I shook my head.

"*Intersections of Belief*?"

I lifted my shoulders.

"Oh, well," he said, in deprecating tones. "They're quite popular in some circles. At any rate, within the UFO community, I'm fairly well-known. No need for cloak and dagger. A federal agent could have come along and picked me up at any time, which leads me to believe my unseen friend is most definitely not working for the government."

I had to admit that argument made some sense. "So if you've never met, how is he going to know who we are?"

"I assume from my book jacket photograph, or the photograph on my website, or—"

Raising my hands in mock surrender, I said, "Okay, okay, get it. You're a big celebrity."

He shrugged. "Well, I don't know about that."

"Big enough. So where are we supposed to meet, exactly?"

Paul smiled then. A few of the women in our vicinity shot him admiring glances, but he appeared not to notice. If he had been one of the other men of my acquaintance, I probably would have said that he affected not to notice, but he truly didn't seem to realize the effect he had on the female half of the population. Too busy looking for aliens, probably.

He replied to my question by asking another one. "Where else but at the Café at the End of the Universe?"

It was far too soon after that omelette to even think of eating anything else, but I did get some iced tea, and Paul bought bottled water so as to justify our taking a table up against one of the bank of windows that gave the café a breathtaking panorama of Hollywood, downtown Los Angeles, and beyond. The overcast had lifted a little, but the breeze coming off the ocean was still brisk.

So soon after opening, the café was almost deserted. Later, after people had worked up a thirst from tromping up and down the Observatory's innumerable stairs, the place would collect quite a crowd. Right then, however, except for a young woman with a laptop and an enormous cup of coffee, and another woman with improbable heels who was nursing a soda and rubbing the ball of her foot, we had the place to ourselves.

A minute ticked by, and then another. I glanced at my watch. The contact was almost ten minutes late.

"What if he doesn't come?" I asked.

"Then I suppose I can take you to a planetarium show," Paul replied imperturbably.

"Seriously."

"I am being serious. I've heard they're very good."

If it had been anyone else, I probably would have given him a good dose of annoyed side-eye. But, despite having slept in the same room together, I didn't feel as if I knew Paul well enough to do such a thing. I settled for scowling and sipping at my iced tea as I stared out at the L.A. skyline. Far off in the distance, I thought I saw the faintest glimmer of gold as the clouds near the coast parted and allowed a few rays of sunlight to catch in the waves off Santa Monica.

"Who's she?" came an unfamiliar voice, and I turned away from the window to see a scruffy-looking individual with a few days' growth of beard and wearing an oversized military surplus jacket staring down at us.

"This is Ms. O'Brien, whom I mentioned in my message," Paul said.

The young man—who was probably in his middle twenties at most, even with the beard—

summoned up a scowl that put mine to shame. "I didn't know you were going to bring her."

"Hi, nice to meet you," I said, and stuck out a hand.

He recoiled as if I had hit him with a stun gun, and instead pulled out the table's free chair so he could sit down. Pointedly ignoring me, he said to Paul, "How do you know she can be trusted?"

Of all the— "I'm right here, you know," I remarked, withdrawing my hand so I could cross my arms.

"We wouldn't know about any of this if it weren't for her," Paul pointed out. Although his voice still sounded level, a little twitch at the edge of his jaw line seemed to indicate he was just a bit irritated.

The stranger shrugged. "Okay, fine." He swung the battered leather messenger bag he wore over one shoulder onto the table. I barely had time to get my iced tea out of the way. A second later, and it would have been splattered all over my front.

A few choice words rose to my lips, but I decided it was probably better for me to keep quiet and not provoke him. No wonder the guy hid out on message boards and forums and didn't get out much—I'd seen better manners from a two-year-old.

He pulled a laptop out of the messenger bag, opened up the computer, and began typing in some rapid-fire commands. What exactly he was doing, I couldn't tell, because the strings of characters that moved across the screen didn't look like anything I'd ever seen before. Not that that necessarily meant much, since my level of computer skills allowed me to set up spreadsheets for my business and hack some basic CSS for the WordPress install on my website, and that was about it.

"There's been a lot of chatter," he said. "You two stirred something up. Sounds like they've got people all over L.A. looking for you."

Wonderful. So much for doing a little Nancy Drew work and then heading home at the end of the day. I knew that Ginger's and my schedules didn't always overlap, so most likely she probably hadn't yet even realized that I hadn't come home last night, but if I were absent too much longer, she'd notice I was missing. And since Ginger wasn't the type to sit around and do nothing, she very likely would call the police.

Or, even worse, my mother.

I shuddered a little and made myself focus on the scruffy stranger—who, I just realized, had never even told us his name.

"Any concrete leads?" Paul asked.

"Not that I can tell. They searched her apartment and her office, but I don't think they've found anything. They're more than a little pissed at the way you disappeared into thin air."

Well, that was something. Who knew I had such a talent for a life of crime? Maybe I'd gone into the wrong line of work. Psychic powers could probably be a big asset when robbing banks or running Ponzi schemes.

"Good," said Paul, with a sort of grim satisfaction. Then, "Persephone, why don't you explain what brought you to see me?"

I really didn't want to, not with the way I could practically feel the irritation pouring off the stranger in waves. Funny how I could sense his emotions so easily, when Paul might as well have been a closed book. That was just how it worked—my abilities ebbed and flowed based on the vibrations of those around me, and Paul was one of those I tended to regard as a neutral energy, one that didn't give off any discernible tells. Unlike this young man, whose name I suddenly knew was Jeff Makowski, and who I also knew ran his underground operations from a ramshackle Craftsman house in the Silverlake district.

"I thought you already told him," I protested.

"Just the bare bones. Go on."

A strong pull of my iced tea to fortify me, and then I said, "Well, *Jeff*, I had a client come to see me yesterday"—he blinked when I said his name, but otherwise didn't react—"And he told me his girlfriend was possessed by an alien...." From there I went into as complete a description of my encounter with Alex Hathaway as I could remember.

When I got to the part where Alex said his girlfriend had changed after getting a spray tan, Jeff held up a hand to stop me. "A spray tan."

"That's what he said."

Jeff drummed his fingers on the tabletop and looked over at Paul. "Thoughts?"

"Not sure."

"Could be something in the tanning spray. Easy way to get into our system, through the pores. The aliens could have infected the spray with a virus that allows them to infiltrate a human's system—"

"You mean like the black oil?" I cut in. It had been a recurring plot device in *The X-Files*, a gooey substance the aliens used to infect people with some sort of mind- and body-altering virus.

Both men's heads swiveled toward me, staring as if I were the one who had suddenly sprouted antennae.

"Hey," I said, "you're not the only ones who watched *The X-Files*, you know."

From Jeff I got a sense of extremely grudging respect, while Paul was still a blank—although he did give me an encouraging nod.

"Okay," Jeff said. "So we've got the possibility of the spray at a tanning salon being contaminated with an alien virus. Do you know which one?"

"Which one what?"

"Which tanning salon she went to." The exasperation was back. He gave me a glance of narrow-eyed irritation, as he added, "Try to keep up."

I didn't have time to count to ten, so instead I sipped my iced tea. That way, I wouldn't risk throwing the cup at his head. "I'm afraid my session with Mr. Hathaway wasn't that in-depth."

"I'll see if I can look him up. You have an address?"

"No. Since I didn't charge him for the session, I didn't get any more information than his name. I did get the impression that he was local, so I'm guessing the salon his girlfriend went to was also in the area."

"I'll look him up, see if I can narrow it down."

He began tapping away again, and I lifted my eyebrows at Paul. He only shrugged, but something in the tilt of his head told me he expected me to show some patience. All right, I'd try to be patient, but if Mr. Makowski started slinging insults again, I wouldn't be responsible for my actions.

"Uh-oh."

Both Paul and I looked questioningly at him. He stopped typing and turned the laptop around so we could both see the screen.

"That your guy?"

I stared at the image, fighting the sick sensation that rose in my stomach. The face was slack and pale, bloodless. At first glance, you barely saw the black hole in his temple, or the ring of livid flesh that surrounded it.

Now I understood why I had sensed that wave of cold when Alex's shoulder brushed mine. I'd known something terrible was about to happen, but that could have meant a variety of things, from a fatal car crash to an IRS audit. And while I didn't feel quite ready to acknowledge the connection between his visit with me and his subsequent murder, it was clear that he hadn't lived more than a few hours after I had spoken with him.

The omelette somersaulted in my gut, and I stood up from the table. I knew I had to get some fresh air or risk being sick right then and there. Without a word, I rushed for the door and then made my way out onto the terrace that ran alongside the west wall of the cafe. A cool breeze, tangy with ocean salt, washed over my face, and I took in deep gulps of air, willing the food to stay down, trying with all my might to keep that image of Alex Hathaway's blank, dead face from my mind. I wasn't very successful at the latter, although the nausea subsided after a few seconds.

"Persephone."

I glanced over my shoulder and saw Paul standing a few feet away.

"Are you all right?"

I nodded. "I'm—well, 'fine' isn't exactly the right word, but I'll manage. It was just—unexpected."

For a few seconds Paul didn't say anything. He stepped toward me, then hesitated. "The police report says he was found this morning, but apparently he was killed yesterday in the late afternoon."

"I know."

A flicker of surprise moved over his features. "You saw the time of death?"

"I didn't have to." I shifted so I faced him fully.

There were a few people out on the terrace, but none of them were close enough to hear what we were saying. "I knew when he left my office that he didn't have long to live."

"You never told me that."

"Because I hoped I was wrong." I shoved my icy fingers into my jacket pockets. "I'm not one hundred percent accurate. I make mistakes. Not often, but I do. And so when I felt the cold when I touched him, I tried to tell myself it was nothing."

"Couldn't you have warned him?" There was no reproach in his voice that I could hear, only a desire to understand my actions.

"I could have—and I doubt he would have believed me, considering I struck out pretty spectacularly during our session. Anyway, if I've learned anything, it's when it's your time, you go. This isn't like giving advice on whether to go out on a second date or buy a certain stock. Death can't be cheated."

Again he was silent. After a pause, he nodded. "All right. Are you ready to go back in?"

"Sure, as long as Jeff doesn't bring up any more show-and-tell. And just how did he get that photo, anyway? It had to have come from the LAPD's servers."

"And I'm sure he'd like to know how you learned his name," Paul replied, looking unruffled. "I suppose you both will just have to acknowledge that you have certain...talents...and leave it at that."

"Fair enough."

I followed him back inside the cafe and resumed my seat. To my surprise, Jeff seemed rather subdued. I'd been sure he'd mock me for my precipitous flight from the table, but maybe even he had his limits.

"Right," he said, as if I hadn't interrupted the conversation at all. "I got the address, and it turns out there are four tanning salons within a quarter-mile radius of Alex Hathaway's apartment. One called SunGold, another called Paradise Tanning, one named Golden Age, and a day spa called Lotus."

I must have let out a little sound of surprise, because both men shot questioning glances in my direction.

"Er—I go to Lotus," I explained, and then, as they sent disbelieving looks at my fish-belly-pale skin, "Not for tanning. I get my eyebrows done there."

"Eyebrows," Jeff repeated, as his own lifted slightly.

"Good eyebrows are very important," I assured him, and he made a sound of disgust.

"So you know the people there," Paul cut in.

"Yes. I've been going for the past two years."

"Good." He reached into his jacket pocket and pulled out his cell phone, then slid it across the table toward me. "I think it's time you made an emergency eyebrow appointment."

CHAPTER SIX

I STARED AT PAUL FOR A FEW SECONDS, THEN BLINKED. "Um, what happened to not using your phone because they might be able to trace it back through one of my contacts?"

"Would they have any way of knowing you've frequented this spa?"

He actually had a point there. Information about my clients could be easily gleaned from the laptop back at my apartment, since I kept fairly extensive records for tax purposes. However, anything personal, whether pertaining to my dentist, my hairstylist, or Ula, the genius at Lotus who tended to my brows, stayed on my phone. So unless the feds—or whoever they were—had been tailing me for weeks, I was pretty certain they had no idea who did my hair, or my toes, or my teeth cleanings. And since we'd already tentatively established that no one had paid any attention to me until Alex Hathaway had showed up on my doorstep, I guessed I was in the clear on this one.

"Probably not," I admitted. "So I make an appointment...and then what?"

"Get a sample of the spray tan fluid," Jeff said immediately. "I have some people who can analyze what's in it if we can lay our hands on some."

"And what if it's not Lotus, but one of the other salons?"

"Then we'll try again," Paul replied. "But it makes the most sense to start with a place that's familiar to you and work our way from there."

That argument made some sense, but I still wasn't thrilled about the situation. Somehow, things had seemed more distant, less real, when all I was doing was hiding out in a motel in Pomona and refraining from using my cell phone or going back to my apartment. But the image of Alex Hathaway's dead face had brought it all back that this was real, that someone—or some*thing*—had raised the stakes pretty damn high. Also, I had a hard time believing that Badri, the stunning Persian woman who owned Lotus, had anything to do with alien plots and government cover-ups. However, I sort of guessed it wouldn't be too hard to slip someone a topical Mickey. After all, Badri didn't even handle the spray-tan side of the operation; her assistants did that.

"All right," I said. An idea had begun to form in

my head, one I thought might just work. "I'll give it a try."

Jeff melted away to his hideout in Silverlake with barely a goodbye. Not that I was too sad to see him go. He made sure to see Paul and me off, as if he didn't want us to know what kind of car he was driving or which direction he would go once he reached the bottom of the hill. I refrained from mentioning that I already knew the number of his house and the name of the street where it was located. Things came to me that way sometimes, in flashes of blinding clarity. At other times, I needed the cards, or Otto.

Otto, who was still conspicuously absent. Maybe he'd decided this one was a little too close to home and so was leaving me to fly solo. But if that were the case, then why had he sent me to see Paul in the first place? If I'd learned anything in my years of being a psychic, though, it was that some questions always remained unanswered. Only time would tell if Otto's disappearance was one of them.

Paul parked our rented Camry a few blocks away from Lotus, down a side street. He'd been silent on the drive over, except to ask for clarification on some of my directions. In the middle of the day, it wasn't quite as difficult to navigate the streets between Griffith Park and West Hollywood, but it had still taken us almost a half-hour to go those few miles. We lucked out by having someone pull away from the curb just as we turned the corner, and he neatly maneuvered the car into the space the much bigger SUV had left behind.

"So what exactly do you have planned?" he asked, just as I reached for the passenger-side door handle. As usual, he sounded calm and unruffled, but something in his expression seemed to indicate he might actually be a little worried about me going into the spa without any backup.

"It's a surprise," I told him, and reached up to adjust my sunglasses with my free hand. "Trust me— I'm just going to work the L.A. angle."

His brows knotted as he apparently attempted to puzzle through that one. While he was occupied, I opened the car door and got out.

The main reason I hadn't wanted to tell him about my plan was that I didn't want him, the double-doctorate with the overwhelming brain power, to start poking holes in it. As it was, I had just enough sheer nervous energy carrying me along to keep me going, down the sidewalk and out onto Santa Monica Boulevard, where I turned to the left and passed a few storefronts before entering Lotus' reception area and waiting room.

Everything there had been carefully designed to be soothing, from the warm cocoa color on the walls to the fountain with its floating lotus blossoms under a glass-block skylight in the far corner. I felt far from soothed, however, as I made my way past two glossy-looking women who were waiting on the buff-colored couches, and on to the reception desk.

Hoping they wouldn't realize I'd gotten my entire outfit off the clearance rack at Kohl's, I removed my sunglasses and smiled down at Paz, the receptionist.

"Persephone!" she exclaimed, widening eyes made even wider by perfectly applied false lashes and cat-eye liner. She glanced over at her computer screen, then typed a few commands and did a quick scroll-up, obviously looking up my account. "I thought you weren't coming in until next Thursday."

"I wasn't, but I've had something very important come up. Is Badri available?"

"Let me check." Paz picked up the phone and dialed what I guessed was the extension in Badri's office. "Badri? I have Persephone O'Brien here, and she needs an immediate consult. Is it all—" She broke off, and then nodded. "Of course." After hanging up, she said, "She'll be right out."

Almost as soon as Paz had finished speaking, Badri appeared. Her age was something she'd managed to conceal from everyone, including me, and could have been anything between thirty and fifty. There was something timeless about her elegant features, and she always wore classic clothing that seemed to transcend trends. In other words, she almost always made me feel like a complete schlump, and my bargain-rack attire wasn't exactly helping at the moment. On the other hand, she seemed to find something fascinating about having a bona fide psychic as one of her clients and always went out of her way to be polite to me.

"Persephone!" she exclaimed, and extended a pair of perfectly manicured hands. "What is it I can do for you today?"

"I need some expert advice on a very important matter." I hesitated, then looked quickly at the women in the waiting room and back at Badri.

She got the message immediately. "To my office. Here we go."

So I followed her down the hallway, past the rooms where women were getting massages or body wraps or facials or any of the myriad services the spa offered to make us all better conform to current standards of beauty. Badri's office was located at the end of the corridor, in a large room decorated in the same exquisite taste as the rest of the facility. Here, though, I saw personal touches in the form of framed Persian textiles on the walls, and sculptures that also must be Persian, though my knowledge of world art wasn't all that extensive and I couldn't be completely sure. She indicated that I sit down, and took her own seat behind a desk of warm mahogany.

"So what is it?" she inquired, with what she probably thought was a surreptitious glance at my left hand. "Should I be offering congratulations?"

I stared at her blankly for a moment, then managed a quick laugh. "Oh, no. Not that. I've, well —actually, I've been offered a reality show."

In any other town, such a pronouncement would most likely have been met with skepticism, if not downright derision. But here, where everyone could be a star if they had the right connections, it probably seemed completely plausible. After all, with the multitude of reality shows currently populating the all those rapidly multiplying cable channels and streaming services, didn't it make sense to have one that focused on an L.A. psychic?

"But that is wonderful!" she exclaimed. "How very exciting for you!"

"Yes, it is," I replied. "However, the producers think—that is, they'd like me to be spruced up a little. You know, a little polish."

"Ah," she said. Of course she was far too polite to say out loud that she agreed with them, but it didn't take a psychic to know privately she concurred.

"One of the things they mentioned was a spray tan," I continued.

"Oh, excellent. That would give you a nice, healthy glow."

"True," I allowed. "I know I'm a little pasty for L.A. The problem is that I have sensitive skin. Really sensitive."

"Not to worry. We use the highest-grade formula, the best—"

"I'm sure you do. But I was wondering...would it be possible for me to get a sample of the tanner you use? I'd really like to take it to my dermatologist, have him test it for me. Just to be sure," I added, as Badri started to open her mouth again, no doubt to protest that their tanning ingredients wouldn't cause a reaction on even the most sensitive skin.

"Well, it is most unusual—"

"I know. And normally I wouldn't ask. But this is a big deal for me, and I really want to do what the producers want. I just don't want to harm my skin."

"Of course," she said, and smiled, although it looked a little stiff. "This I can do for you. If you can give me a moment?"

"Sure," I replied, and waited as she got up from her desk and went out the door. I let out a sigh of relief. Crazy as it had seemed when I first cooked it up, it looked as if my plan might just work after all.

Of course, we could be on the wrong track, and Alex Hathaway's alien-infected girlfriend could have gone to a completely different salon. But, as Paul had said, we had to start somewhere, and I could prob-ably use this ploy at the other places if necessary. And if my life ever got back to normal, and I did return here to get my brows done, I could always say the deal had fallen through. I worked with enough entertainment industry types to know that sort of thing happened all the time.

After a few minutes, Badri returned, holding a plastic vial filled with golden liquid.

"Here it is," she said, and extended her hand. "Make sure you keep it very tightly sealed—Dita said it can stain clothing and upholstery quite badly if it is spilled."

Dita, I knew, was one of the assistants, but I'd never worked with her. Smiling, I took the vial from Badri. "Thank you so much. I've already talked to my dermatologist, and he's going to see me first thing tomorrow morning. So I should know fairly soon if I can set up a tanning appointment."

"Excellent. And if there's anything else—a wrap to firm up, an oxygen facial—"

"You'll be the one I call," I promised, as I tucked the vial into the inner pocket in my purse.

"And possibly a credit on the show?"

"If I can." By that point, I was feeling horrible about all the lies I had told her, but what else was I supposed to do? I had to have that sample, and if the cost was a little false hope, well, I could live with that. Better that than the risk of other people getting infected.

Or killed.

I thanked Badri again and left her office, and nodded at Paz as I passed through the reception area and went outside. I speed-walked back toward the car, purse clutched tightly against me. It would be just my luck to get mugged at this point, although I had to admit the odds for that sort of thing at this time of day and in this neighborhood were pretty low.

But I made it back to the car without incident and slid into my seat, then made a point of locking the door as soon as I could.

Paul had been sending a text on his phone when I entered the car. He continued with the message, tapping away furiously, then closed the phone and turned to me. "Did you get it?"

In answer, I reached into my purse and held up the vial. "Piece of cake."

"You are truly an amazing woman," he said, and it didn't sound as if he was teasing me.

I shook my head, but he continued, even as he turned the key in the ignition and started up the car. "No, really. You've been through things in the last twenty-four hours that would be enough to put anyone off, and yet you seem completely unfazed by it all."

"Oh, I'm fazed," I told him. "Trust me. But I couldn't just walk away from this, could I?'

"Definitely not after that shootout with the agent," he replied, with what looked like an actual grin pulling at his mouth. "Even so, I want you to know I appreciate all the help you've given me."

Compliments had been few and far between as of late, and I really didn't know how to respond to his praise. I just lifted my shoulders and said, "So what now? Meet with Jeff and hand over the loot?"

"Something like that. He wants us to meet him."

"Let me guess. Dodger Stadium."

Paul laughed. "No, someplace a little less public this time. Apparently he has some contacts at a lab out in"—he squinted down at the phone, which was lying in his lap—"Fontana?"

All the way back to where we'd started in Pomona, and then some. I hoped Paul had gotten unlimited mileage on the car. "Keep heading east on Santa Monica, then turn right on Fairfax. I guess we'll have to take the 10 Freeway and hope for the best. Maybe the traffic hasn't gotten too bad yet."

"You make an excellent GPS," he remarked, and pulled over into the right lane.

Maybe not the sort of praise most women would want, but I'd take it. My father always said I had a bump of direction. Might as well put it to good use. "More reliable than the one in your first rental car?"

"Infinitely." He turned the car down Fairfax, eyes fixed on the traffic, thick even at barely two in the afternoon. "But I suppose I should be grateful for that malfunctioning GPS."

"Oh?" I replied, trying to sound nonchalant.

Then he did glance away from the road, just for a second, but that second was enough. The hazel eyes met mine and shifted away. He said, "If the GPS hadn't stopped working, I wouldn't have met you."

A rush of warmth moved through my midsection, and I found myself staring at the choked streets of Little Ethiopia passing by as if they were the most fascinating thing in the world. "Oh, I don't know. Otto might've still found a way to get me over to the Sheraton Universal."

"Ah, Otto. Any advice from the world of the spirits?"

"Absolutely nothing. Dear Otto, it seems, has taken a powder."

"Does he do that often?"

"Occasionally, but usually not as long as this." Again I tried to tell myself that it was just Otto being difficult—something he excelled at—but I was beginning to wonder. He'd always made the spirit world sound as if it were a serene place, for the most part. Not a world where you could be detained or held captive or any of the other awful things that might happen to those who were still corporeal. Most likely, my worries were for nothing, and I was being neglected because one of his other gigs was allowing Otto to hold forth, which would be much more interesting to a being with his sort of ego.

"And you're worried."

"A little. It's probably nothing. I'm not his only psychic."

"Really?" Now Paul sounded almost amused. "I didn't know it worked that way."

We had just approached the on-ramp to the eastbound freeway, so I waited until he had safely maneuvered the car up the ramp and into the traffic. As I'd feared, it was already starting to stack up. L.A. freeways were almost always a nightmare, but Friday afternoons were the worst.

"Some spirit guides speak to only one person, but some have other...clients...for lack of a better word. It's always been like that with Otto and me."

"Do you know who these other 'clients' are?"

"No. Otto won't talk about them, except to make excuses as to why he wasn't around for a particularly important session."

"Do your own clients mind?"

"They usually can't tell." Thank God, or I

wouldn't have been able to build my business to its current levels. Dead sessions, like the one I'd had with Alex Hathaway, were few and far between. "If Otto's not around, I use the cards. And sometimes I can get information through psychometry, or what I refer to as my spider sense, although of course I don't call it that in front of my clients."

"Fascinating," Paul said, sounding positively Spock-like.

I tried not to chuckle. "What about you?" I asked. "How long have you been chasing UFOs?"

Something about him seemed to tense, his fingers clasping the steering wheel a little more tightly than they had only a few seconds earlier. "About six years."

"Is that all?" Somehow, it had seemed to me he'd been doing this for much longer than that. "What, no boyhood dreams of riding around in a spaceship?"

"No more than usual, I suppose." He paused, then said, "I'd always been fascinated by the stars, got my first telescope for my eleventh birthday, but I never saw anything out of the ordinary, even with all the hours I spent watching the skies. Like most members of the scientific community, I thought UFOs were the realm of crackpots talking about abductions and little aliens with big heads. But then—" And he broke off. "Which way am I supposed to go, anyway?"

"Stay to the left. Follow the signs that say '10 Freeway, San Bernardino.'"

He did as I had instructed but didn't seem inclined to continue the conversation. Since the freeway was choked with early commuters, and it was tricky navigating the odd little jump you had to take in East L.A. to continue on the eastbound 10, I thought it better to remain silent until we were safely where we needed to be and headed due east. From that point, all we had to do was keep going straight until we hit Fontana.

"Then what?" I prompted. I hadn't forgotten where he'd left off the conversation.

"Then I was out in the desert. I just gotten a new 200mm telescope, so I wanted to test it out. It was a clear night in March." Again he hesitated.

"And?"

"And I saw it. A huge wedge-shaped ship, with lines of lights shifting through the colors of the spectrum. At first I thought it had to be a new experimental craft—but no manmade object could move like that. It hovered over the desert, then shot straight upward at a speed that should have been impossible."

A little shiver worked its way down my spine. "Were you frightened?"

"I didn't have time to be frightened. By the time I figured out what had happened, it was gone."

"So that turned you into a believer."

He shook his head. "Not right away. But then I saw it again. Twice. And I started doing some research, discovered there were many, many people who'd had similar experiences. I talked to some of them online, met a few in person. And everything I learned, everything I saw, seemed to tell me that something had been hidden for years, something the government really didn't want us to know about. Then I made the mistake of stating some of my views openly."

"Mistake?"

A grim laugh. "I was on the faculty of the astrophysics department at the university. Junior professor, but still. Had a good reception for the papers I'd published, seemed to be on the fast track to tenure."

It didn't take a genius to figure out what had happened next. "I'm guessing the powers that be didn't appreciate your new hobby."

"That's putting it mildly." He didn't quite sigh, but he let out a breath, gaze still fixed on the road ahead of him. "My department head took me aside and informed me that he didn't think I was a good fit for the department after all, that I'd be better off somewhere else. That it would save everyone some trouble if I'd just resign instead of being publicly sacked."

"Jesus." I didn't bother with any expressions of disbelief; my father was on the faculty of a prestigious private college, and I knew just how cutthroat academia could be. "What did you do?"

He shrugged. "I left Albuquerque, then went home and licked my wounds. By then my father was my dead and my mother at the retirement community in Santa Fe. I had some money saved up and had the house free and clear, so my expenses weren't that high. And then someone in the local MUFON chapter asked me to talk at a conference they were hosting, and people seemed to be impressed and asked if I was planning to write a book. I really hadn't thought about it, but I certainly had enough time on my hands, so I did. It met with some success in certain circles, and I was invited to more speaking engagements, and then came the next book, and...here we are."

"On our way to Fontana, with a vial that may or may not have some sort of alien virus in it."

"Exactly." Although his expression had been somber up to that point, I thought I saw a trace of a smile tug at the corners of his mouth. "Which, believe it or not, appeals to me more than facing the prospect of grading a stack of midterms. So I've learned to be Zen about the situation. Or at least as close as I can be."

Having done my share of paper-grading during my stint as a T.A. while I was getting my master's degree, I could sympathize completely. "You're not the only one who did a total career change," I told him, hoping to let him know I understood at least a little of what he'd gone through.

"Oh?"

"I'm a certified MFCC—marriage and family counselor," I added, just in case there had been a shortage of those in the astrophysics department at the University of New Mexico. "I tried it for a few years, but Otto kept pestering me about not following my true vocation."

"So Otto gives career advice, too?"

"Yes, especially if it's unwanted." I gave a rueful little shake of my head, then went on, "But I realized he was right. I thought my…abilities…could help me as a counselor, but I found myself tripping over them more often than not. You're bound by a lot of rules when you're working under a state license. So I closed that business and started another."

"But you're still helping people."

"I'd like to think so." Of course, that "help" varied widely, from finally convincing Susan Yamamoto to leave her abusive boyfriend to convincing Josh Epstein that investing in the latest hot script making the rounds wasn't actually that good an idea after all. One might think such a thing was trivial…except the script in question had turned into the previous summer's worst bomb, with the studio that bought it losing millions. Josh came out looking like a hero, and couldn't praise me enough— and also brought me a whole slew of high-paying entertainment industry clients. Everyone wanted a line to the psychic who could help them avoid the fate of the studio exec who'd backed the losing script. Current word on the street was that he was living out of the back of his BMW.

All during this conversation, traffic had been crawling along, but once we were out of the city limits and moving into the San Gabriel Valley, things seemed to pick up, and we began cruising at almost-normal speeds. We were both silent for awhile, Paul keeping a careful watch on the cars around us. Now that we were actually moving, people were taking advantage of the situation by zipping in and out of traffic, trying to score that extra car length. I wondered what he thought of the immense crush of people here in Southern California. It had to be some kind of adjustment for a man who lived alone out in the middle of nowhere in New Mexico.

"Do you have an address in Fontana?" I asked, a little while after we had crossed the border between Los Angeles and San Bernardino counties. "Because it's not that far from here, and I don't know if we need to jump on the 15 or keep going east on the 10."

"It's on my phone." He lifted it from its resting place on his lap and handed it to me.

The cell phone was still slightly warm from sitting on his leg, and I had to force myself not to hold it more tightly, to feel his body warmth radiating from the plastic. A few compliments and one admiring gaze aside, he hadn't given me any indication that he saw me as anything other than his current partner in crime. Fondling his cell phone would just make me look like an idiot.

So I pressed a button to get it out of "sleep" mode and found the address, then plugged it into my own iPhone so I could use its far more sophisticated map application. It turned out we were headed to an industrial park that would be easier to access off the 15 Freeway, so I told Paul to turn north and then get off almost immediately at Fourth Street. From there, we headed east for a little bit, until I saw the side street that led to this Lampson Labs, whatever that was.

"Turn here," I instructed, and we pulled into the park, following the signs that pointed us to number 162, which was the lab's address.

For a Friday afternoon, the lot for 162 looked pretty empty, in contrast to the other businesses in the industrial park. I saw a silver Prius, so new it still had its paper dealer plates, and then a disreputable-looking older white van. We parked and got out.

The door to the lab facility was unlocked, but no cheery receptionist awaited us. Fact was, the place seemed deserted, cars parked outside or no. A door to the left and behind what should have been the receptionist's desk stood partway open. I could see some lights on, and a stretch of long hallway with bare beige walls—not even any hackneyed motivational posters or improbable beach scenes.

A little chill ran down my spine, and I glanced up at Paul, who frowned.

"Hello?" he called out.

Nothing.

"Are you sure this is the right address?" he asked me, then pulled out his phone and appeared to inspect the text Jeff had sent earlier.

"Yes, it's the right address," I replied. Tension

made my tone a little more waspish than I had intended it to be. "Besides, it says 'Lampson Labs' right on the window. Maybe they're all in the back of the building or something."

With more courage than I was feeling at the moment, I moved past him and down the hallway, which was a real corridor and not just a passageway through a cube farm. Closed doors ranged past on either side of us. I had a feeling all those doors were locked.

The one directly to my right swung open, and I jumped. Jeff's Makowski's unruly head stuck out into the corridor. "You took your time."

My heart must have been going about a hundred beats a minute. "You know what the eastbound 10 is like on a Friday afternoon?" I retorted.

He opened his mouth, but Paul cut in smoothly, "We're here now. Are you ready to look at the sample?"

"Yeah, we're ready." And he stepped aside so we could enter the room.

It was a cavernous space, much bigger than it had seemed from its modest little door. Computers and microscopes and equipment I couldn't begin to recognize covered the built-in lab tables on each wall, and more tables crowded the middle of the room. The place looked as if it could have supported a complement of at least twenty or thirty scientists, but all I saw was one man, who pushed his chair away from a computer with a display almost as big as my new TV. He was short, probably only a couple of inches taller than I, and maybe a few years older, with dark hair already beginning to thin at the temples. Unlike Jeff, he wore a button-down shirt and a dark tie, and a white lab coat over all that.

This stranger glanced from Paul to me and then grinned. "Who's the hottie?"

Well, he might have been older than Jeff, but obviously he'd gone to the same geek school of manners and deportment. "I'm the person with the inside line on a possible alien infestation," I replied, and crossed my arms in the vain hope that it would keep him from looking at my chest. "Who are you?"

He didn't appear offended. "I'm Raymond Lampson. This is my lab."

"We're hoping you can tell us if there's anything strange about the sample," Paul said, in an obvious attempt to guide the conversation back into more productive channels. "Persephone?"

It wasn't worth it to protest that I didn't like this Raymond Lampson and that I had my doubts as to whether he'd be able to find anything in the sample. Sure, Jeff had vouched for him, but what did that mean? It seemed as if Paul had put a lot of trust in someone he'd only just met in person today. Still, since I certainly didn't have any of my own resources, I dug in my purse and pulled out the vial, then handed it over to Raymond. He held it up to the fluorescent lights overhead, squinting a little.

"Looks like cooking oil," he commented.

"Yeah, that's exactly it," I said. "We drove all the way out here so I could bring you a sample of Mazola."

Jeff shot me a withering look, but I really didn't care. It was pretty obvious this Raymond person was going to do the tests no matter what I said.

"We'll see soon enough." Raymond moved away from us and began busying himself with slides and various apparatus.

"You might as well go back to the break room," Jeff told us. "This will probably take a while."

Break room? I wondered, but I just shrugged and followed Paul as he nodded and headed in the direction Jeff had indicated. Sure enough, toward the back of the building there was a pretty well-equipped space with a couple of tables and accompanying chairs, soda and snack machines, and, thank God, a coffee maker. I realized it had been a long time since breakfast. Lunch had come and gone without us even noticing it.

"Coffee?" I asked Paul.

"Sure. It could be a long night."

That comment sounded ominous. I hoped he didn't think we were going to hang around here for hours and hours. Sure, I could live for a few hours on pretzels out of the snack machine, but sooner or later I was going to need something a little more substantial than that.

I busied myself with making some coffee—Lampson had a decent variety from Peet's, so I put together a pot of Kona Gold. There was a row of new-looking mugs sitting in a cabinet above the counter where the coffeemaker lived, and I grabbed two of them and set them down.

It was strange, though. The place had none of the feel of an office occupied by actual human beings. All the mugs were plain white heavy stoneware with a thick glaze. I didn't see any of the motley assortment you'd usually find in a regular company's break room. And the refrigerator, when I opened it, was likewise shiny and clean, occupied by only a single takeout container. It was as if Lampson had the entire facility all to himself.

"Here," I said, setting a mug of coffee in front of Paul, followed by a couple of containers of cream and some stir sticks. I remembered from breakfast how he liked to take his coffee.

"Thanks."

He poured cream, and I sat down opposite him and took my own mug, adding both cream and sugar. I'd never been a huge coffee fanatic, preferring tea, but I knew from my grad school days that coffee would keep me going the way nothing else could.

"Odd, isn't it?" he commented, after he'd finished swirling the cream through his coffee.

"What is?"

"This place. It's set up as if there should be an entire staff working on-site, but I don't see any indication that there's anyone but Lampson here."

So he'd noticed it, too. Of course he had—Paul

Oliver was not stupid. The coffee was too hot for me to drink yet, but I wrapped my cold fingers around the mug, grateful for its warmth.

"No one does work here," I said. "There no food in the fridge, no personal stuff in the the cupboards. And yet—"

"What?" He leaned forward to blow on his coffee, but I noticed the hazel eyes had remained fixed, watching me.

"And yet it doesn't *feel* wrong, even with how obnoxious Lampson was acting." I paused, still holding on to my coffee cup, letting the vibrations wash over me. I didn't sense anything strange, none of the jangling psychic residue of a building that had been hastily evacuated or its occupants told to leave, their business unfinished. I lifted my shoulders and said, "This just feels like it's his place."

"It is," said Jeff, who had appeared out of nowhere to pause at the entrance to the break room. "He owns the building. Likes to work alone. Guess he can afford to—his father developed most of the land around here. So Raymond bought himself a lab. By the way, he sent me over to tell you that you might as well leave."

"Leave?" I asked. Barely ten minutes had gone by since we left him in the lab. "He didn't find anything?"

"On the contrary. He found plenty—he just doesn't know what it is. And he's pretty sure it's going to take him all night to even start to figure it out."

Paul pushed his mug of coffee away from him. "You're sure the sample is safe here?"

"And what could you do to protect it if it weren't?" Jeff responded, and then shook his head. "This place is as secure as anywhere else. I'll stay here. But there's no point in us all hanging around all night."

Some part of me thought abandoning the sample to Raymond Lampson's tender mercies was a horribly bad idea, but another, larger, part thought that getting out of there sounded pretty appealing. Especially if some food was involved.

For a few seconds, Paul hesitated. Then he glanced over at me. I had no idea what he saw in my face. Stark hunger, maybe, because he said, "All right. Text me if you have anything. In the mean-time"—he smiled—"I think I owe someone some dinner."

CHAPTER SEVEN

EVEN THOUGH RAYMOND HAD MADE IT SOUND AS IF HE was going to need all night, Paul didn't want to stray too far away from the lab. So we ended up at Ontario Mills, a sprawling mall only a few miles away. Since our eating choices were pretty limited unless we wanted to fight the crowds at the food court—which neither of us really found too appealing—we went to the Rainforest Cafe, a kitschy spot that seemed to cater to tourists and families with small children. Not exactly something I would have chosen if I had a decent alternative, but I didn't, as the other restaurant that would have allowed us to sit down was located inside an arcade. We decided to take our chances with the ersatz Tiki Room and hope for the best.

I didn't exactly see money change hands, but somehow we ended up at one of the few booths tucked away in a corner, far from the large tables populated with oversized families. The din was a little muted back there, and the faux greenery surrounding the booth and the fish tanks around the corner offered at least a semblance of privacy, if not the actual thing.

What I really wanted at that point was a mai tai roughly the size of my head, but I thought ordering such a thing might not go down very well with Paul. I settled for requesting a glass of chardonnay when the waitress appeared, although Paul only ordered an iced tea.

"It could still turn out to be a long night," he said as the waitress departed, and then I felt vaguely guilty for ordering the wine.

"That may well be, but I have a feeling I'll be spending it asleep in the back seat of the car."

He laughed then, and shook his head. "I'm guessing Raymond at least has a couch somewhere in that building, if not an actual bed. We can probably do better than the back seat of the car."

"Here's hoping. My back would probably have a few choice things to say to me if I did end up sleeping in the car." I reached for the glass of water the waitress had left for me and drank. I hadn't realized how thirsty I actually was, and downed almost half the glass without thinking. Still, I couldn't help pondering Jeff's comment about Raymond definitely finding something of interest in the sample we'd brought him. "What do you think he found?"

"Hard to say." Paul lifted his own water glass but paused, holding it a few inches above the table as he appeared to consider my question. "Biology isn't my strong suit. But we all know that the human dermis is like one big sponge. It can absorb all sorts of things. A topical application of a substance carrying an alien virus—or whatever it turns out to be— makes sense in that it would be absorbed quickly and not leave much trace, unlike something given in a syringe or even orally. But why a spray tan, which would seem to target a certain fairly small segment of the population?"

"I don't know." I thought about it for a minute and couldn't see the reasoning. You'd think if aliens were trying to take over the planet by mind-control-ling certain key figures, they'd be going after members of Congress. God knows some of them were orange and spray-tanned enough to qualify, but even though their actions were often incomprehen-sible to me, I didn't get the feeling that any of them were directly connected to this. Not yet, anyway.

The waitress showed up then with our drinks, and I took a bracing sip of chardonnay. It was sharp and way too heavy on the oak, which was about to be expected in a place like this. I guessed they were more concerned with pushing T-shirts than main-taining an adequate wine list. Something was tickling at the back of my mind, however, and usually when that happened, the best thing to do was just wait and let it come up to the surface.

"Lotus," I said slowly, and Paul dropped a lemon slice into his iced tea and watched me, obviously waiting to hear what I had to say next.

"A lot of industry types go there," I continued. "I only went the first time because of a recommendation from one of my clients. And then I liked the service, so I kept going. But I'd say the majority of their clientele is studio execs, or wives of studio execs, or people connected with them in some way. I'm guessing that Alex Hathaway's out-of-work actress girlfriend was not their usual type."

"So you think that was a red herring?"

"Maybe. I just don't see why aliens would even care about people who work in the film industry. I mean, there's a lot of money that gets thrown around in this town—and I do mean a *lot*—but although humans tend to equate money and power, I don't know if aliens would."

Paul stirred his iced tea in a contemplative fashion, eyes narrowed. "There's got to be some other connection, something we're just not seeing."

"Very likely, but I'm not getting hit with any bolts of inspiration." This came out sounding a little more testy than I had intended. I didn't like feeling this way, as if I was just blundering around in the dark. Otto was going to get some serious words from me when—or if—he ever reappeared.

"Neither am I, so don't beat yourself up about it." He opened his mouth as if to say more, but at that moment the waitress appeared, asking about our order.

I'd barely looked at the menu, so I guiltily scooped it up and ordered the first thing that sounded interesting, which was grilled fish with mango salsa. Paul also ordered fish—blackened salmon—and the waitress took our menus and disappeared in what I assumed was the direction of the kitchen.

It wasn't just the absence of Otto, though, but my utter blankness regarding the entire situation. I knew my spider sense hadn't gone completely away, because I'd certainly gotten strong enough feelings from Jeff and Raymond. Somehow, though, my native abilities just weren't enough to pierce through the veil of obscurity that seemed to have been thrown over the alien conspiracy. If there really was one. Not that I really wanted a visitation from little green...that is, gray...men in the middle of the night, but even the slightest hint that Paul and I weren't on the world's biggest wild-goose chase would have been nice.

A thought struck me, and I set down my glass of wine before saying, "You told me you'd never been abducted."

"That's right." The reply was delivered in a flat tone that didn't seem to invite further questioning, but that had never stopped me in the past.

"Do you want to be?"

"God, no."

I felt my eyebrows shoot up at hearing the vehemence in his voice. "Really? I'd think with your field of research—that is, with all the investigation you'd done, you'd want to have that sort of firsthand experience."

At the moment, he was beginning to look as if he'd regretted not ordering a drink. "I've talked to far too many abductees to want it to ever happen to me. Some view it as a positive experience—or at least they come to feel that way—but for most it's terrifying. It can lead to all sorts of problems...failed marriages, substance abuse. Not to mention the little problem of most of the world thinking you're either crazy or a liar."

"I can see why these UFO groups are so important for people," I commented. "When you feel that alone, you instinctively reach out to people you think have shared the same experience, or at least aren't inclined to disbelieve you from the get-go."

Paul was silent for a bit. He swirled the straw through his glass of iced tea once or twice, then asked, "Was it like that for you?"

"For me?" I stared at him, puzzled. "I've never been abducted by a UFO."

"No." A hint of a smile flickered around the corners of his mouth. "When did you realize you were psychic?"

Oh, that. "For real?"

"For real."

It had been twenty years since Otto first appeared

to me and told me what my "true path" was intended to be, but I'd known there was something different about me for some time before that. "I guess I was twelve. Oh, there were times when I was younger that I got odd feelings about things, or told people that something was going to happen and it did, but Otto first showed up on my doorstep when I was in middle school. He sort of explained what was going on."

"That must have been a shock."

"To put it mildly. As if puberty wasn't tough enough."

He laughed then, just as the waitress appeared with our entrees. She shot an apologetic smile at us, as if she knew she was interrupting.

"Do you need anything else?"

Both Paul and I shook our heads, and she scampered away.

The food smelled amazing, and I couldn't resist just digging in. Paul did the same, so for a few minutes we ate in silence. I could practically feel my depleted tissues soaking up all the protein and Omega-3s and all the other good stuff in that delectable hunk of filet. I had to revise my opinion of the Rainforest Cafe upward a few notches. The place might have felt like the Enchanted Tiki Room on crack, but the food was excellent.

"It's interesting, though," he said after we had done some serious damage to our respective meals. "I've worked with some psychics, and the ones who channel other beings have often said they've been in contact with spirits from other dimensions, or intelligences that claim to be from other worlds. And yet you've never experienced anything like that?"

I shook my head; my mouth was still full of red snapper and mango salsa. After I swallowed, and took a sip of chardonnay to wash down the food, I replied, "No. Otto is definitely an earthly spirit. I've met some other psychics who have said the same thing, that the beings they're channeling are definitely otherworldly in origin, but that's never been the case with me. And I've never had contact with any other intelligences besides Otto. I don't know if that makes me a deficient psychic or what."

There might have been a touch of defensiveness in my last words; over the years, I'd often wondered as well why I only spoke with Otto...and I'd had one or two snippy practitioners make disparaging remarks about my limited repertoire of psychic guides. At the time, I'd done my best to brush them off, telling myself that this wasn't a competition. Even so, I couldn't help questioning these supposed "abilities" of mine and how strong they really were.

Then again, considering the grief Otto was able to cause me all on his own, I supposed I should be glad that I didn't have a whole bevy of spirits hanging around and clamoring for attention.

Paul said, "I definitely wouldn't call you deficient."

That look was back in his eyes, the one I wanted

to think of as admiring. Ginger probably would have looked at him boldly, inviting more. Since I was definitely lacking in flirting skills, instead I glanced back down at my plate and pretended to be gathering up a choice mouthful of mango salsa. After an awkward pause, I said, "One woman I met a few years ago at a New Age fair said I was bottling myself up, that I needed to open myself to new experiences. But I don't agree. When you're dealing with the paranormal, sometimes if you open the door too wide, you risk letting all sorts of bad things in."

"Like those kids who play with Ouija boards."

"Exactly. I don't know if it's the Devil—I've never met the guy—but not all intelligences are benign."

"Apparently not." His expression sobered, and I knew he must be thinking of Alex Hathaway, dead for a reason neither one of us could begin to understand.

At that moment, Paul's jacket pocket began ringing, and he reached in and pulled out his cell phone. "Hello."

Of course, I couldn't hear who was on the other end of the line, but somehow I knew it had to be Jeff, a certainty that had more to do with the fact that no one else had the number for Paul's pay-to-play cell than because my psychic powers had decided to kick in.

"We can be there in ten minutes," he said, and shut the cell phone. He peered past me into the main section of the restaurant. "Have you seen our waitress?"

"No, but we can probably just guesstimate the tab if it's that urgent."

"It's not. Raymond has a few things he found that he wants to discuss with us, but he certainly hasn't cracked the code, as it were."

At that moment, our waitress did appear, probably to do the customary "how are things going?" check-in. She looked a little surprised when Paul requested the bill, but nodded and said she'd take care of it right away.

Maybe she'd seen something in his face that I hadn't, because she did return with greater than usual haste and set the bill down on the table. He and I both reached for it at the same time.

"I said I was taking you out to dinner," he protested.

"And how much cash do you have left?" I countered. "I'm carrying a lot more than you—might as well make yours last longer."

Slowly, he withdrew his hand, but I could tell he wasn't happy.

To mollify him, I asked, "How about I make you take me someplace fancy when all this is over?"

He smiled then, just the tiniest bit. "Deal."

The damage wasn't all that bad; I dug a couple of twenties out of my wallet and tucked them into the leatherette envelope next to the bill. Only a few swallows of chardonnay remained, so I finished off my glass and set it down as Paul drank the rest of his iced tea. We both slid out of the booth and headed toward the parking lot.

California was still a week away from Daylight Savings Time, so full dark had fallen by the time we emerged from the restaurant. The wind had picked up, catching at my hair and most likely making it look wilder than ever. I shivered and wished I'd brought my leather jacket with me.

Paul was quiet as we walked out to our rented car. Maybe he was thinking about what Raymond had found. I found myself wondering the same thing but didn't really feel like discussing it. Whatever he'd discovered, I had a feeling it couldn't be good.

To my surprise, Paul walked me around to my side of the car instead of simply hitting the remote to unlock the doors and leaving me to fend for myself. I didn't have time to ponder this outburst of chivalry, however, because instead of pulling out the car keys, he reached for me and drew me toward him, even as he bent and pressed his lips against mine.

This action was so unexpected—just a further indication that a good part of my psychic talents seemed to have abandoned me—that for a second or two I couldn't even react. But then I realized just how good it felt to have his arms around me, how firm his mouth was, how he tasted faintly spicy and better than I could have ever hoped for. He held me like that for what could have been just a minute or maybe half an hour. It was hard to tell, with the way my head was spinning.

He pulled away a few inches and said, "I probably shouldn't have done that."

"Why not?" I managed, glad I was able to string even two words together.

"With everything that's going on, with what's at stake...." The words trailed off, and he shook his head. "Kissing you in the parking lot like we're back in high school isn't exactly a mature reaction to the situation."

My lips still tingled from the touch of his lips. "So why did you do it?"

His shoulders lifted. "I kept looking at you during dinner, wondering. I suppose some part of me just said the hell with it."

"Then say the hell with it again," I told him, and the words were barely out of my mouth before he bent down and kissed me once more, his hands tightening on my arms, holding me tightly as if he was afraid someone or something might come along and snatch me away.

No chance of that. It would take an act of God to pull me away from Paul, that much I knew. The familiar sensation was back, the one of absolute certainty. Whatever else was going on, and whatever dark forces might have forced us to flee here where no one knew us, I did know I was meant to be with Paul. Crazy, sure—I'd known the man for less than forty-eight hours. But the same still, quiet voice that had guided me through my counseling sessions seemed to have returned long enough to tell me I had finally found the one man who took me as I was and expected nothing more…and nothing less.

His pocket buzzed against my collarbone and I jumped, breaking our contact. He shook his head, then reached in and pulled out his cell phone.

"Yes, Jeff, we're on our way. Just had to…wait for our check." And he closed the phone and stuffed it back in his pocket.

"You are such a liar," I told him, even as he clicked the remote to unlock the car, then opened the door for me.

"It wasn't a complete lie. We did have to wait for the check."

"A whole three minutes." But I got the point, and lowered myself into my seat as he went around to his own side of the car.

Neither one of us said anything as he started the engine and then backed out of the parking space before pointing the Camry toward Fourth Street and Raymond's lab. Somehow, though, it wasn't an uncomfortable silence. The pressure of his lips seemed to linger on mine, and I smiled a little as I stared out the window at the streets passing by. Whatever might still be waiting for us, I knew Paul had feelings for me, feelings strong enough that he'd acted on them, even though logically both of us should have known to keep our libidos in check until we'd gotten the rest of this mess sorted out.

At the moment, I was very glad neither one of us had turned out to be all that logical.

Nothing seemed to have changed appreciably as we pulled into the parking lot at Lampson Labs. The Prius and the shabby white van were still in their respective places, and the front office was still noticeably empty, the fluorescent lights within glaring out through the open blinds. Paul and I got out of the Camry and went in, heading toward the back of the building.

We found Raymond and Jeff in one of the labs, Raymond with his eyeballs apparently glued to a complicated piece of equipment I guessed was some sort of microscope, although it appeared to be an order of magnitude greater in complexity than the sorts of microscopes we'd used when I was in college and taking my required biology coursework. Jeff hovered a few feet away, and shot us an irritated glare as we entered the room.

"Nice of you to drop in," he remarked.

I barely refrained from raising a guilty hand to my lips, as if Paul's kiss had left an imprint there. Which was just silly, since I'd done a quick reapplication of lipstick on the way over.

"What have you got?" Paul asked, his tone mild. You'd have thought he was the one who'd had the calming glass of wine with dinner.

At that point, Raymond lifted his head from the microscope, but slowly, as if reluctant to turn away from whatever he was inspecting. "It's definitely alien," he said.

Paul's eyebrows went up slightly. "How do you know?"

"Are you a biologist?"

"No."

"Well, then," he replied, as if that explained everything.

It was my turn to throw an aggrieved glance in Jeff's direction. "You called us back here because you said you had something important to tell us. So what is it?"

"It's alien," Jeff said, "but it's not exactly biological. That is, it appears to be an engineered virus of alien origin, but in a nanotech delivery system. We've never seen anything like it."

"No one's seen anything like it," Raymond mumbled, his face planted back on the microscope as if pulled there by some irresistible force.

"So what does it do?" Paul asked.

"We don't know yet for sure," Jeff replied after throwing a quick glance at Raymond, as if guessing that the biologist wasn't about to provide the answer. "We just thought you should know it's definitely not spray-tan oil."

No kidding. I didn't pretend to understand exactly what they were talking about, but I could tell from the furrow between Paul's brows that he had gotten some of it...and didn't appear to be precisely encouraged by the news.

"This delivery system," he said. "I assume it's intended for quick absorption through the skin?"

"That's what it looks like."

"But you don't know why."

Right then, Raymond did look up from the microscope. "Not yet. If you think you can do any better—"

"Of course not," Paul broke in. It seemed to me that he'd been mostly thinking out loud, not actually trying to impugn Raymond's research abilities. "Ms. O'Brien and I will continue our side of the investigation," he went on. "Let us know if you find anything else."

"No problem," Raymond replied, sounding sour even for him. "It's not like I'm planning on sleeping tonight."

There didn't seem to be much of a way to reply to that, so I sent him what I hoped was a reassuring look, even as I wondered what the hell Paul thought we could investigate. I'd been under the impression that we'd pretty much hit a dead end...at least, until we got more information out of Raymond.

But I kept my mouth shut as Paul made his curt goodbyes and went back to the car. It wasn't until he'd pulled out of the parking lot and had us headed back toward the freeway that I asked, "So, do you have some hot leads I wasn't aware of?"

"No," he said briefly. "Which way to get back to the motel?"

"North on the 15, and the 210 west."

There was still a good bit of traffic around the on-ramp because of the influx from Ontario Mills, but we made it onto the freeway without incident. A few miles passed by without either of us saying anything. It wasn't until we'd transitioned to the 210 and were headed toward Pomona that I said, "So what do you think that nanovirus is for?"

"I'm not completely sure." He had his face forward, his attention focused on the unfamiliar roadway. "There has to be some connection with the film industry, but I'm just not seeing it right now."

"Film industry?"

"Look at the clientele at Lotus. You yourself said a good number of the people who patronize that spa are individuals with influence in the movie industry. And Alex Hathaway told you that his girlfriend had suffered a complete personality change after going to get her tan. So let's go with Jeff's earlier theory, that the spray tan provides a means to get this nanovirus —if that's what it truly is—into a human host. Maybe you were right when you said earlier that Alex's girl-friend was simply a mistake. It doesn't mean there aren't others being infected, people who have far more power than an out-of-work actress. What do you think they might be trying to control?"

I wanted to tell him that it was silly to believe aliens would really care enough to take over a bunch of studio execs, but a cold little chill somewhere in the midpoint of my spine told me he wasn't just engaging in a bit of blue-sky thinking. It figured my spider sense would kick in just when I really didn't want to hear what it had to tell me. Of course, I didn't have any direct connections with the film industry, but I knew many people who did...and from what I'd heard, the people who ran Hollywood were scary enough on their own without being taken over by aliens in the bargain.

"I don't know," I said. "I mean, it just doesn't make any sense that aliens would care about the movies one way or another. They're just a bunch of flickering images in the dark."

Flickering images in the dark....

It struck me then, the way these things sometimes did, as if they'd been sent down a pipeline by God or the universe or whatever else you wanted to call it. Far more than a notion—a certainty, the inescapable realization that what my mind had just whispered to me was the absolute truth.

I didn't remember making a sound, but I must have, because Paul looked over at me sharply. "Persephone? Are you all right?"

"No," I replied, voice shaking. "I really don't think I am."

He reached down from the steering wheel with his right hand and wrapped his fingers around mine. "What is it? Did you sense something?"

There was a lot to be said for being with a man who just accepted your psychic powers and didn't joke about them or try to exploit them. "I think I know what they're doing."

"What?"

I swallowed against the sick taste in my throat and hoped my dinner would stay where it was. "They're not here to destroy us," I informed him. "They're here to control us."

CHAPTER EIGHT

SURPRISINGLY, HE DIDN'T APPEAR ALL THAT STARTLED. "What makes you say that?"

"I just know."

"How?" A pause. "Is Otto back?"

"No," I replied, sounding a little tetchy. Did Paul really think I couldn't have one flash of intuition without my spirit guide's help? "This one just came to me—as things did before Otto showed up, and still do on occasion. Thank God, since it looks like Otto's permanently relocated to the Bahamas or something."

"So what does your intuition tell you?"

"Just that the aliens are looking for a way to control us, and it's connected to the movies some-how. Or actually, movies and television." I shut my eyes then, drawing myself into the dark. The interior of a car barreling down a freeway at seventy miles an hour was perhaps not the best place for peaceful contemplation, but one worked with the available materials. That sensation was there still, accompanied by a rapid succession of images, some from films I'd seen recently, others snippets from television shows. And from all of them vibrated a sense of wrongness, a flicker at the very edge of perception no one would have ever known to look for. A dissonance began to build in my mind, pulsing at some subsonic level that caused a throbbing pain to build in the bone behind my ears.

Unable to endure it a second longer, I opened my eyes. At once, those painful harmonics disappeared, and I let out a hitching little gasp.

"Persephone?" Paul asked, his tone sharp with worry.

"I'm okay. Get off at the next exit."

He must have heard the tension in my voice, because he only nodded and then maneuvered the car over to the right, pulling off the freeway at Towne. From there, he seemed to recognize where he was, because he didn't ask for any further directions as he headed south toward Foothill and the motel where we were staying.

It was only after he'd pulled into the parking lot and followed me up the stairs to the room we shared that he said, "What did you see?"

At any other time, I might have considered the awkwardness of the situation, of the two of us sharing a room after a kiss that had forever changed the way we viewed one another. Right then, though, I could only think of the painful wrongness that made itself felt in my bones, of the similarly soul-deep knowledge that somehow the very mediums we employed for entertainment were going to be used against us.

"I don't know how they're doing it," I replied. "I don't even know how I know, but I've learned not to question these things. But somehow they're building a—I don't know what you'd call it, exactly—some sort of signal into the movies and TV shows that are coming out of Hollywood."

His eyes narrowed slightly. I watched as he went back to the door and tested the lock, then turned toward me. "A carrier wave. I can see how that might work. But we need to be able to find out how they're doing it—what the wave is composed of, to see if there's any way of blocking or neutralizing it."

"Easier said than done." I sat down on the bed I'd been using and kicked off my shoes. They were more or less comfortable, but almost any pair of shoes needed a breaking-in period, and it had been a long day. What I wanted right then was to lie down and lose myself in blissful sleep for a few hours. My mind, however, had other plans.

The prickly feeling returned, along with the certainty that whatever the aliens' ultimate goal might be, they weren't even in the testing stages yet. Made sense, or Paul and I and everyone around me would have already been turned into a brain-controlled zombie. Well, maybe not Paul; I got the impression he wasn't much of a movie or TV guy. At any rate, luck seemed to have guided us to discovering the plan while it was still in its embryonic stages. But it was beginning to happen, and would continue, if we didn't do something to stop it. What that something would be, I had no idea.

Paul said quietly, "There's always a way."

Who knew a ufologist could be such a Pollyanna? I wished I had some sort of retort to make, but the truth was, I didn't have the energy. The wave of dark sound that had welled up into my brain seemed to have drained whatever reserves I had left. "Well, if you have a plan, I'd love to hear it."

He didn't appear to be put off by my reply, but sat down in the chair by the window and appeared to think for a moment. "What we really need is someone who works in the technical end of the business, but who hasn't yet been affected. As far as I can guess, it seems the actual alien takeover is geared more toward the top level of the studios. There's a possibility that the tech people have escaped unscathed."

I wanted to argue that you'd think the techs would be the first people to be taken over, since one person smelling a rat might be enough to upset the whole plan, but I didn't know that for sure. After all, from what I'd heard, the people in the trenches pretty much kept their heads down and just did their work. There were too many people waiting in line for those jobs for anyone to make waves. One of my clients, who worked post-production, had some horror stories that would make your hair curl—

Of course. Tyler Russo was a sound engineer at a lab out in Studio City. We'd had a session only two days earlier. I found it hard to believe that the aliens had already suborned Tyler—surely I would have noticed if something was wrong. And even if he was on the list, it seemed as if there were a good number of people higher up the food chain who were more in danger of being spray-tanned into mental domination.

"I think I know someone we can talk to," I said, and then, as Paul's eyes lit up, "...tomorrow. I'm pretty sure Tyler would find it odd to have me calling him out of the blue at nine-thirty on a Friday night."

"Tyler?"

"A client of mine. He's a sound engineer. He'd be a good place to start."

"You are a woman of infinite resources."

I laughed. "I don't know about that. I do know a lot of people in Hollywood. That helps. As for the rest—we'll just have to see. Just because he's a sound engineer doesn't mean he'll be able to nail down this carrier wave-whatsis."

"But he might be able to direct us to someone who could."

"Hopefully."

Paul stood up then and stared at the closed curtains for a moment, as if seeing something in the tacky blue and green striped fabric that I apparently had missed. He shifted his weight from one foot to the other, obviously on edge about something.

"What's the matter?" I asked. "Sorry I couldn't come up with a better plan, but—"

"It's not that. I'm just—I suppose I'm not sure how we're supposed to proceed."

"'Proceed'?" I repeated. "Proceed with what?"

In answer, he came over and sat down on the bed next to me. "With this."

I probably should have been more prepared for the kiss, since it wasn't our first, but once again it seemed he had blindsided me. Not that I minded— the second his lips touched mine, a rush of warmth flooded my body, all the way from the tips of my toes to the crown of my head. The wave of heat seemed to push out the weariness that had come over me after my bout in the car, and I pressed against him, feeling the strength of his arms as they tightened around me, hearing the wordless little sigh he gave as we clung to each other.

It seemed the most natural thing in the world to roll over on the bed, to have his weight suddenly on top of me. I held him close, hoping by that contact I was telling him it was all right, that I wanted this.

Apparently I had telegraphed my need to him, because his hands moved lower, tracing the curve of my breasts, pausing at the buttons of my blouse.

I might have breathed a "yes." Or maybe he didn't need any words to know what I wanted.

Whatever the case, those strong fingers of his worked their way down the row of buttons, loosening each one as he went. And he moved lower as well, his breath warm against my throat at first, and then against my breast.

Then I did moan, wanting more, needing to have him touch every part of me. He fumbled a little as he worked the hooks of my bra, even as I reached up to pull at his jacket. It ended up tossed haphazardly onto the other bed, followed by his shirt, which made a distinct *clunk* as it hit the floor.

"Oops," I whispered. "Forgot you had your phone in your pocket."

"The hell with the phone," he said, and then his mouth covered mine again, as his bare torso touched my exposed skin.

That was enough for me to forget the phone, forget the world and alien conspiracies and pursuing government agents. I pressed against him, my fingers loosening his belt, pushing his jeans out of the way. He did the same with me, those strong fingers of his touching me in places I really hadn't expected him to be that familiar with.

It had been a long time since I'd felt this way, with heat flowing out to every part of my body. Hell, I didn't know if I'd ever felt precisely like this. I do know he definitely broke my personal record for bringing me to the fastest orgasm.

Then he paused, and said, "Well, shit."

"What?" I gasped. I was still lying flat on the bed;

at the moment, I wasn't sure if I was even capable of sitting upright.

He raised himself on one arm and ran a hand through his hair. "I didn't exactly think I was going to need protection on this trip."

Oh. Luckily, I had made certain arrangements at the pharmacy when we'd picked up our other supplies; thank God for computerized prescription systems. Life was complicated enough without skipping multiple pills and having to start over from scratch the next month.

I thought about it for roughly a half-second and said, "I don't care. I'm on the pill."

Without moving, he replied, "You trust me that much?"

"As long as you swear you haven't been banging UFO groupies at symposiums from coast to coast."

"God, no." He laughed then. "You do have quite the imagination."

All I wanted at the moment was to show him just how good my imagination really was. "Well, then. And since my last sexual encounter predated my last yearly checkup by at least six months, I'd say I'm in the clear, too."

"If you put it like that…."

"I do."

And he was on me again, mouth against mine, as he shifted his weight and was suddenly just there, filling me, our bodies meeting in a rush of heat and need. I wrapped my legs around him, drawing him into me further, as we rocked in perfect rhythm, drawing ourselves into a timeless circle where nothing else existed except the sound of our cries, the pulse of our blood.

When it was over, he remained on top of me for a long moment, cheek laid against mine. I could feel the hastened beat of his heart, hear his rapid breathing. Then he kissed me, ever so gently, just the lightest brush of his lips against the side of my mouth, before he lifted his weight from mine and stumbled toward the bathroom.

I stayed where I was, breathing in, breathing out. It seemed as if I drifted in a bubble of exquisite warmth and comfort. In a few minutes, I'd have to do my own post-coital cleanup, but for the moment, I was content to remain in place, reveling in that moment of gentle balance. Right then, I wasn't worried at all. I knew Paul and I would find some way to make everything right. He and I fit together, better than I had ever dreamed.

The aliens didn't stand a chance.

We both slept in, still basking in the afterglow. And when we awoke, we both reached for one another, driven by some unspoken signal, and made love again, this time slowly and quietly, as if it was the most natural thing in the world. Afterward, we got into the shower together and then laughed as we tried to negotiate the cramped quarters without getting soap in each other's eyes.

Things got a little more sober after we had dressed and realized we needed to make some sort of plan for the day. Paul checked his cell phone and shook his head at the conspicuous lack of messages from Raymond or Jeff.

"It's probably nothing," I told him, after I scrunched some more de-frizzing serum into my hair and hoped for the best. Trying new products always filled me with trepidation, but the drugstore hadn't carried the high-end salon brand I used. "You saw how Raymond was. He's probably still glued to that microscope. He'll call us when he has more information. Come on—let me buy you breakfast."

He gave a reluctant nod. "You're right. And by the time we're done with breakfast, it should be late enough for you to call this Tyler person."

I glanced at my watch. A little past nine-thirty, but I knew from my interactions with Tyler Russo that he sometimes kept very odd hours if he was in a crunch on a big project. It would have to be a leisurely breakfast. Maybe a call around eleven wouldn't be completely beyond the pale.

Paul and I stopped on the way to the car to pay for two more nights at the motel. It seemed safer to do it in small increments, just so we wouldn't be on the hook for more days than we needed if we had to suddenly pull up stakes and get out of town. This just seemed to be common sense, and not any push from a greater spiritual power, but you never knew. Besides, although my store of cash was still holding up pretty well, I knew that eventually it would run out, and then we'd have to figure out what to do next.

In the meantime, it was a beautiful spring day, and the feel of Paul's hand in mine as we walked to the car was just enough to remind me of the other, more intimate touches we'd shared. And the warmth in his eyes told me he was recalling the same things, with just the slightest glint that indicated he was ready for Round Three whenever we got the opportunity.

I thought I might be, too, but my stomach told me it needed some sustenance after all the gymnastics. Since we had to burn some time, and since Pomona wasn't exactly known for its fine dining, I told Paul to head east into Claremont. I knew of several places in the Village where we could get a killer omelette and dine *al fresco*, maybe pretend that we weren't in the middle of trying to stop a vast alien conspiracy.

Well, a girl could dream, anyway.

Of course, if I'd stopped to analyze the situation, I would have realized that going back to the town where I'd grown up and where my parents still lived and worked was fraught with complications. Because no sooner had Paul and I been seated at an outdoor table and left to peruse the menus than I heard probably the last voice I wanted to encounter at that particular moment.

"Persephone!" my mother called out, stopping on the other side of the planter that separated the restaurant's outdoor dining area from the sidewalk.

Oh, crap. What were the chances, really? My mother ran a travel agency that had managed to survive the internet takeover of most vacation arrangements—through sheer force of will, I guessed —and usually Saturday mornings were fairly busy for her, since a lot of people couldn't make it in during the week. So what the heck was she doing down here in the Village, a good mile from her office up on Foothill Boulevard?

My father used to joke that I looked just like my mother, except someone took me out of the oven before I got properly browned. It was true in some ways, since we did share the same wild curly dark hair, longish nose, and wide mouth. But she was olive-skinned where I was fair, and my eyes were a greenish shade halfway between her brown and my father's blue.

If pressed, I would admit that she looked amazing for her age, the result of relentless exercise and a disciplined diet. People often remarked that we looked more like sisters than mother and daughter.

She pushed her big Jackie-O sunglasses back on her head and gave Paul a frankly appraising stare. "Aren't you going to introduce us?"

Since I knew there was no easy way to weasel out of the situation, I set down my menu in some resignation and said, "Mom, this is Paul." I purposely left off his last name, because I knew if I told her his full name, she'd be Googling it the second she got away and could look it up on her phone. The last thing I needed was for her to set off any red flags that might send the hounds chasing out to Claremont. "Paul, this is my mother, Arianna O'Brien."

He rose and extended a hand. "Very nice to meet you, Mrs. O'Brien."

"Arianna, please."

"Arianna."

She sent me a sideways half-surprised glance. I knew the surprise was less for showing up in Claremont completely unannounced than appearing with such a hunk in tow. Certainly she knew I wasn't seeing anyone special, because I would have mentioned someone like Paul. And I also knew she was doing some other quick mental calculations; after all, most couples who weren't cohabiting didn't go out for breakfast together unless they'd spent the previous night in each other's company as well. Not that it was any of her business, of course, but even at thirty, I still hadn't quite gotten past the weight of my mother's expectations.

"So what are you doing down here in the Village, Mom?" I asked, figuring it was safer to go on the offensive than wait for her to start asking questions.

Not that my abrupt salvo put her off her stride one bit. "Second Saturday—Chamber meeting. I certainly wasn't expecting to see you here."

"I thought Paul should have one of George's world-famous Denver omelettes."

"I suppose it is worth the drive," she said, with another one of those significant glances. "So where are you from, Paul?"

"New Mexico," he replied, looking a bit bemused.

Funny how he could manage alien invasions with aplomb but didn't quite know how to handle my mother. Then again, I really shouldn't have been surprised. Maybe we'd been going about this whole thing all wrong. Maybe all we really needed to do was sic my mother on the aliens and call it a day.

"New Mexico! What brings you all the way out here?"

"Well, I—"

I cut in, "Paul's out here on business. We met through work."

"Work?" she repeated, and pulled the sunglasses off her head so she could tap one of the stems against her chin. I knew that was a warning sign. She'd never been terribly thrilled about the whole psychic thing. It was sort of hard to explain to the other members of the Chamber and her friends at the Women's Club. "Are you a psychic, too, Paul?"

"No," he said, and I saw a little quirk at the corner of his mouth, the one that meant he was trying to suppress his amusement. "I'm an astro-physicist."

"Really?" She sounded almost impressed...and then she squinted a little, as if thinking it over. "I wasn't aware that astrophysicists and psychics had much in common, work-wise."

"Isn't the Chamber meeting at ten?" I asked, even though I knew I sounded desperate. At that moment, however, I really didn't care.

"So it is," she replied, with another of those significant looks. "Guess I'd better be going. Very nice to meet you, Paul."

"Nice to meet you, too, Mrs.—Arianna."

My mother flashed him a sunny smile, then replaced her sunglasses on her nose. "I'll call," she told me ominously before sailing off down the sidewalk.

A silence fell, during which I studiously stirred the lemon in my glass of water and tried to avoid looking at Paul, who was staring down the street in the direction my mother had disappeared.

"I really didn't plan that," I said, once I realized the waitress wasn't going to come rescue me by interrupting to ask what we wanted to order.

He laughed. "I figured."

"Thank you for not running screaming into the night."

With a shake of his head, he said, "After you've sat through two separate dissertation panels, it takes a lot to intimidate you."

"Right. I hadn't thought of that."

And then the waitress did show up to take our orders. I settled for a *café au lait* and hoped it would provide the appropriate kick to keep me going through the day. Tea didn't seem as if it would cut it, given the current situation.

I also reflected that Paul was definitely a keeper. True, my mother had been—somewhat—restrained for her, but it usually only took a few minutes in my mother's company for someone to realize that she might be more of a handful than a man would want as a prospective mother-in-law. And that really was silly of me, because a few days in someone's company and a spectacular night in the sack weren't quite enough to warrant choosing a china pattern.

"Anyone else I should worry about wandering by?" Paul inquired, still with that amused lift to his mouth.   "Father...brothers...sisters...long-lost cousins?"

"No," I retorted. "That is, I'm an only child, and my father tends to spend Saturday morning tinkering with his '67 Camaro. I think my mother started going to Chamber meetings just so she wouldn't have to listen to him playing with power tools."

He appeared to contemplate that for a moment, then asked, "Do you think she'll tell anyone?"

It took me a few seconds to figure out what he was getting at, because at first my paranoia kicked in, and I thought he was worried that she was going to tell the world we were shacked up together. Then I realized he was understandably concerned that she might, in an otherwise innocent phone call, let slip that I'd been seen in the vicinity of Claremont. I had no idea whether anyone was listening in on her phone or hacking her emails, but I knew if I were trying to track down someone who didn't want to get caught, I'd be keeping an eye on all the friends and family just in case.

"I don't know," I said frankly. "She'll say something to my father, I'm guessing, but my mother is definitely the in-person type. That's why she loves going to all these various meetings—that way, she can network with people face to face instead of over the phone or via email or text."

"Well, let's hope for the best."

I nodded, and then the waitress brought our coffee. I busied myself with stirring in the single packet of sugar I would allow myself. Otto had always advised me to follow an Ayurvedic diet, as that would have better freed up my psychic abilities, but I didn't have that sort of discipline. About the best I could do was watch it with the refined sugar and not indulge in too many carbohydrates.

Run-ins with my mother aside, I found myself enjoying the fact that Paul and I had somehow managed to avoid the whole "morning after" self-consciousness. In similar situations in the past, there had too often been mumbled assertions of future phone calls...calls that never materialized...or at the very least, those strange interludes where you'd look over at your companion and think, *Holy crap, I was doing all sorts of unspeakable things to that person not twelve hours ago.*

But with Paul, there didn't seem to be any of that

awkwardness. Oh, sure, he threw a significant glance in my direction from time to time, the sort of look that sent happy little tingles down my spine. However, for the most part, we were just going along, moving forward as best we could, only with the added wrinkle of a layer of intimacy that hadn't existed twenty-four hours earlier.

He smiled at me then, just before he lifted his mug of coffee to blow on it. Something inside me turned over, and I knew I was in trouble. Because I really did want to start ordering china patterns, or at least the emotional equivalent. Never mind that I had no idea what the rest of this day was going to bring, or how the hell we were really going to succeed at what seemed like an impossible task. All I seemed able to think about was how Paul made me feel in a way that no one had ever managed to do before, and how at the moment I really didn't care what happened, just as long as I could be with him.

Luckily, he seemed to understand that I was in a contemplative mood—or maybe he thought I needed some time to recover from our unexpected encounter with my mother. Whatever the case, he appeared content to watch the people pass by on the street, and to take his own meditative sips of coffee, until the waitress arrived with our omelettes.

After that, there was some healthy digging in, because if nothing else, we'd both worked up fairly massive appetites after the previous night and this morning. It wasn't until roughly half of his omelette had disappeared that he set down his fork and said, "How well does this Tyler Russo know his stuff?"

I thought for a moment, my own fork dangling from my fingers as I contemplated his question. "Pretty well, as far as I know. He's been working as a sound engineer for about fifteen years now, I think. The company he works for gets a lot of the big contracts—if there's a blockbuster, there's a good chance it's going to end up passing through Topanga Digital at some point."

"And you think he'll be honest with you?"

"I don't see any reason why not." I picked up a toast point and spread some blackberry jam on it while I contemplated Tyler Russo. Probably the last guy you'd expect to visit a psychic, as he seemed a very nuts and bolts sort of person, but he'd come via a recommendation from a friend and had stuck with me for the past few years. Mostly for relationship help; he didn't have much luck in that area. I guided him as best I could, although I knew his real trouble was that he worked insane hours much of the time, and, short of finding a woman who was an airline pilot and so was never around as well, he'd probably continue to strike out.

"Unless the aliens have gotten to him during the past few days," I added, and waited to see if any sort of twinge or chill might follow my statement. None did, which meant either Tyler was still in the clear, or my spider sense had packed its bags and left for the Bahamas so it could meet up with Otto.

"But you don't think that's the case."

"No—but how did you know?"

"Maybe some of your powers are rubbing off on me."

Or it could be that I had the world's worst poker face. I glanced down at my watch. Ten forty-five. If Tyler wasn't up by now, then he was sleeping in after an all-nighter, which meant it really didn't matter what time I called—anything would be inconvenient. "Let me borrow your phone."

Paul reached into his shirt pocket and pulled out the little prepaid cellular. I had to hope Tyler would pick up, even if he didn't recognize the number; on occasion, he took side gigs in addition to his regular job at Topanga Digital, and so it wasn't in his best interests to ignore a call, even if it came from a phone number he'd never seen before.

I did power up my own iPhone, but only to get Tyler's number from the address book. His phone rang once, twice, three times. I bit my lip and began mentally composing a message in case it rolled over to voicemail, but on the fourth ring, I heard a sleepy-sounding male voice say, "Hello?"

So I had woken him up. Knowing there wasn't anything to do but forge ahead, I said, "Hi, Tyler. This is Persephone O'Brien."

"Persephone?" A pause, and then, "Did I miss an appointment or something? It's been kind of crazy lately—"

"No," I broke in. "Nothing like that. I actually just wanted to ask you a couple of questions."

"Questions?"

"About your work. If you don't mind."

"Well, I've got to be back at work in about an hour—"

There went any plans of seeing him in person. I'd have to do this over the phone and hope for the best. "Oh, that's fine," I said hastily, and glanced across at Paul and raised my eyebrows, as if to ask whether it really was okay. He responded by lifting his shoulders and giving me a somewhat resigned nod. "I'll make this fast. You say you've been really busy lately?"

"Well, yeah."

"Have you noticed anything unusual about the projects?"

A note of suspicion entered his voice, but it felt like normal caution to me, not any real attempt at a cover-up. "Unusual how?"

I sent a pleading look in Paul's direction. How was I supposed to ask the right questions when I really didn't know what we were looking for?

Paul leaned across the table and murmured, "Ask him if he's noticed any anomalies in the upper bands of the digital tracks. They might have caused a distortion that he'd have to compensate for across the other bands."

My knight in shining armor. "Any anomalies in the upper bands? They might have caused distortions that you'd notice, and have to compensate for."

A long pause. Then he asked, "How'd you know about that?"

I could practically feel the uncertainty and worry pulsing across the ionosphere and working its way down into the cell phone I held. All very human emotions, though...I still didn't sense anything odd or otherworldly about him. So Tyler was apparently still Tyler. "Um—something another client spoke to me about. I told him I had someone I could ask. Confidentially, of course. I didn't give him your name."

"Oh." Another one of those hesitations, but somehow I knew that, more than thirty miles away, Tyler had relaxed slightly. "Well, yeah, I actually have been seeing stuff like that for the last few weeks. It's really making my life miserable. I even went to my bosses with it, said that we were getting junk from the studios and that the mix wasn't going to be clean, but they told me to just do what I could and leave it alone. So I did."

Which could mean the bosses were controlled by aliens...or just too used to taking their orders from the studios, which of course were everybody's bread and butter in this town. I knew that things in post-production were often worked on up until the last minute, so the material that had been hitting Topanga Digital and playing havoc with Tyler's carefully cali-brated equipment was probably going to be in multiplexes within the next few weeks, if even that long. We didn't have a lot of time.

"Thanks, Tyler," I said, and tried to sound breezy and unconcerned, as if all I'd been doing was collecting data for someone else and not trying to figure out what I was supposed to do to keep the alien hordes from enslaving the entire planet. "That helps a lot. Sorry I woke you."

"No prob. The alarm was going to go off in ten minutes anyway. Have a good one."

He hung up, and I snapped the phone shut and handed it back to Paul.

"There's already a lot of 'infected' material in the pipeline," I told him, and his brow creased.

"Damn. I was hoping we might have gotten a jump on things."

"Well, all is not lost." I thought furiously, trying to dredge up all the minutiae of the technical side of the film industry that I'd mentally shoved aside, not thinking it would ever be of much use to me. Guess you just never knew. I went on, "I know all that data has to be stored someplace. And I know actual film also has to be stored, even though more and more places are fully digital these days. But we don't have much of a lead, that's for sure."

Paul was still holding the phone in his hand. It went off, chirping away in the annoying standard ring tone he'd never bothered to change.

I probably would have startled and dropped the

thing. But he merely opened it, scanned the number quickly, and lifted the phone to his ear. "Jeff."

That syllable was followed by a silence of about half a minute, while the line between Paul's eyebrows deepened and his mouth tightened. Finally he said, "We'll be there in fifteen minutes."

Immediately, I started looking around for our waitress so I could have her bring the bill. "What is it?"

"New developments. Jeff wants us there as soon as possible."

"What sort of developments?"

"He didn't want to say. Just told me it was urgent."

Great. After craning my head to survey the other end of the patio, I locked eyes with the waitress and beckoned her over. Luckily, she had just finished dropping off someone's order, because she came over almost at once.

"Anything else for you?"

"Just the check."

Bless her, she had it in the pocket of her apron, and so was able to extract it and hand it to me on the spot. I thanked her, pulled the money out of my wallet, and handed it over to her. "Keep the change."

Her eyes widened a bit; she'd probably gotten about a thirty-percent tip, but it wasn't worth waiting for those couple extra dollars. "Hey, thanks!"

"My pleasure."

Paul got up and I rose as well, stuffing the wallet back into my purse at the same time. Without speaking, we hurried out the little gate that led from the patio to the street, and then on to the parking lot half a block down. It wasn't until we were back on the freeway, speeding eastward, that I spoke. "Did it sound bad?"

"I didn't get any details. But he sounded...strained."

In which case, it probably wasn't good news. I fiddled with the strap of my purse and stared out the window as the carefully landscaped freeway embankments slid by. Reapplying my lipstick seemed like a frivolous use of my time, but I didn't have anything better to do, and Paul didn't seem inclined to conversation. Too bad that the lipstick reapplication took roughly thirty seconds, while the trip to Fontana seemed to drag on forever.

It was a bright, sunny day, much nicer than the one before, and yet as we drew closer to Lampson Labs, a chill began working its way down my spine. I knew that sensation, and it wasn't a good one.

I said, "I don't know if this is such a good idea."

"What makes you say that?"

"A feeling. Something bad is waiting for us."

He let out a breath and frowned as he turned off Fourth into the little industrial complex where the lab was located. "We already know it's bad. It's an alien virus."

"It's more than that," I told him.

"Could you provide a little more detail? A nebulous 'bad feeling' isn't all that helpful."

I knew that just as well as he did, but at the moment, I didn't have anything else to offer. "Sorry. That's it for now."

"We'll just have to be careful, then."

Meaning he might be a little extra wary, but he wasn't about to turn the car around. I forced down a few deep breaths, trying to calm myself. True, my having a raging case of the heebie-jeebies meant more than it did with most people. However, I knew Paul was determined to meet Jeff and hear his news, so there wasn't a lot I could do, short of making him stop the car and let me out.

I knew I wouldn't abandon him, so I knotted my fingers around my purse strap and bit my lip as we turned the corner and pulled up in front of Lampson Labs.

Nothing seemed to have changed. Jeff's shabby van and Raymond's shiny Prius still occupied the same spots, which made sense, if they'd pulled an all-nighter. True, the rest of the lots around the building were pretty much deserted, but it was a Saturday, after all; not everyone was as dedicated as Raymond.

We pulled into the empty space next to the Prius and got out of the car. By then, my heart was slamming so hard against my ribcage, I was surprised Paul couldn't hear it. However, he strode toward the door, chin lifted, and if he had any misgivings about going into the building, he sure wasn't showing them. I followed a pace or two behind.

As before, the front office was deserted. We headed on back down the hallway toward the lab where we'd left Raymond and Jeff the night before. Sure enough, both of them were still there, although Raymond had apparently abandoned his electron microscope for the time being.

The chill I'd felt on the way over intensified, sending a wave of cold down my back and through my limbs. I looked down and saw the hair on my forearms standing straight up.

"Good," said Raymond, and although I barely knew him, still I heard something wrong in his voice, wrong as the dissonance that had filled my ears the night before.

I stopped in the doorway, but Paul continued forward until he was only a few steps away from Raymond. I wanted to scream at him, to tell him to back away, but something seemed to be constricting my throat, preventing me from making any sound.

"Glad you could get here so quickly," Raymond continued. "Better to get this all cleaned up, with no trouble. Humans really should learn not to stick their noses in where they don't belong."

Humans…?

Paul caught it, too, and took a step backward. "What's going on?"

"Nothing you'll need to worry about." He nodded at Jeff, who looked as glassy-eyed as someone who'd spent all night smoking some really premium weed. Jeff lifted a hand-held radio of some sort and pushed the red button on it.

From nowhere—or maybe everywhere—Otto's voice thundered in my head.

Run, Persephone! Run now!

I can't leave Paul—

You'll do him no good if you're captured as well!

Captured?

The door on the opposite side of the lab flew open, and out of it poured men in black jumpsuits, men with what looked like assault rifles held in their hands. Paul glanced back at me, face filled with agonized worry—not for himself, I realized, but for me.

A grip of iron descended on my arm, and without thinking, I raised my other hand and smacked my assailant directly against the temple with my purse. It must have hurt like hell, considering the bag was loaded with emergency supplies. He let out a muffled oath, and I took advantage of that one second of surprise to turn and bolt down the corridor.

This way! came Otto's voice again, and I zigzagged down a short side hall that ended in an emergency door. The alarms began to shriek the second I pushed it open, but it hardly seemed to matter at that point.

Fleetingly I thought of the car, but I didn't have the keys, and there was no time to hot-wire the thing even if I'd known how to perform such a procedure. Instead, I darted between two buildings, hoping the maze of the industrial complex would be enough to hide the direction I'd gone. From behind me, I heard shouts and the pounding of booted feet, and I increased my pace, thanking God for all those dance classes with Ginger and their cardio benefits. I also thanked God for my little Kohl's flats.

To the street, instructed Otto, and I turned toward what I hoped was Fourth Street. Sure enough, I emerged just a few seconds later—only to see a city bus fast approaching.

Did you arrange that?

Just get on!

I raised my hand, and, wonder of wonders, the bus paused, even though I wasn't anywhere near a designated stop. Trying to keep from panting too heavily, I dug the correct change out of my purse and then staggered back to the first empty seat, where I dropped onto the worn cushions and tried to wrap my brain around what had just happened.

I was safe for the moment, but Paul was in the hands of the enemy.

CHAPTER NINE

I KEPT WATCH OUT THE WINDOW, SURE THAT A PHALANX of black SUVs would descend on the tired Omnitrans bus at any moment, but it seemed I had shaken off my pursuers, at least for the time being. My hands began to shake, and I clenched them around my purse and willed myself to be calm.

As usual, Otto, your sense of timing is impeccable, I thought sourly.

Otto's mental voice sounded almost sheepish. *My apologies for abandoning you, but there are greater things happening than you can possibly imagine.*

So I gathered. What now?

A long pause. *You must go forward on your own. I have helped you this once, but the way ahead is your own path to forge.*

At first, I didn't quite get what he was saying. I

blinked as comprehension slowly dawned. *What, you mean you're not going to help me?*

I cannot help you further...not now. Not more than I already have done. But you will have help. Just remember to keep your heart and mind open, and it will come to you. Another of those hesitations. *Trust your instincts. They have served you well in the past...they will serve you now.*

And then he was gone. I couldn't exactly explain how I knew he had left when he had never materialized in the first place, but I sensed a sudden absence, a lightening of a pressure I hadn't even known was there until it disappeared.

Trust your instincts. I didn't know how helpful that advice was, considering at the moment my first instinct was to break down into some noisy and much-needed hysterics. But that wouldn't solve anything, and would only result in my being thrown off the bus.

Instead, I shut my eyes and took a few of the centering breaths that always prefaced my meditations. Not that I was planning to meditate, but now more than ever, I needed a clear head. If I panicked, I'd never see Paul again.

Just for reference, it actually was possible to take mass transit all the way from the Inland Empire to Burbank...if you were willing to give up three or four hours of your life. By the time I limped off the bus and headed toward the long-term parking lot at Burbank Airport, I was beginning to wonder whether I should have parted with some of my dwindling cash reserves to get a cab, or maybe called an Uber.

Somehow that didn't feel right, just as it seemed the right thing to do to reclaim my car. Probably the last thing my pursuers would be expecting was to have me jump back into my red Volvo. But it was familiar to me, and if I was going to have to do any evasive driving in the near future, better to do it in a car whose reactions I knew as well as I knew my own.

Because I'd begun to feel something, some sort of force that wanted to drag me eastward. I knew, without knowing exactly how I knew, that I needed to head east, that it was somewhere beyond Ontario and even past the borders of California where Paul had been taken. In the past, I'd learned to trust these feelings, to let them guide me where they would. No, on the surface it didn't make sense, just as picking up the Volvo, paying off the attendant, and heading down into L.A. didn't make a lot of sense. But although I still had some cash on me, I didn't have as much as I thought I might need, and I knew I had to turn to the one person who would take care of me without question...all right, without *too* many questions.

"You're what?" Ginger demanded. She'd just finished her Saturday afternoon salsa class, and her bright red hair stuck to her temples and the back of her neck. She picked up a flyer for an upcoming ball-room dance competition and fanned herself with it.

"I'm driving to Arizona, and I don't want to pull the money out of my own account. You know I'm good for it."

"That's not the point." She frowned, but deli-cately, so as not to overly crease the professionally filled skin between her brows. "You disappear for two days, don't leave word with anyone, there's these men poking around—"

"What men?" I demanded, more sharply than I had intended.

"Men in suits. They looked like government types, but they flashed their I.D.s so fast I didn't have time to see what branch. Not police. I've dated a few policemen in my time, and these guys had a totally different smell."

I should have expected as much, but still, the verbal confirmation that they had been snooping around my friends and my business made my stomach clench. "What did they want?"

"Wanted to know if I'd heard from you, if you'd left any information as to where you'd gone." Her mouth quirked. "I told them I had no idea but that I hoped you'd hooked a hottie and gone off for a lost weekend somewhere."

"Ginger!"

A lift of her perfectly toned shoulders. "Well,

what was I supposed to say? It was the truth. So did you?"

"Did I what?"

"Hook a hottie," she said. "Because unless my eyes are deceiving me, that's a fairly decent hickey you've got there on the left side of your neck."

My hand rose of its own volition to touch the spot she'd noticed. I had seen it in passing that morning as I'd gotten ready, but as my hair hid it most of the time, I had deemed it not worth covering up. Most people probably wouldn't have even seen it, but Ginger had eagle eyes when it came to that sort of thing.

"I, um...I did meet someone. But believe me, it's safer if you don't know anything about him."

"Oh, really?"

"Yes, really. And he's in trouble, and I need to help him. So are you going to loan me the money or not?"

"Don't get your panties in a bunch." She moved away from me to step behind the reception desk of her studio. From the lanyard around her neck she selected a key, then bent down to unlock the bottom desk drawer, which I knew was where she kept her cash box. She opened it and rummaged through the bills inside, then extended a handful to me. "I've got about fifteen hundred here. Think that'll be enough?"

"It has to be. Thanks, Ginger." I shoved the money into my purse, and leaned across the desk to give her a quick hug, which of course she brushed off. Ginger wasn't big on genuine shows of emotion.

"Enough of that," she said with a wave of her hand. "Just do what you have to do—and then come back here and give me all the juicy details, because I want to know all about Mr. Mysterious."

"I will. I promise." I flashed her a grin and hurried for the door. After my bus ride to get out of Ontario, I didn't have much change left, and I hadn't dared to use my debit card on the meter. This visit was by necessity a quick one.

As much as I wanted to go to my apartment and grab some clean clothes, I knew that would be a huge mistake. Just the thought of it made the hair stand up on the back of my neck, which meant my sixth sense was still humming along just fine. Probably there were several agents surveilling the property, just in case I went back there for some reason.

But I didn't get the same hinky sensation when I considered stopping by the motel in Pomona, and at least I did have some clothing and other items there I could collect. Besides, it was on the eastward route out of town, and so I'd be losing very little time.

That matter apparently settled, I pointed the Volvo toward Highland and hoped the traffic wouldn't be too bad. Yes, it was a Saturday after-noon, but in L.A. that didn't necessarily mean much. As it turned out, though, the trip back to Pomona went more smoothly than I had hoped, and it wasn't quite five when I pulled into the parking lot of the

Route 66 Motel. Since I didn't have all that much to pack, I had the room cleared out in less than five minutes. And I carefully folded Paul's few articles of clothing and stowed them in one of the Kohl's bags, then wrapped his toiletries in another shopping bag.

My throat went tight as I performed these tasks. Was this all just an exercise in futility? He could be dead...or worse, already infected with the alien virus.

No, the universe told me, and my shoulders loosened just the smallest bit. Whatever they were doing with him, it wasn't that. Not yet, anyway. The need to head east was strong, but not so much so that I should be panicking yet.

I settled up the bill at the motel using my own money; Ginger's cash infusion was insurance, but I wouldn't dip into it until all of my own funds were depleted. And then, since there was nothing left to hold me, I got back into my car and drove east.

For some reason, I'd thought I'd drop down to the 10 Freeway and head toward Arizona along that route, but something told me that was not the way to go. Instead, I headed northward and then east along the 40, driving over territory that would take me parallel to the old Route 66 and over the Colorado River before moving on to Arizona's high country.

I'd never been that way before, and I looked around with interest. Well, interest at first, anyway— after the first hundred or so miles of monotonous desert, my attention began to flag. Also, the sun began to set behind me, at once obscuring the landscape with odd gray-blue shadows and illuminating the sky at my back with a bloody light I sincerely hoped was not a harbinger of things to come. Then night fell, and all I could see were the taillights of the vehicles in front of me and the occasional illuminated road sign.

Maybe it was crazy, driving out into the darkness like that. I'd looked at I-40's route through Arizona on my phone, but that didn't give me much information, not even a ping to tell me if I was on the right track. About all I could do was keep heading east and hope for the best.

The markers told me Flagstaff was 400 miles away, then 350. I didn't know if the mountain town was my destination or not. Midway through the journey, I stopped at a wide spot in the road to get gas and noted it was almost a dollar a gallon cheaper than in California. And I realized, with a sort of abstract curiosity, that I was hungry, and pulled into a Wendy's to get a burger and some iced tea. Funny how the body can give you those reminders even when otherwise it seems as if the world is falling apart around you.

Somewhat refreshed, I pushed on. Small towns flashed past...Seligman...Williams...Ash Fork. Pools of light in the surrounding darkness, little flickers to remind me I wasn't alone in the universe.

I crossed the city limits into Flagstaff and waited for the twinge, the one that would tell me I had come to the right place. Nothing, and I drove on, my fore-head creasing into a frown. Had I been wrong? Was I supposed to continue on into New Mexico, to some hidden base in Paul's own home state?

And then I saw the sign that said "89A Sedona," and the surge that went through me almost made me swerve off the road. I gripped the steering wheel, following the road to an odd roundabout-style turn-off, and then swung onto 89A, which turned out to be only a two-lane road headed down into almost absolute blackness.

No one followed me, and I saw no taillights on the highway ahead of me. True, it was past eleven o'clock, but Los Angeles on a Saturday night was barely waking up at that hour. I got the distinct feeling I wasn't in L.A. anymore, though.

The first stretch, probably at least five miles or so, went smoothly enough. Then I saw a sign that warned me of a twenty-five mile-per-hour speed limit, and I slowed accordingly. That wasn't nearly enough, though; the road switched back on itself like a demented pretzel, and I slowed far below the recommended speed. Thank God there wasn't anyone behind me to protest my glacial pace. My headlights did little to illuminate the route, showing only patches of rock, scrubby trees by the side of the road, an improbable pale flash of something that might even have been snow in a forgotten little meadow. Then I saw a portion of hillside covered by some sort of net—presumably to prevent rock slides, and I slowed even further. If they were putting up nets to keep the hillsides from sliding, then the whole area couldn't be all that stable.

Somehow I twisted and slalomed my way down into Sedona, fingers wrapped in a death grip around the Volvo's steering wheel. I had to hope that the universe didn't intend for me to end up a wet smear on the narrow canyon road, but I also had to question its wisdom in sending me down such a route in full dark.

When I finally reached the town, the transition was almost shocking in its suddenness; one moment I was banking cautiously through a narrow canyon, and the next I had emerged into what looked like a fairly civilized street, with shops and restaurants and pedestrians.

All right, not very many pedestrians, not at that hour. Still, even that minor sign of life was enough to reassure me, and I drew in a shaky breath as I made my way down what was obviously Sedona's main drag. All of the shops and even the majority of the restaurants seemed to have closed for the night, but there was just enough foot traffic to let me know I wasn't completely alone in the world.

I didn't know where I was headed. I had to let the instinct within guide me as I continued down the street through the heart of the town, and hope that whatever I was seeking, it wouldn't be too late for me to find it.

Then I saw a modest building off to my left, one

with a brilliant neon green sign that proclaimed it to be the "UFO Depot." I slammed on the brakes and made a precipitous left. Lucky for me, the traffic was pretty thin at that hour.

I pulled into the poorly paved parking lot and stopped. My heart had begun a quick, irrational beating, but I tried to ignore it as I slid out of the car and faced the storefront.

Of course, the shop was closed. I could tell that at once, from the darkened windows and complete lack of any other vehicles in the lot. What else had I expected? It was well past eleven and pushing on toward midnight. Most shops in Los Angeles wouldn't have been open at that hour, either. Restaurants and clubs, sure, but not retail establishments... not even the ones that catered to a fringe population.

The sign at the door had one of those little clock faces, the ones with the hands you could move to represent the hour of your return. This one said, "We'll be back at ten."

All right. I didn't like to wait, felt the weight of those intervening hours like a stone on my back, but I knew I didn't have much choice. The universe had told me Paul would be all right for now. I had to trust its communication, have faith that the intervening time wouldn't make a difference. What else could I do?

There was a motel down the street, one where they were happy enough to take my cash and enter my name on an old-fashioned ledger at the front desk. No computers, a fact for which I was profoundly glad. Computers could give away my location. I still had that sense of being compelled, of being shown the path to follow, but there was no point in taking chances. I couldn't risk making a foolish mistake that might reveal my position.

Somehow, I knew that my strength lay in being unknown, undetected. With any luck, they wouldn't know what hit them.

Amazingly, I overslept the next morning. Or maybe that wasn't so amazing; after all, I'd had a fairly exhausting day, and the bed in the motel was more comfortable than it had any right to be. And just maybe the universe was allowing me that rest, knowing I had even greater ordeals to face in the day ahead.

At any rate, by the time I'd showered and dressed, it was well past nine. I stepped out of my motel room and then stopped, mouth agape.

I'd come into town in utter dark and hadn't seen anything except the lighted storefronts along Highway 89A. Oh, of course I'd heard how gorgeous Sedona was. But those casual mentions—usually accompanied by exhortations that a professional psychic should make the pilgrimage there at least once—had done nothing to prepare me for the reality of the place.

Red rock bluffs soared off to the east and to the north as well, framed by the lacy green of cotton-woods and the darker, duskier hues of junipers and pine. Here and there on the highest peaks, I thought I saw a pale flash of unmelted snow. The sky was an achingly deep blue, the sort of lapis hue you never saw in Los Angeles. And the air that touched my skin, though cool, felt soft and welcoming, as if it had come there to personally greet me. The winds were alive, filled with shimmers of energy that seemed to draw me in, to guide me.

I walked down the street to a charming little café where the proprietor greeted me as if she'd known me all my life, and where I was served the best coffee and eggs I'd ever had. By the time I was done, it was ten, and I somehow knew the UFO store would be ready to meet me.

I went to my car and drove back to the shop, then pulled into a space at the far end of the decrepit parking lot. Sure enough, the sign was off the door, which stood open. I went inside.

It was a cramped space, filled with the sort of bric-a-brac you'd expect a store like that would carry to entice tourists—T-shirts, DVDs, books, stuffed plushie aliens with big heads and almond-shaped eyes. A TV overhead showed *The Day the Earth Stood Still*. I wished the aliens I was dealing with were even half as appealing as Michael Rennie.

A woman around my age, maybe a little younger, sat behind the counter, typing away at a computer keyboard. Since the monitor was pointed away from me, I couldn't really see what she was working on.

Now that the time had come, I felt strangely reticent. I pretended to be interested in the merchandise, even picked up a few books and DVDs and made myself look as if I were reading the blurbs on the back covers. But I knew I couldn't procrastinate any longer. The universe had sent me here, and if it wanted to make me look like a complete idiot, so be it.

I set a copy of *The Day After Roswell* back on the shelf and turned to the woman behind the counter.

"Excuse me."

She lifted her head. For a UFO nut, she looked pretty respectable, actually—expertly streaked hair, makeup applied with more precision than mine. "Can I help you?"

"I hope so."

Her head cocked to one side, and she watched me steadily. I noticed that her eyes were a deep, clear blue, almost the same shade as the cerulean skies that had greeted me as I left my motel room.

"This might sound sort of crazy," I began, then paused and shook my head. Nothing ventured…. "Actually, it's going to sound completely crazy. But I was sent here for help, and so I'm asking. I have a friend who was, well…abducted."

"Abducted?" she echoed, and at once her glance slanted upward.

"Oh, not that kind of abducted," I said hastily.

"That is, the people who took him might have been in league with them"—and I sent a quick look heavenward as well— "but they were definitely human. It's just that I know they brought him here."

"Here."

"Well, somewhere in this area. Some secret base or something." Her expression didn't change. I didn't know whether that was a good or a bad thing, since I wasn't getting much of a read off her. Doggedly, I went on, "I know this must sound absolutely insane, but it's the truth. Paul and I were on the trail of this alien conspiracy—"

"Paul who?" she interjected.

"Paul Oliver."

"*The* Paul Oliver?" she demanded. "The astrophysicist? The author of *Investigating the Unknowable*?"

"The same. I met him at a MUFON symposium in L.A.—"

"Hold up." She lifted a hand to stop me, then reached out and picked up the handset of the phone sitting on the counter, dialed a number. "Hey, Kiki. I've got a situation here. Get the team together, and be at the shop ASAP." A brief silence, during which she seemed to be listening to the person at the other end of the line. "Yes, Lance, too. Especially Lance."

She set down the phone, and I asked, "Who's Lance?"

"A friend."

Her friend...or mine? Since I didn't know quite

how to respond, I said, "My name's Persephone, by the way. Persephone O'Brien."

"Kara Swenson." She put out her hand and I shook it, feeling more than a little awkward. Then she went on, "You came to the right place, Persephone. Something must have been guiding you here."

I lifted my shoulders. "Oh, well, that's probably because I'm a psychic." Somehow, it seemed the most natural thing in the world to tell her that, even though I was usually still reticent to admit my profession to others even after all these years.

"For real?"

"For real." I fished a card out of my purse and handed it to her.

She took it from me and scanned it briefly, then said, "Los Angeles? You're a long way from home."

"Tell me about it."

A smile, showing teeth so perfect they could have belonged to one of my TV-executive clients. "An alien conspiracy, huh?"

"Unfortunately, yes."

She laughed then. "Well, we specialize in those. And just so you don't think you're crazy, my team has been tracking down information on the hidden base out in Boynton Canyon for months. Actually, most people think it's Boynton where everything's going on, but it's really up in Secret Canyon that the real action is taking place."

Shaking my head, I said, "I've never heard of

either of those places. Hell, I didn't believe in any of this stuff until I had a client who was mixed up in it...." I trailed off, paused, and added, "No, that's not right. He wasn't mixed up in it, just had it thrust on him. And now he's dead."

To my surprise, Kara didn't look at all shocked. "There are more dead than you realize. Or those who have disappeared, so we have no idea what really happened to them. It's what happens when you get too close. They dismiss us because we pass ourselves off as all part of the tourist attractions—hell, I run UFO tours that carefully keep people away from anything that might be too dangerous—but we keep digging. And we're in possession of some information I'm pretty sure certain operatives wouldn't be too happy to learn we know."

"But they don't stop you?"

"I'm pretty visible." She waved a hand around the store. "And I try to make myself visible in other ways—our website, my blog. People would notice if I suddenly disappeared. Besides, I'm harmless. I sell T-shirts and DVDs to the tourists. Who's going to suspect me of doing anything underhanded?"

"Anyone who knows you well," came a new voice, and I looked over to the front door, where a pretty woman—girl, really—with long, flaxen-blonde hair and Kara's bright blue eyes smiled at me.

"My sister, Kiki," Kara said. "And Adam, her boyfriend."

I gave a half-hearted wave at a tall, brown-haired

young man who leaned out from behind Kiki and sent a grin in my direction.

"And Michael Lightfoot, and Lance…well, it's just Lance."

These last two still stood outside the door, but I could see Michael Lightfoot was clearly Native American, older than Kara and me by several decades, his iron-gray hair pulled back in a ponytail, his dark eyes calm but appraising. A sense of quiet, of stillness flowed from him, a sensation that was immediately reassuring. With him along, I thought we might actually have a chance.

I couldn't see Lance clearly at first, as he was blocked by Michael Lightfoot's broad shoulder. Then he shifted, and I found myself looking up into hard, chiseled features, the sort of face I would have expected to see behind a pair of mirrored lenses as it leaned down to ask me if I knew how fast I was going. But more than that, I sensed the power flowing out from him, power that struck me almost as a wave. I staggered backward, and put out a hand on one of the shelves behind me to steady myself.

He said nothing but stared down at me, face impassive, as if taking my measure. After an interminable second or two, he nodded. "She's not making it up."

"As if I would!" I said, indignant that he would even make such a suggestion. Did he have any idea what I had gone through the past few days—what

Paul had gone through? Surely the truth was frightening enough without adding any embellishments.

"You'd be surprised."

Kara waved a hand. "We don't have time for this. Paul Oliver is in trouble—"

"*The* Paul Oliver?" Kiki broke in, eyes shining. She had a turquoise blue streak in her pale blonde hair, which was pulled into a pair of Swiss Miss braids. If she was a day over twenty-one, I'd be shocked.

I reflected that I would never have known a few days ago that the UFO world had its own rock stars. And I also wondered what the hell I was doing, dragging these people I didn't know into my own personal nightmare. Kiki and Adam were just kids, and although you certainly couldn't say that about Lance or Michael Lightfoot, still, they were strangers. Maybe this had all been a terrible mistake.

But then I heard Otto's voice, strong and sure, in my mind. *You will have help. Just remember to keep your heart and mind open, and it will come to you.*

I nodded, although whether in response to Kiki's question, or as an affirmation of my spirit guide's remembered words, I couldn't really say. My voice was firm as I responded, "Yes, *the* Paul Oliver. And he—and I—need your help."

CHAPTER TEN

It didn't take as long as I had thought it might to recount the story to them—how Alex Hathaway had come to see me at my office, how Otto had commanded me to go see Paul at the Sheraton Universal. The chase by the agent in the parking garage. Our growing discovery of the conspiracy. The subjugation of Raymond Lampson. Paul's capture.

By the time I was done, Kiki's blue eyes—so like her sister's—were almost as big as the saucers she hunted in the night sky. Adam similarly appeared far more excited than worried or nervous. Michael Lightfoot's expression was grave, and as for Lance, well, he didn't have wear much of an expression at all. Kara seemed more intrigued than anything else, although her excitement was more muted than her sister's.

She turned to Lance. "Secret Canyon?"

One nod. His gaze flickered in my direction for the barest fraction of a second. He asked, "Have you seen him?"

"What?"

"You're a psychic." There was just the smallest hint of contempt in the word. "Haven't you tried to see him, made an attempt to find out where they've taken him?"

I almost pulled out my "psychics are not one size fits all" speech, then decided it wasn't worth the effort, since I had the distinct impression Lance knew very well that his question was guaranteed to irritate me. Technically speaking, I wasn't a clairvoyant. If Otto wasn't giving me outright advice, then most of my readings came from hunches, or feelings...like the one that had brought me here to Sedona in the first place.

"No," I said. "I just know he's still alive, and still all right...for now, anyway."

Lance's flat stare didn't flicker. "Maybe you should try."

The middle of the UFO Depot, with a group of people I barely knew looking on, was perhaps not the most ideal situation for attempting that sort of feat. But he had put me on my mettle, and I had done such a thing once or twice before. I just had no idea whether it would work this time, especially when I hadn't had any time to mentally prepare myself for such spiritual exertions.

Without bothering to reply, I shut my eyes,

closing out the faces of the people watching me, the cluttered shelves of the cramped store, and eased into a calm blankness. The sound of the film playing in the background became tinny, then died away to nothing.

I thought of Paul, of the quick flash of his smile, the green and gold glints in his hazel eyes. The way his mouth had felt on mine, the warm scent of his skin. All the thousand and one little details I hadn't even realized I was noticing at the time, but which had been carefully filed away in my mind. I built an image of him in the darkness behind my eyelids, and suddenly, he was there.

Or rather, I was there with him. I saw him clearly as he sat on a mean little cot with a thin Army-issue blanket in a room with dark gray walls. He seemed to be alone. A fresh bruise showed clearly along the fine bones of his jaw, and he was sporting a pretty spectacular black eye. But his gaze as he stared at the metal door of the chamber seemed sharp enough, and I knew he was still Paul, no puppet of the aliens. How long he would remain that way, I had no idea, but at least I knew the universe had told me the truth.

Oh, Paul.... Seeing him like that made the need clench in my stomach. I almost reached out to touch him, even though I knew such a gesture would be futile. He was still miles away, maybe even farther than that.

His head went up, and he looked around his prison cell, eyes wide. "Persephone?"

He couldn't have heard me. Impossible. But I mentally sighed his name again, and once more his head moved from right to left, as if he could somehow find me within the confines of that stark little room.

My throat tightened, and the hot, sharp edges of tears began to prick at the corners of my eyes. So we had made some sort of connection, even in the short time we'd spent together. It wasn't all wish fulfillment and foolish dreams. I'd never been able to make contact like that with anyone else.

But then a strong, cool hand touched my wrist, and a deep voice said, "Persephone."

My eyelids snapped open. Michael Lightfoot stared down at me, his dark gaze not quite as imperturbable as the last time I had looked at him.

"Why did you do that?"

His eyes narrowed. "You were gone for almost fifteen minutes."

Fifteen— "*What?*"

"You totally tranced out," Kiki supplied. "Lance said to leave you alone, but Michael finally decided if we didn't do something, you might be standing there all day. You already scared off a couple of customers."

I blinked, and realized that my left foot had gone to sleep. Fifteen minutes. I'd never done anything like that before. Jesus.

Lance asked, "Did you see him?"

Again, that constriction squeezed my throat, a burden born of need and fear and doubt. I nodded, since I wasn't sure how well my voice was working.

"Details?"

His tone was too even to be called outright annoyed, but I could tell he didn't have much patience with me.

I coughed, and forced the words past the thickness surrounding my vocal cords. "He's in a small room. The walls look like rock. There's nothing in there except a cot. He's not bound, but it looks as if he's been roughed up a little. But he's alive…and still himself."

He nodded. "We'd better not waste any more time, then." A quick, sharp glance at the rest of the group, and he added, "This could get dicey."

"I live for dicey," Kiki said immediately, while her boyfriend nodded. I felt a sharp thrum of worry from Kara, but she only said, in resigned tones,

"Guess I'll be holding down the fort once again."

"Your role is valuable as well," Michael said, and she gave a little shrug, even as a sense of resignation drifted from her in waves.

"I keep telling myself that."

Kiki grinned. "I'm driving!"

The first true emotion I'd seen so far passed over Lance's face. His eyebrows creased. "Oh, shit."

We all trooped outside, except for Kara, who had turned back to her computer in a vain attempt to look as if she really didn't mind being left behind. I stopped dead in my tracks when I saw what was waiting for us in the parking lot.

"You really think you're going to be inconspicuous in that?"

The van was black and had "UFO Night Tours" painted across the sides in an acid green almost the same hue as the shop's sign. An alien with huge teardrop eyes stared at me from directly above the wheelwell.

"Protective camouflage," Kiki responded cheerfully. "Everyone's used to seeing tour buses and vans all over town. No one takes it seriously. Even the MIBs pretty much ignore us."

"MIBs?" I echoed.

"Men in black," Lance said. "Not to be trifled with. Get in—time's wasting."

I wondered who, in one of my exes' pithy terminology, had pissed in his Wheaties, but decided it wouldn't be prudent to ask. Instead, I climbed into the back of the van, since Adam had already taken the shotgun position. There were three rows of seats, and I settled myself in the one directly behind Kiki, while Michael Lightfoot sat down next to me. Lance, of course, went all the way to the back, where he stared out the window as if expecting a squad of MIBs to descend on us at any moment.

Kiki didn't wait to see if we'd all fastened our

seatbelts, but instead squealed out of the parking lot in a scatter of loose gravel. I clung to the armrest and decided that Lance, despite his sour mood, hadn't been exaggerating about her driving.

There was a good deal of traffic on the main drag, despite it being a Sunday morning. To take my mind off the way Kiki was weaving in and out of the cars, SUVs, tour buses, and vans not terribly unlike our own, I leaned toward Michael and asked in an undertone, "So what's the deal with Lance?"

He smiled, the lines around his eyes seeming to make them almost disappear for a moment. "Ah, Lance. His way has not been an easy one."

"He was part of Project Stargate," Kiki chimed in.

"What?"

"Project Stargate. The army's remote viewing program," she added, sounding a little impatient, as if everyone should know what that was. "But he left even before they disbanded it. The whole thing does seem to have made him a little cranky."

"Can you stop talking about 'him' as if he wasn't in the same vehicle with you?" came Lance's sour tones from the back of the van.

I risked a quick glance over my shoulder and saw him leaning forward in the space between the two headrests. To my surprise, he appeared far less irritated than his comment would have indicated.

"'Remote viewing'?" I repeated, curious despite myself. I didn't really expect him to answer me, but I couldn't help asking, "Why did you leave?"

"Saw more than I should have," he said, and shot me a narrow-eyed look. It was almost as if he got some perverse pleasure in providing me with a reply when I clearly had been predicting that I would get none. "More than I wanted to." A jerk of his leather-clad shoulder toward the red rock–rimmed canyon toward which we were headed. "And it was up there."

Even though the country around me was beautiful—staggeringly gorgeous, actually—I shivered. Something waited out there, that much I knew. What exactly that thing was, whether aliens, MIBs, squads of Army Rangers, or what-have-you, I got the distinct impression it wasn't going to be rolling out the welcome mat for the motley crew inside the UFO Night Tours van. And how we were supposed to get into what I guessed had to be some sort of heavily fortified facility, I hadn't the slightest idea.

"How is that possible, anyway?" Adam asked, turning in his seat to look back at Lance. At the same moment, the paved road abruptly gave way to dirt and gravel. The van lurched a bit, and I hung on to my armrest grimly and hoped the vehicle had decent tires and a sturdy suspension.

Lance's gray gaze shifted to Adam for a second before moving straight ahead once again. Although otherwise I couldn't get a clear read off him, I did sense that Lance didn't have much patience for Adam. "How is what possible?"

"How can they be hiding some big operation up there, right under all our noses?"

"Classic obfuscation. Most people think Boynton's where the action is—as if the shadow government would be stupid enough to let someone build a resort right on top of its base—so no one pays attention to Secret Canyon."

"Shadow government?" I said.

Lance threw another sour look in my direction. "You really don't know anything, do you?"

"Well, not having spent the past five years hanging out on conspiracy theory websites—"

Michael broke in, his clear, deep tones overriding my rebuke. "The evidence does seem to indicate that there are elements within the government working independently of its charter. These elements have their own agenda."

"Including colluding with aliens?"

A grave nod. "If it suits their purpose."

Maybe I was just being naive, but I couldn't understand how people in the government would be willing to betray their fellow human beings. After all, this wasn't like selling secrets to the Russians or something. "So you're trying to tell me that people funded by our taxes are working behind the scenes to enslave their own people? That doesn't make any sense to me."

"Obviously, you don't get out much," Lance remarked. "There are plenty of people in the government who don't think the American public has the smarts to wipe its own ass. They'll sell them out in a heartbeat if it means gaining more power or furthering their aims."

"Don't forget about the technology—you know, like the Aurora Project," Kiki put in from the front seat. At least she had her gaze more or less directed forward, but I still worried that she wasn't paying enough attention to the road. "The aliens trade bits of technology for access and staging areas—like the hidden base up in Secret Canyon."

It would have been nice if she hadn't kept bringing up all this stuff as if it was supposed to be common knowledge. I remarked, my tone a little sourer than I had intended, "It can't be that secret if you all know about it."

Lance shrugged. "We spend our time digging. Most people don't. And it's not as if Secret Canyon is off-limits. People hike there, but it's a rough trail. And more often than not, they don't make it all the way up the trail."

"Too steep?" I asked, even though I knew that probably wasn't the reason.

"Let's just call it bad vibrations. That's something a psychic can relate to, right?"

Something almost made me respond that if he had been in the remote viewing program, then he must be a psychic, too, and what was with all the sarcasm? But then I realized the last thing we needed was to keep sniping at each other. Too much was at stake. We had to work as a team...even if Lance was as prickly as one of the cacti that lined the road around us.

So I just lifted my shoulders and stared ahead as well, watching as we bounced and jounced over the unpaved track and slowly climbed higher. On every side, the red rocks seemed to close in, as if looming over us. I hated to admit it, but Lance was right. Something about the place just felt wrong, and we weren't anywhere near our destination yet. It was beautiful, yes, but beautiful in a deadly way, like the web of a black widow spider.

I wondered if we'd be able to escape that web.

None of us spoke for a minute or two. Maybe they'd all sensed the same thing I had, or maybe they were just picking up on what was a galloping case of the heebie-jeebies.

"What did you see?" I asked Lance finally. "What made you quit?"

Surprisingly, he grinned. The expression changed his whole face; I realized he wasn't as old as I had originally thought he was...maybe ten years or so older than I. "You don't beat around the bush, do you?"

"Haven't got the time."

"Fair enough." Lance paused, and I could actually feel the consciousnesses of the other passengers in the van focusing in on him. I realized then that they'd never heard the whole story, either, that Lance had never been one to reveal much of himself.

"I suppose it's only fair you know what you're

heading into," he said. "I don't need to go into the whole story—let's just say that remote viewing is all about staying extremely focused, about finding the target. But after I'd been in the program for a couple of years, I started breaking focus, tracking someplace I shouldn't have been looking. I don't know why. Up until then, I'd been one of the program's top agents. You weren't supposed to do what I was doing."

"Which was?" Kiki asked from the front seat. Her eyes were shining as she looked back over her shoulder at Lance.

"Eyes ahead," he admonished. "If I'm going to die today, I don't want it to be because you ran this crate off the road."

"Fine." But although her tone was sulky, she did as he directed and pointed her gaze forward, over the increasingly treacherous dirt-paved lane, which was barely large enough for one vehicle at that point. God help us if some hikers were coming down Dry Creek in the opposite direction.

"Anyway," Lance continued, "I kept seeing some sort of facility, apparently underground. Scientific base, I thought—there were a lot of white lab coats. Didn't think much of it at first…until I got a better look at the men who were guarding the base." He paused, eyes narrowing as if at some unpleasant memory. "They all had the same face."

He couldn't have meant…. Twisting in my seat so I could look at him more or less directly, I said, "You don't honestly expect me to believe— "

"Yeah, I do. Clones. They could have been the same man sent through a photocopier or something. At first, I just thought I wasn't seeing correctly—remote viewing's not really like watching a movie projected in your head, you know—and I thought I was giving them all the same face because I wasn't getting enough detail. But it kept happening over and over, and I started seeing more, and I began to understand what was going on. They weren't men. They were hybrids."

"Human-alien hybrids?" Kiki demanded, and bounced up in her seat like some middle-school girl who'd just been told the latest teen heartthrob was coming to visit her homeroom class. "For real?"

"Both hands on the wheel."

"They are!"

For some reason, I had the urge to burst out laughing, the juxtaposition between her girlish excitement and Lance's dour revelations was so extreme, but I managed to hold it in. I doubted Lance would be encouraged to continue if I began giggling uncontrollably.

Still, I couldn't really believe what he had just said. Sure, I knew aliens existed, and were plotting against us, but there were lines where the borders of complete insanity were crossed, and as far as I was concerned, we had just driven over one of them. "Really? This isn't *The X-Files*."

"I'm well aware of that." He sent me another one of those sideways irritated stares. "I'm telling you what I saw. And what I saw wasn't human. The hybrids were just part of it."

"You saw...*them?*" Adam asked. Unlike his girl-friend, he had no need to watch the road, so he had turned around in his seat so he could more or less see the rest of us directly.

"Sometimes. But even those occasional glimpses were enough to tell me they were involved, and heavily. Took me a while to figure out where all this could possibly be going down, and once I'd gotten what I thought was the truth, I knew I had to leave the program. Couldn't risk my supervisors learning what I'd seen. I had to let them think I'd just burned out." Another one of those shrugs, somehow eloquent in its resigned simplicity. "So I took off, but I kept researching what I could. And it became clear pretty fast that the times I'd seen aliens at the base were the times that correlated with high levels of UFO activity in the region. They can cover their tracks a lot of the time, but there are just too many eyes looking at the sky in this part of the world."

"Wow," Kiki breathed, even though she'd appar-ently learned enough not to glance back. "So they're holding Paul Oliver in a base full of aliens and hybrid clones?"

"Probably."

"That is so cool."

I wished I shared her appraisal of the situation. About all I could hope for was that this happened to be one of the times when our little gray friends weren't hanging around. Hordes of blank-faced clones were bad enough without tossing a bunch of aliens with unknown powers and abilities into the equation.

"And we're all just going to go barreling in there in our Scooby van and save the day?" I asked.

For a minute, Lance didn't say anything, but only stared past me, his gaze turned curiously inward. Then he smiled again, but this time the expression didn't reach his eyes. "No. It'll be just the three of us when the time comes—Michael, and me…and you."

My stomach dropped to somewhere in the vicinity of my feet—which were still covered in my Kohl's flats and not hiking boots, unfortunately. But I made myself think of Paul, alone in that cell, with that inky bruise distorting his eye and the livid traces of another contusion painting his jaw, and I knew I didn't have any choice.

For Paul, I was willing to risk everything.

The road ran out a few minutes later, and Kiki limped the van over to a hiding place behind a clump of scrubby juniper trees. I shoved my purse under my seat and hoped I'd be in a position to retrieve it when this was all over.

Everyone climbed out of the van, and I could tell by Kiki's furrowed brow that she was less than thrilled about being left behind.

"Adam and I can help, you know. I've hiked these hills—I know what I'm doing!"

"This isn't just a hike, Kiki," Lance said. For some

reason, his tone sounded almost gentle. "Besides, what would I say to Kara if something happened to you?"

"And what am I supposed to tell Kara if something happens to you?" she shot back.

I never thought I'd see Lance looking embarrassed, but he did appear distinctly uncomfortable. "Hopefully, you won't have tell her anything."

"Hmph."

It could have been my imagination, but I thought Adam, who hovered a few inches behind Kiki's left shoulder, seemed almost relieved about being left behind. I guessed his enthusiasm for chasing UFOs didn't extend to infiltrating underground bases staffed by human-alien hybrid soldiers.

I couldn't really blame him.

Michael had been silent for some time. Now he stood a few paces away from the rest of us, watching the looming red rock cliffs with intent dark eyes, as if he saw something hidden there that the rest of us had overlooked. "I know the way."

"I figured you would," Lance said.

The older man didn't smile, but only nodded. "Forty years of climbing these hills helps."

Of course, I didn't have that sort of background. I didn't think the few times I'd gone hiking in the Hollywood Hills with one of my exes counted as experience with this sort of expedition. I tried not to look down at my completely inadequate footwear, instead brought up the mental image of Paul in that cramped little cell.

"Lead on, then," I said, a little more heartily than I'd intended. I guessed I wasn't fooling anyone.

"You're brave. That's good." And Michael turned and began moving.

Brave? That was a laugh.

Lance looked almost as if he was about to comment, but instead just shook his head and followed in Michael's footsteps. I noticed how both men seemed to find a way to jog from scrub brush to scrub brush, effectively hiding their movements. I certainly wasn't trained in the field, but at least they were giving me a good example to follow. I moved after them, then paused for a second to turn back toward Kiki and Adam.

"Keep the motor running," I said, and Kiki, who'd been looking rather sulky, flashed me a grin.

"Aye-aye, captain."

The ground sloped upward at a somewhat alarming angle. I'd known we'd have some rough terrain to climb, but I hadn't realized how quickly it would grow treacherous, how soon the relatively flat land where the road had ended would transform itself into rough slopes cut into gullies by years of rain and weather, how the rocks would give way under my feet, leaving me scrabbling toward the next semi-level spot before I lost my balance completely.

True, I was making the climb in more or less practical flats and not a pair of Louboutin platform pumps, but it was all a matter of degree. Once or twice, Lance's hand shot backward at the last moment before I slipped completely and went ass over teakettle; I couldn't help noticing that both he and Michael wore heavy-treaded hiking boots, the sort of things my friends and I had derisively referred to as "waffle-stompers" back in our middle-school days. Still, I could see they were a necessity here, allowing the two men to find purchase in the scree, and I was definitely thankful for Lance's helping hand.

And all along, that sensation of cold seemed to work its way up my spine, a perception of some wrongness that plucked at the very molecules in the air. For all his insouciance, I could tell Lance felt it, too. His brow furrowed more than ever, and droplets of sweat that had nothing to do with the chilly day glistened across his brow. And Michael, who climbed as quietly and methodically as a machine, also appeared to be sensing it as well, because once or twice he stopped and thrust his chin upward, as if scenting the air, and then shook, for all the world like my shepherd-mix Elsie used to do back when I was a kid and she crossed a smell she didn't like on her evening walk.

For myself, I would have liked to say I was concentrating so hard on not falling off the side of the mountain that I didn't have time to sense any bad vibrations or evil vapors or whatever you wanted to call them, but that was far from the truth. The day was cool but not cold, and I should have worked up a sweat with the way I was exerting myself. Instead, my hands trembled from a chill I couldn't shake, and the back of my neck was a prickled mass of goose-flesh. The chill I'd sensed emanating from the hybrids back in Raymond's lab seemed to be intensified tenfold now that I was in the heart of their territory. Whatever we were climbing toward, it was something that every sense in my body—including my sixth one—told me I should be trying to avoid at all costs.

But the heart never listens to common sense, so I pressed on, ignoring the waves of cold flowing over me, the sensation that seemed to build as if an actual physical force pushed back against my every step.

Michael paused and looked back at Lance and me. "You feel it?"

Wordlessly, we both nodded.

"They're powerful." Again, his chin went up, his profile craggy as the red rocks against the mottled spring sky. Incongruously, he grinned. "But so are we. This way."

He led us down a narrow little ravine dotted with wind-ravaged juniper, manzanita, and small pincushion cacti. It narrowed as we approached, and then the sky was blotted out as gnarled evergreens met overhead, effectively enclosing us in a living cave.

"Hope you know where you're going," Lance commented, his breath sounding a little ragged. I didn't know whether it was from exertion or from the oppressive atmosphere around us. Maybe both.

"You can't assault the front gates with only three soldiers," Michael said. "And so—the back door."

And that's just what it was—a metal door set into the hillside, halfway obscured by a particularly tenacious manzanita specimen that had taken up residence directly above its lintel.

"And I suppose they've just left it unlocked," Lance said, with a curl of the lip.

"No need," Michael replied, and looked over at me.

"What?" I said, not sure what he was asking.

"You must open it, Persephone."

I fought back the urge to laugh. "Um, Michael, I hate to break it to you, but I'm a psychic, not a Jedi Knight."

"I know that," he said imperturbably. "And it doesn't matter, as long as you believe in your need to free this man."

When he put it that way....

I approached the door and stared at it for a long moment. It looked like something left over from a Cold War–era fallout shelter, with one of those metal wheels in the center that you're supposed to turn to get the door to open. Only I knew it had to be locked from the inside. Who builds a top-secret base and leaves the back door open?

Might as well humor Michael...not that I had any alternatives to present, besides going around to the front entrance—wherever that was—and inquiring whether they were done with Paul Oliver and if I could have him back, please?

On that note….

I reached out and grasped the wheel firmly at the nine and three o'clock positions, and tried to turn it. Predictably, nothing happened.

It would have been better if Lance had laughed at me. As it was, I had to force myself to ignore his eyes boring into the back of my neck, as if willing me to fail.

All right, fine. I tightened my fingers on the wheel again and tugged. Still nothing.

Focus. I needed to focus. For a few seconds, I shut my eyes, bringing to my mind once again that vision of Paul in his cell, waiting with a sort of hopeless patience. And I thought of how much I wanted to hear his voice again, to feel his arms around me and the touch of his mouth against mine. How I was damned if I was going to let some stupid piece of metal stand between me and the man I loved.

Loved. I really was in big trouble.

Metal gave way with a horrifying screech, and the wheel began to turn. Startled, I lifted my hands, and Michael called out,

"Don't stop!"

I clamped my fingers around the cold, rusted metal and turned. The ground beneath my feet seemed to shake, and the door slowly swung open—

not by much, but enough to let the three of us squeeze past.

"Well done."

I turned to look back at Michael. "How—what—"

"You don't need to question what happened. I knew you could do it. Come— Paul is waiting for us."

He pushed past me and into the opening, followed by Lance, who smiled slightly and said, "Come on, Alice. Time to go down the rabbit hole," before he disappeared into the side of the mountain as well.

For just a second I hesitated. If anything, the flow of cold and ill will seemed to have increased once the door was open. But I'd just shown myself that I had gifts I didn't even know I possessed. I'd have to pray they would come to my aid once again.

I took a breath, and followed the two men into the darkness.

CHAPTER ELEVEN

At first, I couldn't see anything. I blinked, eyes straining against the black around me. Then I tried to tell myself that the cool, silent darkness should be reassuring. After all, it would've been a lot worse if we'd stumbled into a main hallway populated by blank-faced hybrid guards.

I bumped into something hard and lumpy and smelling vaguely of sweat. Lance's voice snapped at me, "Watch it!"

"Sorry," I mumbled.

Michael sounded infinitely more at ease. "Lance, we need you now. You saw this place. You know more of it than either Persephone or I."

I heard Lance expel a breath, followed by a faint scratching noise, as if he had eased his way along the wall a little ways and the zipper of his jacket had caught on the rock wall. "Give me a minute."

"Of course."

I wished I had some of Michael's tranquility or, failing that, even slightly less jumpy nerves. The dark and the oppressive air around us probably had something to do with it, although it seemed that—for the moment—no one had detected our presence inside the base.

The silence was almost absolute. If there was any activity at the facility, human or otherwise, it had to be a long way from where we now stood. Although that notion should have reassured me, instead it just reminded me that we'd only taken the first step, that we were still a long way from finding Paul or getting him out of here.

Then I heard Lance say, in a low monotone unlike his usual speaking voice, "Ten levels. Five entrances —six, if you count this one, but no one uses it." A long pause. "Detention areas are on the eighth level. There's a bank of elevators north of here...two hundred yards."

"Elevators?" I demanded. He couldn't be thinking of us just marching into an elevator and sailing down to the eighth level. Just because there weren't any guards in evidence up in this forgotten corner didn't mean the elevators wouldn't be crawling with guards.

"Shh," said Michael.

Lance took in a breath. "Stairs...fifty yards from here. Not used much."

"Now, that's more like it," I muttered. Maybe we

could get in and out without anyone noticing us. Right. I was willing to believe there could be forgotten stairways tucked into unused corners of the base, but I sort of doubted the detention level would be unmanned. No, there were probably guards and security cameras and laser alarms and God knows what else.

And that was only if we actually made it all the way down there without someone—or something— discovering us.

"Show us," Michael said, and I heard rather than saw Lance slip past the older man, going farther into the tunnel. "You next," Michael added. "I'll bring up the rear."

Fine by me. I wasn't afraid to admit to a bit of cowardice. Besides if some alien-human hybrid got the jump on us from behind, Michael Lightfoot was far better suited to fighting him off than I would be. The man might have at least twenty years on me if not more, but he looked tough and solidly built, whereas I had never even mustered the energy to take the self-defense classes Ginger had advised I take—"a girl can never be too careful," she'd told me, and I had to admit she was probably right. Then again, I sort of doubted she had envisioned the sort of mess I currently found myself in. More likely, she'd been thinking of fighting off purse snatchers in the parking garage at the Beverly Center.

The tunnel or hallway or whatever it was sloped downward somewhat, but other than that, I had absolutely no idea which way we were going. Apparently, my bump of direction didn't work so well underground.

Luckily, I wasn't the one in the lead, and Lance did seem to have some idea of where to go. After a few minutes, he stopped. "Here." And I heard the creak of a door opening, followed by a flood of light.

All right, it was actually more of a trickle. But after the complete gloom through which we'd just been traveling, even the wan fluorescent lights in the stairwell seemed blinding. I blinked and followed Lance down the stairs, with Michael's footfalls behind me impossibly soft, even though he wore heavy hiking boots and the steps were made of diamond-patterned steel, the sort of thing you saw sometimes on heavy-duty truck bumpers.

I kept count as we descended, and so I knew when we hit the eighth level. The steps continued below us—of course, since Lance had said there were ten levels to the facility. And that was frightening in its own way, that something as big and as complex as this base had apparently been built right under the noses of the local population, with no one but the most extreme of the alien theorists and UFO chasers even guessing at its existence. How many layers existed in this conspiracy? How in the hell had I ever thought I could do something to stop it?

As far as I knew, I didn't say anything, but Michael laid a quick, reassuring hand on my wrist.

"We only need to focus on the task at hand. The bigger picture can wait."

Great, I'm just surrounded by psychics. I managed a wan smile, though. Maybe that was exactly what this mission required—a group of three, each with his or her own skill set. I knew I couldn't have gotten this far without Lance and Michael, and conversely, they wouldn't be here without my help. After all, I was the one who had somehow managed to get us past the heavy door at the end of the canyon.

"So what now?" I asked. "Because I'm pretty sure we can't just open that door"—and I jerked a thumb toward a gray-painted structure that looked as if it might have worked at Fort Knox in a past life—"and go sailing in there."

"Lance?"

He'd been standing near the doorway, head tilted to one side, eyes half-closed. "I'm not getting much. There's someone—or something—out there, but I can't get a grasp on it. I don't think I ever saw this level, but only the upper ones where they do the research."

"All right." Michael turned toward me. "You try."

"Me?" I shook my head. "Look, I've already said I'm no clairvoyant—"

"And yet you saw Paul, were taken away so strongly that you lost almost fifteen minutes in the vision. You can do this."

It must be nice to have such an unshakable faith. But he was right—I had done something similar, and less than an hour earlier. Maybe my proximity to Paul would help, would strengthen my inner eye and allow me to see even the things with which I didn't have a direct connection.

Drawn by some instinct, I moved closer to the door but didn't touch it. Instead, I stood there, only a few inches away from its metal surface, and thought of Paul, who was now so very close. I closed my eyes, and saw.

His cell was on this floor, at the far end of the level from the stairwell where we were currently hidden. I could feel his energy, sense it pulsing outward, so very different from the other men who populated the floor.

Men. That was using the term loosely, because although they looked human, it was their vibrations that seemed to be the source of the wrongness, as if the very air was offended by their existence. Whoever the original "donor" had been, he was good-looking enough...and yet seeing those regular features duplicated over and over seemed to distort them, twist them away from their original symmetry. And even in a high-security facility such as this, you'd think that men stationed on guard duty together would have some contact with one another, some sort of conversation. Not these; they were silent as if carved from stone, and yet I could feel their energy pulsing beneath the surface, darkly, vibrantly alive. I knew then that they were communicating, just not verbally. And if one of them knew some-thing, then all of them would.

I swallowed. This wasn't going to be easy.

"He's there," I told my two companions. "Other end of the floor...of course. There are ten of those hybrid guards on this level, and more on the floors directly above and below. I'm not sure how many. I suppose it doesn't matter all that much, since ten are too many for us to deal with anyway. And if even one of them raises the alarm, then we're done."

"Any ideas?" Lance asked, and for once he didn't sound mocking. Just worried.

Well, he must be worried if he was asking for tactical advice from me. Obviously a full frontal assault wasn't going to work, since we weren't armed, and even if we were, it wouldn't have mattered much, since it was ten against three and I didn't even know how to shoot a gun, let alone take out a bunch of trained soldiers enhanced with alien DNA.

What we did have, though, were three people with some highly unusual talents, talents that we could possibly put to use in this situation. Although I had sensed intelligence in the hybrids, I hadn't sensed much in the way of individuation. Ants and bees weren't known for having distinct personalities, and I thought that possibly the same sort of dynamic was at work here. If we could fool one of them, maybe we could fool them all.

I'd heard of psychics who were able to use the

sheer power of their mind to fool others or coerce them into doing things they would never have contemplated if they'd been in full possession of their faculties. That was a very gray area in the paranormal world, and of course one I'd never done much in the way of investigating. My talents really didn't lie in that direction, even if I'd had the inclination to abuse them in such a fashion. However, I didn't have much compunction about using them on the hybrids. I wasn't sure you could even count them as true people. Besides, I wasn't going to try to make them jump off the building, or light themselves on fire, or even squawk like a chicken. No, I just wanted them all to be otherwise occupied for the next few minutes so they wouldn't notice a prisoner being sneaked out right under their identical noses.

"I have no idea if this is going to work," I said. "But I'm going to try to distract them. Just be ready."

"Ready for what?" Lance asked. For once, I didn't see anything in his face except worry. He was probably thinking I'd bitten off more than I could chew.

Well, I was feeling approximately the same way, but I knew I didn't have much of a choice, since we hadn't armed ourselves with knockout gas or Uzis.

It probably would have been better if I could have stayed behind and worked from the stairwell; it was always easier to concentrate when I was alone. However, since Paul probably didn't know Michael and Lance from Adam—and because I knew I didn't want to have to wait a second longer than necessary to see him again—I inched out in front of the two men and paused for a second, focusing on the oddly pulsing sensations from the hybrids who waited only a few yards away from us.

As I'd sensed earlier, there were ten of them. Two stood directly in front of the door to Paul's cell. Three more were clustered in the center of the detention level, where I thought the elevators were located. A single guard waited at the far end of that floor—near a service elevator, from what I could tell. The other four were ranged up and down the corridor, one of them so close, I probably could have hit him with a well-placed softball throw.

But I wasn't armed with a softball. All I had was my mind and my will and my need to have Paul returned to me.

I took a breath, then another. All I needed was a distraction, something to pull them away long enough that we could get to Paul's cell. I had a flash then of the cell door, of the key card–operated lock next to it. Wonderful. All right, a distraction that would also make at least one of them drop his key card.

Thoughts were energy. Brain waves could be measured. Simple electrical pulses. The trick was making those pulses have an effect in the physical world.

As one, the hybrids' walkie-talkies began squawking. "Code red! Code red! All units investigate possible intruder on Level Seven!"

Both Lance and Michael stared at me.

"What are you looking at?" I snapped. "This is only going to work until they figure out there's nothing going on up on Level Seven."

And in my mind's eye I saw them converging on the elevator.

Key card, I thought, and that same inner eye showed me one of the guards stumbling, a piece of plastic falling from what should have a secure pocket of his jumpsuit. Perfect.

"Let's go!"

I didn't wait to see if the two men were following me. Time was wasting, and the elevator doors had just shut on the ten hybrids. Our window of opportunity had already begun to close.

Breaking into a run, I headed down the corridor to the spot where I knew Paul's cell was located. A brief pause to bend down and pick up the dropped key card, and then it was on to the end of the hall, to the blank steel door with the card reader glowing red next to it.

One swipe, and the door opened. Of course it would. At that point, no one knew anything was wrong.

I burst in, closely followed by Lance and Michael, and saw Paul standing in front of his cot. The look of wariness on his face melted away into utter shock.

"Persephone? How—" He looked past me to my two companions. "Who—"

"We don't have time for that," I broke in. "These are friends."

"Hi, I'm Luke Skywalker—I'm here to rescue you," Lance said, with an evil grin.

"And we really don't have time for that, either," I snapped. And as much as I wanted to run to Paul and wrap my arms around him, I knew that would take up far too many precious seconds.

In fact, we were already running out of time. The low-level dissonance of the hybrids in the back of my mind shifted to sharp spikes of frustration and anger.

"They know they were sent on a wild-goose chase. We've got to go now!"

"Back to the stairs," Michael said.

We all headed for the door and turned to go back in the direction we'd come. A wave of cold hit me, and I said, "No—they're already coming back down the elevator. We'll never get past in time."

To my astonishment, Paul remarked, deadpan, "When you came in here, didn't you have a plan for getting out?"

"Call me the brains, and I'll kick your ass," I told Lance, whose gray eyes had taken on a glint I'd already begun to recognize. "To the service elevator." And I pointed back along the corridor, past Paul's now-empty cell.

"Do you know where it comes out?"

"No," I admitted. "But it's better than just standing here, right?"

"True." He moved closer, took my hand in his.

Just the feel of his fingers around mine was enough to reassure me that somehow we'd be able to get out of this mess. "Let's go."

We all jogged to the service elevator, which also had key card access. I swiped the card and, thank God, it worked. The four of us piled into the elevator. Some instinct told me to press the button for Level Three—I had no idea why, but my spider sense had done a pretty good job so far of keeping me alive, so I was going to follow its lead on this one.

The elevator ascended quickly. We were all silent, watching the red LED numbers flash as we moved from level to level. The unease and worry boiling off the three men was practically palpable. I knew all of us were wondering exactly when the hybrids would figure out where we had gone and would take steps to shut down the elevator so we'd be stranded mid-level, just waiting for them to come along and collect us all.

Miraculously, the elevator made it to Level Three without incident. The doors opened, and I saw we had entered an area that seemed to be some sort of motor pool; various black-painted Hummers and SUVs in a range of sizes filled the space.

"How did you—" Paul began, then stopped. "Never mind. Which one?"

"Whatever's closest," Lance said, and jogged over to a glossy Suburban.

"Fair enough."

We all began to follow him. A wash of cold went

over me then, and I looked off to the left and saw a pair of blank-faced hybrid guards beginning to run toward us.

"Better hope the keys are in the ignition," I called out.

At least there wasn't any testosterone-fueled bickering over who was going to drive. Since Lance was in the lead, he headed to the driver's seat, while Michael fell in beside him and Paul and I ran for the back seats.

No keys, though. Even as I fastened my seatbelt, I watched Lance slide under the steering column and pop off the protective plastic panel, then start mucking around with the wires he had exposed.

"They're getting closer," I said, trying not to sound too urgent.

"I know. I can feel the bastards, too." A sputter, then a roar as the engine kicked over. Lance extricated himself from under the dash and slid into the driver's seat in one fluid motion. I found myself wondering how many times he had done this sort of thing before.

The Suburban surged forward. I gripped the handle above me and shot Paul what I hoped was a reassuring smile. He actually grinned back, the black eye making the expression particularly rakish.

"Interesting friends you found."

I could only lift my shoulders. Then I felt the smile fade from my lips as I saw two guards converging toward the hood of the SUV.

"Oh, my God, they're right in fr—" And then I stopped, because I both heard and felt a sickening crunch as Lance barreled all five thousand pounds of the SUV headlong into both men.

I'd seen those sorts of things in the movies, but I hadn't been prepared for the wet thud of a human body hitting several tons of speeding steel, nor the way it would bounce up and off the hood, flying backward over the roof of the Suburban. A second series of thuds told me the other soldier had met the same fate as his companion. With an involuntary wince, I pressed close to Paul, and he reached out and held me as close as the restrictive shoulder belts would allow.

"Jesus, Lance," I said.

"What does it matter? They're not human."

True, I knew that intellectually and emotionally, but my eyes were telling me that Lance had just cold-bloodedly run over two men.

"He's right," Paul said. His mouth looked very grim.

"You—you knew what they were?"

"Well, it's sort of a giveaway when you see more than a dozen men with the same face."

Despite myself, I smiled a little, then abruptly sobered as we approached the entrance to the motor pool, which was a huge steel door at least fifteen feet high, and apparently locked. Very locked.

"There's got to be a remote," Lance said. "Look in the glove compartment."

Immediately, Michael opened the glovebox and started rooting around, but apparently turned up nothing. Well, no remote. He did find a pistol of some kind and removed it with an air of grim satisfaction.

"Nice," Lance commented after a quick sideways glance at the pistol. "But I doubt it's up to shooting holes in steel doors."

At once, Michael reached up to the sun visor, but no remote was to be had there, either. Prickles of cold ran down my spine, and I turned in my seat to look out the back window. A squad of black-clad men poured out of the service elevator, heading in our direction. They could have been the ones we lured away from the detention level. Difficult to say, when they all looked the same.

Shit.

Then Michael pulled up the lid of the center console between the two front seats and pulled out a thin black box. "Got it."

He pointed it at a device mounted to the cave's stone wall next to the door, and miraculously, the thing began to roll up and out of our way. Sunlight hit us all full in the face, and I blinked. It was a little shocking to realize it was still the middle of the afternoon, after all the darkness inside the secret base.

Something ricocheted off the back of the Suburban, and barely a second later, the rear window exploded in a shower of glass particles.

"Down, get down!" Michael commanded, and

Paul and I both huddled together, as flat against the seat cushions as we could make ourselves.

Would the seats really be protection against bullets? Somehow I doubted it, but our current position was still better than sitting upright so our heads could be blown apart like ripe melons by the hybrids' assault rifles.

With a tremendous jolt, the SUV roared out of the entrance to the motor pool, and we began bouncing down a steep mountain road—well, path—as flying gravel shot out in every direction. For a second, I thought for sure we were going to drive straight over the edge of the switchback and flying out into the canyon below, but somehow Lance managed to wrestle the bulky vehicle so it was more or less in the middle of the road, descending at a rate of speed that at any other time would have had me screaming in protest. Right then, though, I was so glad Lance could manage a level of stunt driving I hadn't seen since Paul busted us out of the Sheraton Universal's parking garage that I happily kept my mouth shut.

The volley of bullets ceased abruptly. Of course, the hybrids wouldn't waste their ammunition when we were so clearly out of range.

My relief was short-lived, however, because only a few seconds later, I heard an ominous thudding noise, and a shadow passed over the Suburban.

"Copter," Michael said, and Lance gritted,

"Yeah, I know."

The road in front of us erupted in dust and flying

gravel as a line of machine gun fire etched the dirt. Lance swerved, one tire slipping off the narrow track, and then somehow he managed to keep the vehicle more or less hanging on as we dropped down another switchback.

"Guess they're not too concerned about catching us alive," Paul murmured.

I reached out and took his hand—no easy task, with us both crouched down against the seat. But I needed to feel him, needed to know he was there, even if we didn't have much longer together. "Guess not."

Because of our position, I couldn't see as clearly as I wanted to. Another volley of bullets hit the ground just behind us, and then a sharp *ping* sounded just a few inches past my cheek, and a puff of dust came up from the upholstery as the projectile tore up the stuffing.

Paul's hand tightened around mine. "You all right?"

"Yes," I managed, surprised I could still speak. "That was a little close."

And then the ground seemed to drop out from beneath us. I let out a frightened little squeak and clung to Paul's hand, listening as rocks bounced up and hit the sides of the Suburban, and what sounded like manzanita or juniper scraped along the sheet metal. Obviously Lance had given up on the road as being too exposed, even though I couldn't see where he was heading.

An enormous jolt shuddered its way along the vehicle, and Lance swore.

"What?" I asked.

"Blew out the rear tire. Luckily, I don't give a shit what happens to the axle. Hang on."

If anything, our speed increased, Lance obviously trying to push what he could out of the Suburban before it broke down completely. I risked a quick peek upward and saw that we were barreling through a narrow canyon, its sandy floor broken up by more of the ubiquitous manzanita and juniper. Since the sun was now in our eyes, I guessed we were still heading westward, more or less in the direction of Dry Creek Road and the spot where we'd left Adam and Kiki.

Whether they were still there was anyone's guess. The men or hybrids or whatever you wanted to call them who staffed the base had to have been surveilling the area. If we were really, really lucky, they'd dismiss the UFO Night Tours van as just another bunch of tourists. But if our luck ran out... well, I decided I'd worry about that when the time came.

The helicopter still hovered overhead, even though we were in enough cover now that it would be much more difficult to see us. From time to time, I heard staccato bursts of machine-gun fire, but it sounded almost petulant, as if whoever was operating the weapon was just taking potshots because he could and not because he actually had a bead on us. I supposed I should be grateful.

Incredibly, the Suburban slowed to a stop under a particularly large pine tree. Lance said, "Get out."

"What?" Paul and I both demanded simultaneously.

"There's good cover from here almost all the way back to the road. Follow the dry creek bed, and you'll be all right."

"What about you?" I asked, although I thought I already knew the answer.

"Oh, Michael and I will draw them off. They're looking for a black SUV, right?"

For a few seconds, I didn't say anything. Logically, splitting up in such a way was the best thing to do. But leaving Lance and Michael still seemed like a horrible betrayal. "What am I supposed to tell Kiki?"

"Tell her I'll see her and her sister back at the shop in time for cocktails. Now get going."

I sat up and looked from him to Michael, who watched me with grave dark eyes. "It's time for you to go on ahead. You know this."

Yes, I did, but that didn't make the situation any better. "See you back at the ranch."

He smiled. "You bet."

Then I reached down and unfastened my seatbelt, and slid out of the back seat. Paul did the same, hiding in the shadow of the Suburban for as long as he could. We met up at the back of the vehicle, which more or less looked like Swiss cheese. He glanced at me, and I nodded.

Running then, running from scrub bush to scrub bush, sliding on the scattered rocks in the creek bed. I didn't even glance back when I heard the Suburban's engine roar and the lumbering SUV take off in the opposite direction from where we were headed. At one point, Paul reached out to take my hand after I slipped on a particularly nasty patch of scree, and with his firm grip to guide me, the way did seem a little easier after that.

Still, my shoulders kept hunching, my body tense from thinking that at any moment a squad of hybrids would show up and shoot us right in the back. But I kept running, feet pounding at the rough ground in my completely impractical shoes. How they managed to stay on my feet, I had no idea.

Finally, after what seemed like two or three hours had passed but was probably more like twenty minutes, we struggled our way up out of the creek bed and saw the black shape of a vehicle only a hundred yards or so ahead of us. For a second, my heart seemed to lodge itself in my throat, and then I realized it was the UFO Night Tours van, not one of the secret base's black-painted SUVs.

We hurried forward then, and I saw Kiki start upward from where she had been leaning against the rear quarter-panel of the van and move toward us.

"Persephone!" Her gaze shifted to Paul. "Dr. Oliver! Can I just say what a huge fan—"

"Um, can that wait until later?" I asked. "I think we need to get out of here. Now."

She seemed to catch herself, and then looked past Paul and me to the empty expanse of scrub and rock. "Where are Lance and Michael?"

"Creating a diversion. Lance said to tell you he'd be back in time for cocktails."

At first, I was afraid she was going to argue or ask more questions, but then she nodded and jogged over to the driver's side door. Paul and I climbed in the back; it seemed Adam had been dozing in the front seat, but he snapped awake as soon as Kiki slammed her door.

"Wha—" he began, but Kiki said,

"Later."

She turned the van around and pointed us to the south and west on Dry Creek Road, heading back toward civilization. After a minute or two, the rattle of gravel under the van's tires gave way to the smooth rumble of asphalt, and I let out a sigh of relief and leaned my head back against the worn upholstery.

It appeared—at least for the moment—that we had actually managed to escape.

CHAPTER TWELVE

My relief lasted for exactly ten seconds. That ominous thudding sound filled my ears again, and I called out, "Helicopter!" just as another line of bullets bit into the road a few feet ahead of us.

"Yeah, kinda figured that out!" Kiki shouted back. The van swerved to the left, then over to the right. She continued, "We just need to hang on for a minute more. We're almost back to civilization—after the next cross street, it's all houses all the way back to 89A. No way they can continue their pursuit with that many witnesses around."

Apparently, the occupants of the helicopter had figured out the same thing, because another volley of bullets broke up the asphalt only a yard or so in front of us. I smelled the acrid scent of heated tar and spent creosote as we blew through the cloud of smoke.

The van continued to slalom back and forth. I was no expert, but Kara and Kiki had to have installed some pretty impressive modifications to the vehicle's suspension, because there was no way a Dodge Ram van had ever been designed for that sort of maneuvering. We careened all the way to the right, the van tipping slightly, and I reached out to take Paul's hand. If we were going to perish on this stretch of lonely road, I wanted to at least die while feeling a little less alone.

That proved not to be necessary, because in the next second, we came up on a stop sign and blew through it, and then to either side of us, the walls of newish-looking developments lined Dry Creek Road, leaving the scrub of the desert behind. The sound of the helicopter above didn't decrease, but the shooting had stopped. I pressed my face against the window and slanted a glance upward. I saw the helicopter a hundred feet or so above us, matching our pace.

"Bastards are going to follow us wherever we go," Kiki called back over her shoulder. "Time to go to Plan B."

She reached down to her center console and picked up the handset to a CB radio. "Magellan, this is Phobos. We have a Code Red. Repeat, Code Red."

The CB crackled to life. A man's voice with a definite Texas twang said, "Copy that, Phobos. What is your status?"

"We have a MIB bird in active pursuit. Need immediate evac."

I felt like commenting that Kiki had watched *Black Hawk Down* one too many times but decided it wouldn't be exactly tactful, given the circumstances. Besides, it appeared that her time playing alien hunter had at least prepared her for this situation.

"Phobos, use diversionary plan Liquid Gold. Backup will be waiting."

"Copy that, Magellan. Thanks."

Next to me, Paul glanced over, and all I could do was shrug. I had no idea what Liquid Gold meant, or who this Magellan was. Clearly, though, he was a friend of Kiki's, and if he had a plan for getting us out of here, I wasn't going to argue with it.

The sound of the helicopter seemed a little less deafening, and I risked another look out the window. At first, I couldn't see our pursuers at all; I had to unroll the window and stick my head out before I could see that they had risen another few hundred feet and were following from at least fifty yards behind us. Still....

"Isn't someone still going to notice a helicopter flying over their development?"

"Not really," Adam put in, as Kiki rolled through a truly spectacular California stop at the next four-way intersection, pausing so briefly it wasn't really a pause at all, but only a beat or two where the van barely moved. "There are helicopter tours of Sedona going on all the time. They're supposed to stay away from the residential areas as much as possible, but not everyone toes the line. No one's going going to give it a second thought."

Great. The back of my neck prickled in anticipation of another volley of bullets, as I thought maybe our pursuers in the helicopter would get just a little bit impatient and decide to start shooting anyway. Oddly, though, I sensed none of the cold associated with the hybrids. Whoever was up in that helicopter was as human as we were.

We stopped at the light where Dry Creek Road ran into 89A. I noticed that Kiki was turning left, heading back up into town. Surely she wasn't going to take us back to the UFO Depot, was she? That didn't seem like a very good idea to me.

I should have known better. We hadn't been on the main road all that long before she turned again, this time into another residential area of older but still well-maintained homes on large lots, most of the houses in some form of the Southwest adobe style, with carefully xeriscaped front yards. I guessed the water rationing here in Sedona would make the limitations back in L.A. look like a joke.

The van made another turn, and I wondered if Kiki was trying to lose the helicopter altogether. If that was the case, she wasn't having much luck, as I could still hear the thrumming sound of the chopper's blades as it hung in the sky above us like some overgrown, horribly determined wasp.

We pulled past a wooden sign that told us we were entering a state park. It was my turn to glance over at Paul, but he appeared just as mystified as I was. A minute later, I thought I understood at least part of Kiki's stratagem; as we pulled to a stop next to a ranger's booth so she could flash some sort of pass at the young woman manning the kiosk, the delicate green of tall cottonwood trees blotted out the sky above us. To the helicopter, which would have had to ascend even more to avoid the greenery, we were now more or less invisible.

Kiki drove past people unloading kids and dogs from the backs of their SUVs, or hauling picnic equipment out of the trunks of their cars. She found an empty space at the edge of one lane and pulled into it.

"Might as well get out and stretch our legs," she said, then turned off the engine and pulled the keys out of the ignition.

"'Stretch our legs'?" Paul echoed, sounding incredulous. I couldn't blame him—he sounded about the way I felt.

"Magellan will be here in a minute or two. And those helicopters can't see us—even if they're watching on infrared, how're they going to be able to tell which signatures are ours?"

She had a point. The parking lot had its share of vans, and most of the vans had several people in them. Who was to say which one was ours?

Besides, getting out of the van and grabbing a bit of fresh air while I could seemed like a great idea.

I undid my seatbelt, reached under the seat to

retrieve my purse, and then slid open the door to the passenger area, with Paul following me just a second or two later. A fresh breeze caught at my hair. Beyond the sounds of people laughing and talking, I heard the soothing rustle of moving water and somehow found myself drawn eastward, through the parking lot, and on past a stand of trees.

The creek was wide at that season, full of snow melt from the high country. It chattered over the stones, catching sparks of stray sunlight. Overhead, the cottonwood trees sheltered me from prying eyes. At the edges of my hearing, the helicopter droned away, but somehow it seemed as insignificant as the buzz of a fly against a screen. Somehow, I knew I was safe here.

Despite everything, a sensation of soothing warmth wrapped itself around me. The light shifted to green and gold, flickering with energy. This was what we were trying to save...our planet, our people. We had done so much to destroy it ourselves, and yet I knew it wanted to protect us, to surround us in its healing energies. I drank them in, letting the peace and the light and the calm, flowing strength of the water move through me.

Even though my eyes were shut, I knew the second that Paul had come to stand next to me.

I asked, "Do you feel it?"

A silence, during which I sensed him watching the water as well, breathing the air, clean and

untainted by factories or six lanes of rush-hour traffic. "This may sound crazy—but I think I do."

I opened my eyes and blinked against the
dazzling diamond-bright flashes of sunlight on the
water. Then I turned to Paul, body humming with all
the energy I'd just absorbed. "I'm ready for the next
stage."

"And what is that?"

With a smile, I replied, "I don't know—I just
know I can handle it. We, actually."

His hazel eyes were almost pure green in the
reflection of the cottonwoods' leaves. "You sound a
lot more confident than I am. There's still a helicopter
circling up there."

"I know." What I didn't know was how much
time we had. But I wanted to use what little
breathing space we did have for something useful.
"Did they question you? The hybrids?"

"No. They're not much for talk. But there was
someone else—some kind of agent, I guess. Human.
He was inquisitive enough." A muscle tightened in
Paul's jaw, and he glanced away from me, over
toward the stream.

That sounded ominous. So there really were
humans in league with the aliens. Some part of me
had wanted to deny that such a thing could be true,
but Paul had been there, had seen it for himself.

I opened my mouth to reply, then paused, still
adjusting to the heightened awareness the surround-
ings seemed to have brought out in me. Another

presence, a friendly one, had entered the parking lot. "He's here."

"He who?"

"Magellan."

And I turned and made my way back to the parking lot. Kiki and Adam had left the van and now stood next to a tall gray-haired man who had just gotten out of a shiny silver Mercedes station wagon. He turned toward Paul and me as we approached.

"This is my cargo?" he asked.

Kiki said, "Dr. Oliver, Persephone, this is Matt Forrest. He's going to get you out of here."

Matt Forrest extended a hand, and Paul shook it. "Thanks for the rescue, Mr. Forrest."

"Call me Matt," he replied, in the Texas drawl I recognized from the CB exchange just a short while earlier. "Happy to oblige. But we'd best get going—don't want to keep our friends in the sky waiting too long." He had keen blue eyes bracketed by deep lines, the eyes of a man who'd spent a good deal of his life looking into the distance. He addressed Kiki next. "You know what to do."

"Yeah." She turned to Paul and me. "You can trust Matt. I just wish—I just wish I could go, too. And Dr. Oliver—"

"Paul."

"Paul." To my surprise, she flushed a little and said, "Well, Kara and I would have loved to have you come to the shop. We—"

"Hey," I said. "We're not going away forever.

Besides," I added, "my car's still in your shop's parking lot. Keep an eye on it for me, could you?"

Her eyes sparkled. "Absolutely!"

Adam said, "We should probably go, Kiki."

"Right. I know." She gave an awkward little wave, then headed back toward the van.

"We'll give them a minute," Matt Forrest said. "Want to make sure that helicopter goes with them."

I didn't like the sound of that very much. "What, we're just going to let them be decoys?"

"You didn't seem to have much of a problem letting those other two men do the same thing," Paul pointed out.

"I know, but Kiki and Adam are just kids—"

"They'll be all right," Matt said. "Kiki's got a good head on her shoulders. Besides, all she's going to do is drive the van back to the store. The MIBs know that Kara and Kiki are always out poking around. They'll decide they were following the van for no good reason."

"You hope," I returned, although truthfully, I didn't get any negative sensations from contemplating Kiki and Adam going back to the store. Surely if that was a terrible idea, it would have felt wrong to me.

"I know." He lifted his head and watched the shimmering leaves of the cottonwoods overhead. "They're gone. Time for us to get going just in case they decide to circle back."

Since I couldn't really argue with that, I just

nodded. It made more sense for Paul to ride shotgun, since he was definitely the taller of the two of us, so he got in the front seat while I climbed into the back behind him. I wondered if we were going to be heading straight out of town, and which route Matt planned to take. Incredibly, I was starting to feel hungry. Or maybe it wasn't so incredible; I'd been running around like a madwoman, and it had been almost seven hours since breakfast.

Then again, I knew I could go a lot longer than seven hours without food if I had to, and of course the important thing was to get out of town and back to Los Angeles. Now that I had Paul back, I knew we had to complete our unfinished business there.

Matt started the Mercedes and moved out of the parking lot, then turned down the same road Kiki had used to get us here. At the next intersection, though, he turned left, heading south and west. I didn't recognize any of the streets he was taking. From what I could tell, he was purposely using side streets through residential areas, keeping off the main drag. Eventually, though, he turned onto a larger street I saw was called Airport Road, and began climbing higher.

"So where exactly are we going?" I inquired.

"Airport," he replied. "Safest way to get you out of here is fly you out. They'll be watching the roads."

"Your plane?" Paul asked.

"Yep. I do a bit of ferry service when the need

arises. Can you reach in the glovebox there, get out the placard for me?"

I watched as Paul opened the glove compartment and extracted a piece of card stock, which Matt took from him and deposited on the dashboard near the driver's-side corner of the windshield.

To my surprise, there were pedestrians suddenly all around us, moving from a parking lot higher up the bluff down to a promontory on the west side of the mesa, where a scenic overlook was located.

I must have made a questioning sound, because Matt said, "Everybody comes here. They say there's a vortex. Don't know about that, but the views are pretty incredible. Too bad we'll miss sunset, but them's the breaks, I guess."

Vortex. That would explain the rapidly building sense of pressure deep within my breast, as if something contained inside me wanted to burst out. It was a very different energy from what I had felt by the creek, but no less powerful for all that. I'd read about the vortexes, of course, but reading about them was far different from experiencing them for myself. At the moment, it seemed as if I had absorbed enough power to take on a squad of hybrids single-handed—not that I really wanted to try.

"Where're we going?" Matt asked.

I made a surprised sound, and he grinned.

"We try to say as little as possible over open channels. Now, I can't fly you to Paris—'less you're going to Paris, Texas—but I should be able to get you where you're going. But I got to gas up first. So how far are we going?"

"Los Angeles," Paul said promptly, eliciting another one of those grins.

"That's easy enough. Whereabouts?"

I thought furiously. Santa Monica was the closest general aviation airport to where I lived...not that I was planning to go home any time soon. There was also Van Nuys, but I didn't know the area very well, and somehow I sensed it was important that I be closer to L.A than stuck out in the middle of the San Fernando Valley.

"Santa Monica Airport," I told him.

"Nice airport. Convenient, too, because we've got some helpers in Venice who can come and get you sorted after you land."

Paul raised an eyebrow. "Helpers?"

"We've got quite the network. But I suppose they'll explain more to you when we get to Los Angeles. Go on up to slip 22A—I need to get a few things out of the car."

Since there didn't seem to be much else to say, we both nodded and followed where he pointed, climbing up toward the top of the mesa, past the small terminal, and on to an area where everything from a sleek Gulfstream jet to a vintage biplane were parked. At 22A, we found a small, neat twin-engine plane.

"Piper Seneca," Paul said, and ran an admiring hand under the belly of the aircraft.

"You fly?" I asked, curious. I wouldn't be surprised if he did; Paul seemed to possess an astonishing number of talents.

"No. Always wanted to learn, but there never seemed to be enough time. Or money."

He spoke unself-consciously, with just the smallest of self-deprecating shrugs. I hadn't expected that; there were very few men of my acquaintance who would openly admit to not being exactly flush in the pocketbook.

"And it'll get us to Santa Monica?"

"Definitely. Take maybe four hours if he's being conservative. It's a good plane."

"Glad you approve," came Matt Forrest's voice. He patted the underside of the Seneca. "We need to fill up, but it won't take too long. I just figured you all might as well get aboard, since the fueling station's on the other side of the mesa."

It was a little awkward to climb up into the passenger compartment, but Paul gave me a boost. Inside, the cabin was decorated in soothing tones of blue. I settled myself into one of the seats directly behind the cockpit, and Paul sat down next to me.

I started a little as Matt revved the engines.

"You ever been up in one of these things?" Paul asked.

"No. I went on a hot air balloon ride once."

In answer to that comment, he just grinned and shook his head.

The engines were louder than I had expected,

even though all we were doing was taxiing across the tarmac over to the fuel depot. Once there, Matt climbed out and entered some negotiations with the attendant on duty, who picked up the nozzle for the pump and began to fill the plane's gas tanks. Apparently, full service wasn't completely dead.

Fascinating as that exchange was, I couldn't help looking through the window and scanning in every direction, eyes straining for any sign of the MIBs, as Kiki & Co. so affectionately called them. I didn't see anything suspicious, though—just a series of light aircraft lining up for take-off and then ascending into the achingly blue skies. From our current vantage point, you could see all of the valley, with the red rocks thrusting skyward everywhere you looked.

"It's beautiful, isn't it?" Paul asked, and I turned back toward him.

"I'm surprised you'd say so."

He lifted his shoulders, then ran a contemplative hand along the bruise on his jaw. "Just because I wasn't given the courtesy tour doesn't mean I can't appreciate beauty when I see it. Funny...I always heard people talk about how stunning Sedona was, but I never had the chance to make it out here. I know it wouldn't be smart to stick around and sight-see, but...."

"Something in you doesn't want to leave," I finished, and he nodded, looking a little startled. "I feel the same way. Well, maybe after we kick the aliens' asses, we can come back here for a spa weekend."

A flash of white teeth. Thank God the hybrids or MIBs or whoever had given him that impressive shiner hadn't seen fit to knock out a few of his teeth while they were at it. "Deal."

Matt returned then and climbed into the cockpit. "We're ready to go. Once we're in the air, I'll make a few calls."

"You've got a phone in this thing?"

He gestured toward a clunky-looking device he'd just dropped on the front seat next to him. "Satellite phone. Very difficult to trace. Not that they'd even know who they're supposed to be looking for."

With that, he began taxiing the little plane down toward the runway, taking its place in the queue behind some kind of sleek private jet. With one of those, we could have been back in Los Angeles in half the time, but I wasn't about to look a gift plane trip in the mouth.

And then it was our turn, and the Seneca glided smoothly down the tarmac, pointed south, and we lifted into the air. Sedona fell away beneath us, red rock formations and dark evergreens and the slow winding curve of Oak Creek resolving themselves into a serene landscape. The town had seemed far more populated when I was down in it; from up here, I could see how little space the developed areas actually occupied.

The dark shape of a helicopter appeared off to our

left, and I let out a little yelp. Paul leaned past me and squinted out the round porthole window. His hand closed around mine.

"It's all right," he said. "Look closer."

It was my turn to squint. I saw letters on the side of the helicopter, letters that resolved themselves into the words *Arizona Helicopter Adventures*.

"Okay, now I feel like an ass."

"Don't. I think it's all right to be a little on edge after having a bunch of guys in a helicopter trying to shoot you up."

I was silent for a few seconds. "Do you really think Kara and everyone will be okay? That helicopter—"

His fingers tightened around mine, and he stared out the window as if considering his words before replying. "We have to hope they are. Matt doesn't seem too worried, so that's something. And it's clever of them to be so visible. If you're a fixture in the community, there's a far greater chance that someone's going to notice when you go missing."

Even though I still wasn't totally reassured, I knew there wasn't much else we could do at the moment. Besides, we had our own business to deal with.

I said, "Paul, I'm so sorry I left you at Lampson Labs. I didn't know what else to do—"

He cut me off. "Don't. You did the right thing. I would've loved some video of you hitting that one commando upside the head with your purse, though.

That was the stuff of legends." His smile faded. "I was just glad you were able to get away."

"Weren't—weren't you scared?"

"Of course I was scared." One corner of his mouth lifted, ever so slightly. "I'm an astrophysicist and lecturer, not James Bond. I didn't know what those men were going to do to me. And after seeing what happened to Raymond...." He let the words trail off.

A shiver passed through me. Raymond Lampson, while not exactly the sweetest guy on the planet, definitely didn't deserve to be suborned by an alien intelligence. "It could have been a lot worse," I said.

"Exactly. As it was, well, I struggled a little—who wouldn't—but one guy hit me in the jaw with the butt of his gun, and another got me in the eye...just before they dropped a bag over my head and threw me in the back of one of their Hummers. Then they moved out—bringing me here to Sedona, although of course at the time I didn't know where we were going. It's hard to keep track of time when you're stuffed in the trunk of a Hummer with your head in a bag."

"I would imagine," I said, outraged sympathy flaring in me at the way he'd been treated.

"Once I was at the base, they started asking questions—how I knew you, what Alex Hathaway had told you, but I wouldn't say much. I didn't have a serial number to give them, since I'm not in the service, but I think I did rattle off the ISBN for my last book."

I laughed then. "Wonder what they made of that."

"They weren't amused. I could tell they were holding back, though. I'm not an expert, but it could've been a lot rougher than it was. I got the impression they were waiting for something…or someone."

Another of those little shivers trickled down my back, although this one didn't have anything to do with the presence of hybrids. "Good thing we got there when we did."

"That's for sure." He paused, then watched me carefully. "How did you know where I was?"

I gave a nervous little laugh. "What, you still don't believe in my psychic powers?"

"I didn't say that. But still…this wasn't exactly like tracking down somebody's lost dog."

No, it wasn't. At first I didn't say anything, but only watched the sere desert landscape passing far beneath us, obscured from time to time by a passing cloud. "I had a feeling. No, it was more than that. A compulsion. Something drawing me eastward. I didn't even know where I was going until I saw the road sign for Sedona. The rest…just sort of fell into place. I was told I would have help, and I did."

Those keen hazel eyes missed very little. "The absent Otto put in an appearance?"

"Well, I wouldn't really call it an appearance, since he never materialized, but he did show up to give some timely advice. For all his faults, he's never steered me wrong. I had to trust him—and the universe—and follow my gut."

"That explains how you got here. But how did you get past all those guards?"

That was a question I didn't really have an answer for, since I still couldn't entirely explain it to myself. I knew I had done something to make those walkie-talkies come to life with false commands, but I wasn't sure exactly how I had done it. And Paul, for all his credulity when it came to aliens and conspiracies, would probably have a hard time swallowing the fact that somewhere along the way I'd picked up a Jedi mind trick or two.

"Luck of the Irish," I told him.

"I thought you said you were Greek."

"Half."

He stared at me for a moment, apparently nonplussed, and suddenly let out a chuckle, right before he leaned in and planted another one of those unexpected but entirely welcome kisses on my mouth. A quick one, with a shift of his gaze toward the cockpit where Matt Forrest was sitting, but still, it was enough to send a rush of heat through me, right down to my toes.

"Guess you can tell me later," Paul said, with a weight of significance in his tone.

Later…when we're alone.

I hoped we'd have a chance to have that private

conversation once we got to Santa Monica. Or maybe "conversation" was the wrong word for it.

Roughly three hours later, we landed at Santa Monica Airport. By then, the sun had almost set, and thin trails of fog were drifting in off the ocean. When we alighted, the air seemed far too damp and heavy, laden with salt. Odd that it would seem that way to me, since I'd been breathing in L.A.'s sea breezes for the last fifteen years, ever since I left Claremont to attend UCLA.

A woman was waiting for us at the airport, a stranger, of course. But she was probably the last person I would have ever expected to be mixed up in an alien hunters' underground—I was no expert, but her suit looked like Chanel, and the diamonds in her ears and on her perfectly manicured fingers had a wicked glitter that told me they were genuine.

"Bettina Croft," she told us. "Dr. Oliver, I have to say this is such an honor—"

"We're just grateful for the help," he said, after shooting me another one of those embarrassed little sideways glances.

I repressed a smile. By this time, I was pretty much inured to the adulation.

"And your eye—do you need to see a doctor?"

"I'm fine, Ms. Croft. Really, I think all Ms. O'Brien and I need is a place to regroup."

"Well, I have the perfect thing for that. I'm sure you're on urgent business, but I think you could use a decent night's sleep." She looked past us to Matt Forrest. "Are you staying?"

He shook his head. "Got to get back, make sure those girls haven't gotten into any more trouble. Besides, I was never one for the big city. You take care of them, Bettina, and my thanks."

With that, he gave us a wave and got back into the Seneca's cockpit.

"As I thought," Bettina Croft said. "But I do always like to ask. Now, where was I? Oh, that's right. I've set you up in a bungalow at the Fairmont. I hope that will be all right?"

"All right?" Paul said faintly.

"It sounds lovely," I put in. More than lovely. The Fairmont was definitely above my pay grade but not, apparently, Ms. Croft's.

"Excellent. Well, best be going."

Feeling a little shell-shocked, we followed her off the tarmac, through the small terminal, and out to the parking lot, where a driver in a dark suit waited next to a massive black vehicle that my befuddled mind belatedly realized was a Bentley limousine. As soon as Ms. Croft approached, he opened the back door, and we all climbed in.

The smell of expensive leather surrounded me. I took a deep breath and decided a girl could get used to this sort of thing.

"So…erm…Ms. Croft," I ventured, as the car glided away from the curb and headed northwest toward the ocean and the hotel, "how do you know Matt Forrest?"

"Oh, I've been part of the network for a long time, and so has he." Her blue eyes twinkled beneath eyelashes coated with what I guessed was the most expensive mascara money could buy. "My husband always thought I was a complete lunatic for being interested in these things."

"Thought?"

"Oh, he passed away three years ago. Since then, I've done what I can to keep busy. Supporting the network is just part of it, but I have to say it's far more interesting than planning another charity luncheon!"

I smiled wanly at that comment, since she seemed to expect some sort of response. The next leg of the journey passed in relative silence, although I couldn't help wondering who the dead husband had been. Judging by the car, either a Rockefeller or the Sultan of Brunei.

The Bentley sailed majestically down Ocean Park Boulevard before turning north on Pacific Coast Highway. From there, it was just a slight jog to where the Fairmont was located. Before I knew it, the Bentley had pulled up in front of an impressive lobby.

"The room is reserved for a Mr. and Mrs. Anderson," Ms. Croft said, sounding almost apologetic. "I just thought it would be simpler that way. They're expecting you."

"Thank you so much, Ms. Croft," I began, but she waved a manicured hand, her diamonds flashing under the dome light in the passenger compartment.

"My pleasure. But it seems you don't have any luggage?"

I looked down at my purse, which was the only personal belonging I had with me. "We had to travel light."

She looked at me and then Paul with a practiced eye. "I'll send some things along. Size eight, right?"

I nodded, and hoped she wouldn't reveal my bra size while she was at it.

"And Mr. Oliver—thirty-eight long, if I'm not mistaken."

"Um—that's right. But really—"

"Nonsense. If there's anything I love more than sticking a monkey wrench in those traitors' plans, it's shopping. Consider it done. Good evening—and good luck."

Although I really didn't remember getting out of the car, somehow I found myself standing on the sidewalk outside the lobby, Paul next to me, as we both watched the Bentley pull away.

"What just happened?" he asked.

"I have no idea," I replied. "But let's check in and figure it out later."

"Good plan."

As stated, they were waiting for us. And no mention of asking for a credit card...and the hotel clerk kept referring to us as Mr. and Mrs. Anderson. Neither Paul nor I decided to contradict him.

The bungalow turned out to be a cozy little getaway roughly three times the size of my apartment, with two floors and French doors that opened out onto a secluded patio. I unlocked the doors to let in the ocean breeze and stood there for a moment, breathing in the salty air and feeling it ruffle my hair.

"Can we just stay here for awhile?" I asked. "The aliens can wait, can't they?"

In answer, Paul came to me and took my hand in his, then stood facing the ocean without saying anything.

"Um…I take it that's a no."

He smiled. "Persephone."

"I know, I know, we have to save the world. It's just that I'm so damned tired."

Then his arms were around me, pulling me close, his mouth on mine. Despite my comment seconds earlier, I knew I wasn't so tired that I would push him away. I kissed him back, quite thoroughly, then pulled away just far enough that I could look up into his eyes.

"You sure you're up for this? I mean, those guys did a pretty good number on your face."

"Indiana Jones got dragged behind a truck and beaten up by at least five men and still was able to have sex with Marian afterward."

"How do you know they had sex? The movie just faded to black."

Paul raised an eyebrow.

"Oh, all right, they had sex. But—"

And I couldn't say anything after that, because he was kissing me again, tasting me, his hands cupping my face. No reason to resist the flood of heat that came over me—after all, hadn't I fought my way past armies of hybrid alien soldiers just so I could be in Paul's arms again?

Well, when you put it that way…

"Race you to the bed," I said.

CHAPTER THIRTEEN

I OPENED AN EYE. FOR A SECOND, I COULDN'T THINK where I was. Certainly the Route 66 Motel didn't have sheets with a thread count so high they felt like silk against my naked skin, or windows that opened out onto a foggy beachside morning.

Oh, right. Fairmont.

Holding a wad of sheets and down comforter against my bare torso, I sat up. Paul was nowhere to be seen, but the sound of running water and a somewhat off-key baritone from the vicinity of the bathroom told me he hadn't gone very far.

A determined search turned up my panties from under the foot of the bed, while my other clothes, including my bra, had somehow gotten strewn across one of the armchairs. I didn't bother with anything except the panties, and went to retrieve one of the terrycloth robes from the closet.

I'd just finished tying it shut when a knock came at the door. Despite myself, my heart started pounding a little bit more quickly, but I told myself that was just silly. There was no way anyone could know where we were. Well, anyone who wished us harm, at any rate.

When I opened the door, I saw a valet standing there with one of those wheeled luggage carts, the type you can hang garment bags from. Only this one wasn't carrying garment bags, but instead a series of plastic bags, each enclosing its own article of clothing. Below them was a set of matched Louis Vuitton luggage. Bettina Croft had apparently made good on her threat to make sure we were outfitted.

"The front desk said to send this up," the valet offered.

I closed my mouth. "Oh—okay. Right. Um…just put it in the closet."

He shrugged and did as I had instructed, then paused by the empty luggage cart. It took my brain a few seconds to realize he was waiting for his tip.

"Oh, right." Thank God my purse was in plain sight on a side table; I hurried over to it and extracted a twenty from my wallet. I hoped that would be adequate. I didn't have much experience with the tip scales in five-star hotels.

He seemed pleased enough with the twenty, though, and I barely held in a sigh of relief. I shut the door behind him, and went to inspect what Bettina Croft had sent over.

It looked as if she'd raided every boutique in Beverly Hills after dropping us off. I wasn't sure why she thought I'd need a black cocktail dress for chasing aliens, but hey, I was not about to turn down free Prada. A little more digging revealed slightly more practical articles of clothing—jeans and shirts and sweaters, expensive underwear and shoes. Not to mention a small bag filled with toiletries, including the entire line of La Mer facial products, which alone must have set her back about a grand.

"Hey, Paul!" I called out. "Take a look—it's like Christmas out here."

He emerged from the bathroom, drying his hair with one towel, another wrapped around his waist. In the light from the bathroom, I could see bruises on his arms and legs and back that of course hadn't been visible the night before as we made love in the darkness.

The extent of the damage made me wince inwardly, although I kept my tone light as I said, "Those guys weren't fooling around, were they?"

For a second or two, he just stared at me quizzically, and then he glanced downward. "Oh, well. I probably got worse on the thirty-yard line during a home game back in high school."

Paul had played football? I tilted my head and said, "I thought you were supposed to be a science nerd."

"I was. But my high school was small enough that

just about every guy taller than six feet ended up on the football team."

I supposed that was part of the fun of getting to know someone—you never knew when you'd stumble across something new and exciting. "I was on the debate team."

"Why does that not surprise me?"

"Hey," I began, then caught the twinkle in his eyes.

Was it supposed to be like this—feeling so comfortable with someone you'd only known for a few days? I guessed the movies and books said it was, but I'd never experienced anything remotely similar in any of my past relationships. Then again, none of those men had had the advantage of trying to bond with me while chasing down aliens and government conspiracies.

"Anyway," I went on, "Bettina seems to have burned a hole in her platinum Visa for us, which is just as well, because I think those poor flats from Kohl's have decided they're not up for hazard duty. You done with the bathroom?"

He nodded, and I went on in. The air was still steamy and damp from his shower. I breathed in the moisture, then climbed into the shower and turned my face up to the hot water. Sometimes a hot shower was the only medicine you needed.

Eventually, I climbed out and wrapped myself in a towel, and twisted another one around my head. Paul was standing in the dressing area, scrunching his face this way and that as he shaved with a shiny new electric razor—another bonus from the Bettina Croft care package.

I watched him carefully for a moment, then said, "We're going to have to do something about that."

"About what?"

In answer, I pointed at the blue-black bruise surrounding his left eye. "About that. If you go out looking like you were just in a bar fight, you're sure to attract attention...and that's the last thing we need."

"So what do you propose? A bag over my head?"

"Bettina the ever-resourceful thought of that, too." I reached past him to the vanity top and pulled out a tube of Dermablend.

"Makeup?" he asked, sounding about as horrified as if I'd asked him to go outside wearing the Prada cocktail dress Bettina had gifted me.

"Well, technically, but it's made for covering scars, that sort of thing. It's not as if I'm proposing you put on lipstick and false eyelashes."

Obviously, Paul was no metrosexual, because he continued to give me the side-eye. Still, he didn't say no, so I unscrewed the cap from the concealer and squeezed a bit onto my index finger, then sidled up to him and began dabbing it around his eye. He endured these ministrations in stony silence, although I could actually feel his jaw clench as I moved lower and smoothed a bit along his jawline, where another contusion stood out in shades of dark red and purple.

I worked as quickly as I could, even though there was something intoxicating about standing that close to him, surrounded by his clean shower smell, feeling the heat radiating from his body. If we hadn't spent a good chunk of the previous evening making love— and if we still didn't have that pesky alien problem to deal with—who knows what I would have done next? What I really wanted to do was drop my towel and see what happened, but....

"There," I said, hoping I didn't sound too breathless. "No more bar fights."

He leaned closer to the mirror, inspecting my handiwork. "Doesn't look too bad."

"It's supposed to look natural, you know."

In response, he gave the barest of nods, then went to the closet and ruffled through the items Bettina had sent over, selecting a button-down shirt in a dark green-gray that looked great with his eyes, along with a pair of jeans and some sturdy-looking lace-ups. I took the cue from him and also grabbed some jeans, and a cardigan and tank. Judging by the skies outside, it was going to be one of those days where the marine layer never lifted completely, and Los Angeles would be covered in a bank of thick gray clouds.

Since I wasn't going to worry about impressing anybody, I kept the makeup to a minimum, and scrunched some frizz-taming serum into my hair so I could let it air-dry. I'd just finished zipping up a pair of flat ankle boots—I figured I could probably use the support in case I ended the day running away from commandos or clambering through a ravine—when the phone rang.

Paul and I both looked at each other.

"Did you order room service?" he asked.

"No."

Another ring.

"Guess I'd better answer it," I said. "It's probably just Bettina checking in on us."

"Probably."

Still, my heart thumped a few times before I picked up the phone. After all, it was entirely possible the MIBs had somehow managed to track us down here. Then I told myself not to be silly, that if they'd really discovered where we were, they wouldn't be calling politely.

I put the handset up to my ear. "Hello?"

"Persephone! It's not too early, is it?"

It took me a couple of seconds to recognize Kara's voice. "Hey—Kara. How are you?"

"I'm fine."

Thank God. "And Lance and Michael? They made it back okay?"

"Oh, yeah, sure. They had to dump the Suburban in a ravine and hike back into town, but they're all right. We all went out for tequila shots at the Javelina Cantina afterward."

And there Paul and I had both been worrying

about them…not to mention being careful teetotalers last night, since we wanted to make sure we were as sharp as possible today.

"Well…that's good. So what's up?"

Kara's tone became a bit more businesslike. "Oh, we've got contacts there in L.A. who're ready to come over and pick you up, but we wanted to make sure you were up for it."

"Contacts? Bettina?"

A short laugh. "No. Bettina's a great facilitator, but she really doesn't get out in the field and get her hands dirty, if you know what I mean. No, their names are Justin and Troy, and they can be there in about fifteen minutes if you're ready."

"Well, we haven't eaten anything yet—"

"Even better," she said. "You guys can discuss the next stage over breakfast. I'll send 'em on over. Just be out in front in fifteen."

"But—"

"Good luck!" And she hung up.

Feeling just a teensy bit blind-sided, I set the receiver back in the cradle and turned toward Paul. "We're meeting Justin and Troy out in front in fifteen minutes."

"Who?"

"Our L.A. contacts. But at least they're buying us breakfast. I think."

"Okay, good…I guess."

"Come on," I said, and went to retrieve my purse. "It'll be an adventure."

"Haven't we had enough of those?"

In response to that question, I could only shrug.

Somehow, the names Justin and Troy had conjured the image of a couple of surfer dudes who would pull up in a grungy '70s van, but my instincts in that case proved dead wrong. A Lexus SUV waited for us at the curb, and a thin-faced man in his forties peered out the passenger window.

"Dr. Oliver—and Ms. O'Brien?"

I resolved then and there that at some point I'd have to take Paul to a psychic convention just so he could be the one tagging along with the rock star for once. Oh, who was I kidding? Not that many people knew about me; I guessed "psychic to film editors and studio accountants" didn't have quite the same ring as "psychic to the stars."

"That's us," I said, in resigned tones. "Troy?"

"Justin, actually. Justin Cole. Come on in."

Paul opened the door for me, and I got in on the passenger side behind Justin while Paul went around the back so he could take the seat behind the driver, a tall black man, also in his forties, who presumably was Troy.

"We thought we'd take you over to the Coast-side Café for brunch," Justin said. "Plan our strategy."

"About that," Paul said. "We don't really know

what the strategy should be. We've pretty much been winging it this whole time."

"All the more reason we should have a planning session," Troy put in. "Kara filled us in a little bit about the entertainment business angle in all this. That's partly why she called me and Justin."

"Oh?" I asked.

"I used to work in the distribution arm at Universal. You need someone to help you track down where these tainted films and TV shows are being stored, right?"

"Right," I said. Of course the logical thing would be to keep that material as far away from the public as possible. Then I added, "Used to?"

Justin grinned and patted Troy on the arm, and I realized in that moment their relationship was a little closer than just a couple of guys who teamed up to assist the UFO underground. "Troy played the Lotto for years. I always teased him about it. Last year, he won big—so now we're living a life of leisure, fighting for truth, justice, and the American way."

I glanced sideways at Paul to see how much of that he'd absorbed, and I could tell by a brief lift of his eyebrows that he'd figured out the situation as well. I found myself holding my breath, wondering if my newfound soulmate was going to turn out to be a secret homophobe. But he just smiled a little, as if to himself, before commenting, "Well, that's handy. I'm sure Kara, et al. appreciate having someone full-time on the ground here in Los Angeles."

Troy practically beamed. "It's been convenient, that's for sure. Of course, we never had anything quite as hot as this before, right, Justin?"

"No, nothing."

It would have been better if the situation weren't quite so "hot," in my humble opinion, but you had to play the hand you were dealt.

We pulled into a parking lot then, and Troy maneuvered the Lexus through the narrow aisles and past groups of pedestrians, finally finding an open space at the edge of the lot, almost back out on the street. I wondered about him bringing us someplace so public. Then again, sometimes having a lot of witnesses was a good thing.

I didn't know if Troy or Justin had called ahead to get us a table or whether they were favored regulars, but either way, we were ushered to a table almost immediately, earning us some evil looks from the people waiting in the reception area. If I'd been in their position, I probably would have been irritated, too, but as it was, I was just happy at the prospect of tea and something a little more solid in my near future.

The waitress came and took our drink orders. We all waited until she was safely away.

Paul said, "So, do you have a plan?"

Troy nodded. I noticed he had diamond studs in both his ears. "As I said, the best thing to do is block the films and shows at the distributors. There's no way we can get to everything—too many indies out there these days—but my guess is that our friends upstairs aren't interested in the art-house stuff. No, they're probably more interested in getting their signal on the latest blockbusters and new install-ments of reality programming."

That made sense. Even narrowing the field, though, it seemed like a fairly daunting task. "What do we need to do?"

A pause as Troy frowned and looked over at Justin, whose own expression was far from sanguine. "Well, it's going to be complicated. There are six major studios in town, each with its own subsidiaries. And sometimes the subsidiaries have subsidiaries. Added to that, some stuff's digital, while some is still on film reels. The TV shows are mostly digital. That's a whole hell of a lot of hard drives we have to crash. It's not as if we can just drive to a central warehouse, throw in a couple of Molotov cocktails, and have done with it."

Of course, the waiter had to show up right at that particular moment. I got the impression that he'd heard the Molotov cocktail remark, but luckily, all he did was set down our respective tea, coffee, and lattes, then ask in the most neutral tone possible if we were ready to order.

I hadn't even opened the menu, but I grabbed it and gave it a quick once-over as Troy and Justin saved the day by placing their orders first. By the time the waiter got to me, I'd recovered enough to calmly ask for a Belgian waffle with fresh strawberries and a side of scrambled eggs.

He departed, and Paul said, "So I'm guessing this isn't the sort of operation the four of us can pull off on—" He stopped and gave Justin, who'd been staring at him with the oddest expression on his face, a quizzical look.

"What?"

"Dr. Oliver, are you wearing makeup?"

"He's got a shiner the size of Rhode Island," I said calmly, stirring milk into my tea. "I thought it better to cover it up."

"Oh, right. Of course," Justin returned, while Paul shot me a classic stink-eye. Well, I'd only been trying to help.

"As to the matter at hand," Troy forged on, with the air of someone who'd spent a lot of time dealing with Justin's digressions, "yes, it's going to take a lot of people. We've got a decent-sized contingent here in Southern California, but—"

"How many?" Paul asked.

"Twenty, thirty I can really trust. A lot more hangers-on, people who like the excitement but who I wouldn't want to rely on in a pinch, if you know what I'm saying."

"Is Jeff Makowski one of your inner circle?"

Justin, who'd been pouring an extra dollop of milk into his latte, paused. "You know Jeff?"

Uh-oh.

"Yes," Paul said evenly enough, but there was an

edge to his tone that I'd begun to recognize. "Unfortunately, Jeff is compromised. Kara didn't tell you that?"

"No. I don't think she knew." Justin set down the little ceramic pitcher of milk and frowned in my direction. "Why didn't you tell her?"

"I was a little pressed for time," I replied, and wished my stomach hadn't knotted itself quite so badly. "Look, I told them the basics. We needed to get going and rescue Paul. If I'd known Jeff's involvement was so important, I would've said something."

No one likes a fallible psychic, but even psychics were only human. We made mistakes. We didn't know everything. If you met a psychic who said she had all the answers, she was lying. Yes, we had a better feel for the pulse of energy or knowledge or whatever you wanted to call it that drove human affairs. But even that heightened awareness didn't allow us to make all the right decisions all the time.

Paul reached under the table and gave my hand a reassuring squeeze. Just a quick touch, so fast I might have imagined it, but enough to let me know he was there, and he understood.

"Piling on Persephone isn't going to help," he said. "She's done an amazing job so far. I'd be dead if it weren't for her. So let's focus, all right?"

"Right." Troy glinted the briefest of sideways looks at his partner, as if to let Justin know it was time to back off. "Anyway, Jeff was the core of the network here. If he's compromised, then there's a good chance the conspiracists know the identity of everyone in the Los Angeles group."

For a few seconds, everyone was silent. I swallowed some tea and said the words everyone was thinking and no one wanted to voice aloud. "Including you two."

Troy's voice was steady as he replied, "Including us two."

I turned away from him to look out the window. Our table faced out on Ocean Avenue; I could see the dull gray of the Pacific, the swirl of the morning mists as they began to thin. And then, heading southbound on Ocean, a trio of black SUVs.

"Paul," I said in warning tones and stood, scooting my chair backward over the tile floor with an ear-piercing screech. All around us, diners stopped to see what had made the noise.

He looked over my shoulder and nodded, his expression grim. "Gentlemen, thanks for the coffee— and the information. But I think we'd better be going."

"Here," Troy said, and tossed a set of keys to Paul, who caught them neatly. "There's an exit down the hall by the bathrooms that lets you right out in the parking lot."

We didn't bother with any thanks, but just moved as quickly as we could through the restaurant and out the back door Troy had described. Luckily it faced away from Ocean, with the bulk of the restaurant between us and the street. I had to hope the

MIBs would pull up in front and not waste time with a parking lot. After all, they had no reason to believe we knew they were on to us.

Once we were out of the restaurant, Paul and I gave up any pretense of nonchalance and ran for the Lexus. He hit the remote when we were still yards away, and the doors unlocked, allowing us to jump inside and get moving without an appreciable pause. Since the vehicle had been parked at the far end of the lot, close to the side street that ran alongside it, we were able to pull out and head into the quiet residential district that lay in the blocks beyond Ocean.

I twisted in my seat and looked backward. Almost at once, I saw a dark SUV, but I had to force my heart out of my throat as I realized it was dark blue, not black, and had very unMIB-like surfboard racks installed on the roof.

"Any sign of them?" Paul asked, turning down yet another side street.

"No." I twisted in my seat so I was more or less facing forward. "Do you know where you're going?"

"Not really. Does it matter?"

"Well, if you want to get out of Santa Monica, turn right on Lincoln so you can head back to the freeway."

He didn't reply, but wrenched the Lexus around the right I had indicated. The little glow-in-the-dark alien head hanging from the rearview mirror dangled wildly.

"Paul?" I ventured. His jaw was set, his profile as

he navigated down Lincoln Avenue grimmer than I had ever seen it. "Are you okay?"

Silence again. I held my tongue as he waited at the interminable light that would allow us to turn left to get on the eastbound freeway.

Once we were moving again, he finally spoke. "No, Persephone, I'm not okay. Every time we take one step forward, it's two steps back. Now the network that was supposed to help us is all but useless. All we can hope is that our enemies are so bent on finding us that they won't waste their time with people like Justin and Troy. Or Bettina Croft."

I'd almost forgotten about Bettina. I tried to reassure myself that they wouldn't bother with her, that her money and her obvious position in society would protect her, but I didn't know that for sure. Nothing told me I was wrong, no twinging of my funny bone or odd ache in my gut. I didn't find that terribly reassuring, though. My instincts had been off more than I cared to admit.

"So what do we do?" I asked. "Give up? Turn ourselves in?"

"Don't be ridiculous."

Only one of the most condescending phrases in the English language...and one I'd heard often enough throughout my life that I'd come to heartily hate it. "Well, with you talking like that, I'm not sure what to think."

He sighed then. "I'm sorry, Persephone. I don't like feeling as if I don't have the answers. But in this case, I truly don't. And it seems we never get enough time to go anywhere and think."

Well, that was true enough. The three days since I'd met Paul seemed to be a blur of traffic and streets and freeways. Moving, always moving, and yet we barely managed to stay a jump ahead.

"I know someplace," I told him. "Keep heading east."

Surrounded by the tranquillity of the Japanese gardens at the Huntington Library, it was hard to believe that such things as aliens and men in black and government conspiracies even existed. Paul and I found a garden bench near a wisteria arbor and sat down. Because it was a cool, pearly gray kind of Sunday, the gardens weren't as crowded as they would be later in the year, when tourists would flock to see the roses and all the exotic plants. Right then, we could almost pretend we were the only two people there.

I wouldn't say the weight had entirely gone from Paul's shoulders, but some shadow of care seemed to lift from his expression as he sat down next to me and stared off into the distance at the graceful arching bridge and sorrowful shapes of the weeping willows.

"You could always take up a second profession as

an L.A. tour guide if the whole psychic thing doesn't work out," he remarked.

"Are you saying I'm not good at being a psychic?"

"You know that's not what I'm saying." Again, he reached out and gave my hand one of those reassuring little squeezes. "I just meant that you've done an amazing job of navigating us out of trouble."

"Well, I *am* a native," I said, a bit mollified. "I just wish I could have done more to get us farther along. Thank you for being understanding, for realizing that just because I have some powers the general population doesn't share, it doesn't mean I'm the Great and Powerful Oz."

"I've met my share of psychics." He smiled then. "Almost impossible not to, in the circles I've been traveling in lately. The more sure they were of everything they said, the bigger charlatans they turned out to be. If you think I'm angry or disappointed, I'm not. Well, not with you, anyway."

I nodded, a warmth that had nothing to do with the absent sun moving through me. At least Paul understood, and really, his was the only opinion I cared about at the moment.

"So what next?" I asked. "Storm the gates of Sony, Universal, Disney, et al.?"

He smiled, but wearily, as if he wanted to acknowledge my quip but didn't see all that much humor in the situation. "If I thought it would do any good. Unfortunately, I doubt we'd get past the security guards."

"It's pretty horrible, if you think about it." I hugged my arms against myself and stared out at the misty vistas of the formal gardens. So much for sunny Southern California. "I mean, even if Troy and Justin had been able to rally the troops and somehow destroy all that film and all those digital files, it would have been ruinous for Hollywood. It would have taken years for the studios to recover financially."

At my remark, he shifted toward me on the bench. The hazel eyes regarded me carefully for a few seconds. This close, I could see the faint layer of cosmetics in the one eye socket, with just the faintest smudge of bruise showing beneath it.

"I didn't even stop to think about that," he said.

I lifted my shoulders. "Well, I have a lot of clients who do the behind-the-scenes stuff. They're always the ones who get hurt when there's a strike or some kind of downturn in the business. People tend to think if you're working in Hollywood, you're in clover, but it's really not like that. Not for everyone, anyway."

His expression was still pensive as he nodded. "And it's a consideration I suppose we'll have to keep in mind…whatever we end up doing next."

"What about Kara and the rest of the gang in Sedona? I'm sure they'd come out here if we asked."

"It's a possibility, but I'm certain they're being

watched. If they headed out to California, they'd just lead the conspiracists here."

I supposed he had a point. "There must be other groups—maybe up in the Bay Area—"

"I'm sure there are, but how are we supposed to contact them? I don't—I didn't know anyone in the California network except Jeff. And he was the one who reached out to me—I'm really not that active in those communities. It's sort of frowned on, actually."

"Frowned on?" I inquired, not sure what he was getting at.

Surprisingly, he smiled. "I'm sure the general public views the UFO community as one undifferentiated mass of nutcases, but, as in any other community, it has its own hierarchies. Those of us who are working to legitimize the field, who publish and do speaking engagements, tend not to get down in the trenches with the conspiracy theorists and the tinfoil-hat wearers. Jeff and I opened a dialogue a while back because he had some interesting ideas, but, as I said, he sought me out. I didn't know who any of his colleagues were. And even if I tried to locate some, I'm sure there are agents looking for just that sort of communication right now."

"So basically we're screwed, no matter what we do next."

"In a nutshell."

I wanted to say something, give him some reassuring words, but I found I had none. Instead, I stood up, partly because the bench was beginning to feel a little damp, and partly because a restlessness had taken hold of me—born, I guessed, from the dead end in which we'd apparently found ourselves.

That restlessness turned abruptly to icy fear as I took in the landscape around us and saw three sets of men in dark suits converging on our location. No one wore a suit to the Huntington, not even on a cooler-than-normal March day.

"Paul," I said.

Something in my voice must have alerted him, because he stood up immediately, his face paling beneath its tan as he took in the ominous shapes of those black-suited men. "Back toward the museum. Now."

And he grabbed my hand and dragged me after him as he took off at a run, those long legs propelling him forward along the gravel path. I didn't look back, didn't do anything except pour every ounce of strength I possessed into forcing my own feet to keep up, to will myself to a speed I didn't know I could manage.

In fact, I was so busy concentrating on following Paul that I didn't notice the one agent until the last minute. A heavy hand wrapped around my upper arm, and something brutally heavy crashed into the side of my skull.

The world went black.

CHAPTER FOURTEEN

AT FIRST, ALL I NOTICED WAS THE SICK TASTE IN MY mouth and a dull thudding behind my right ear. Then harsh white light invaded my world as I opened my eyes.

An unfamiliar voice said, "Ms. O'Brien."

I blinked, and saw a man wearing one of the familiar black suits standing a few feet away from me. We were in a room very similar to the cell I'd rescued Paul from—rock walls and floor, narrow little cot. I lay on the cot now, although I had no recollection of how I'd gotten there. A hybrid soldier stood guard at the door.

"Ms. O'Brien," the man said again.

He had the sort of face you might pass in a crowd and not look at twice—not young, not old, not ugly, not handsome. His eyes were pale, his hair dark.

I struggled to sit up, and nausea swirled through

me. Digging my fingers into the edge of the cot, I managed to say, "I think I'm going to be sick," before I was, right there on the floor of the cell.

Some of it splashed against the man's wingtips. He gestured, and the soldier came over, pulled a handkerchief from the pocket of his uniform, and wiped down my face. These ministrations were oddly gentle, all things considered, although his touch made me want to go take a bath. Once the hybrid was done with me, he left me propped up on the cot while he bent down to clean away the specks of vomit from the agent's shiny black shoes.

"Get her some water," the agent said, sounding more than a little irritated. In a way, I couldn't really blame him. I probably would have felt the same way if I'd been in his shoes. So to speak.

The hybrid went over to a table I hadn't noticed before and poured some water into a cup from a plastic pitcher, the kind they use in hospitals. He came back and handed me the cup. I took it and allowed myself a cautious sip. It tasted like water.

"There's nothing in it, I assure you," the agent said, as the guard resumed his position by the door. "There are far easier ways to drug you."

"What do you want?" I asked, since I couldn't really think of how to reply to that particular statement, delivered in a matter-of-fact way that made me guess he'd drugged more than one person in his career. "Where's Paul?"

"He's safe…for now."

"That's not an answer."

"I think, Ms. O'Brien, that you don't fully appreciate the gravity of your situation. I'll ask the questions…not you."

Oh, I appreciated the gravity of my situation, all right. Now that I was slightly more awake and aware, my instincts told me the agents had brought me right back to their base outside Sedona, which meant I had to have been out for several hours—a good deal more than that, if they'd driven me here.

Us, I thought then. Somehow I knew Paul was here as well, that he hadn't managed to escape. That he hadn't even tried, I realized with one of those flashes of intuition so clear, I might as well have witnessed it with my own eyes. That he'd stopped and turned to see me struck by the one agent, that he'd gone down swinging until they'd administered some kind of knockout drug to him.

And he was here, very close. Possibly even in the next cell, although I couldn't be entirely certain of that.

Somehow the thought cheered me, even though I knew things had gone from bad to just about as worse as they could possibly be.

"Ask away," I told the agent blithely. "Although I'm guessing there isn't much I can tell you that you don't already know."

He frowned at that statement, pale eyes narrowing. "All right, Ms. O'Brien. What exactly did you think you were going to accomplish with all these cloak-and-dagger maneuvers?"

"Were they cloak and dagger?" I asked, all innocence. "I just thought of what we were doing as trying not to attract attention."

His expression didn't change. "How did you manage to free Paul Oliver?"

Ah, so I had stumped them with my little trick with the walkie-talkies. I found the realization perversely pleasing, even though I guessed I wouldn't be able to pull off the same maneuver again. "Your little clones aren't the sharpest crayons in the box. It wasn't that hard."

Lips compressed, the agent regarded me in silence for a moment before asking, "Why do you think they're clones?"

"Well, unless women have started having babies in litters, it's kind of hard to come up with a dozen men who all look exactly the same."

An odd noise, somewhere between a chuckle and a throat-clearing, seemed to emanate from the hybrid guarding the door. The agent shot him a glare of extreme annoyance, while I filed that one away for future reference. Maybe the clones weren't quite as one-size-fits-all as I had thought.

"Moving on," the agent said, now sounding distinctly testy. "How did you find this facility?"

Perversely, I was almost beginning to enjoy myself. "You mean, besides the phrases 'Boynton

Canyon' and 'secret underground base' being scattered all over the Internet?"

"Yes," he ground out. "Besides that."

"Well, I *am* psychic."

Another one of those long pauses. He crossed his arms—a sure sign I was beginning to get under his skin. "You don't really expect me to believe you're truly a psychic, do you? Save that for the rubes you bilk out of their life savings."

His sour tone made me wonder if he'd gotten a bad palm reading at the fairgrounds once upon a time. Still, I wasn't about to let him know that he'd offended me. My tone deliberately breezy, I said, "Oh, absolutely. I mean, if you already believe in aliens and clones and secret underground bases, then you're already halfway to your six impossible things, right? Although I do admit that we're a long way from breakfast."

The word made me realize how hungry I really was, now that the nausea had dissipated. I'd never had a chance to have brunch, and if they'd driven me back here in one of those SUVs, it had to be close to dinnertime now. I knew better than to ask for a meal, though…just in case it might be my last one.

Again he was silent. Then he said, "It will go better for you if you cooperate, Ms. O'Brien."

"I thought I was cooperating."

No answer to that. The agent merely turned from me, saying to the guard, "Watch her," and then swiped his card through the reader and stalked out.

The hybrid and I watched each other for a moment. This was the closest I had ever been to one, and although his wrongness seemed to thrum against some deep chord in my subconscious, I didn't feel any real threat coming off him. The dark eyes that watched me were calm, and maybe even a little sad.

"So," I said, almost daring myself to engage him in conversation. Know thy enemy, I guess. "How do you like being an alien hybrid soldier? Do you get a dental plan with that?"

Incredibly, the corners of his mouth lifted. Almost imperceptibly, but still. "Persephone," he said, and I startled. How had he known my first name? I know the agent had never mentioned it.

"Because I am not what you think I am, child," he told me, and came closer.

I forced myself to stay where I was on the cot, not even moving when he reached out to touch my cheek. "Who are you, then?"

"So you don't recognize me, even after all the years we've spent together? I think I should be hurt."

The inflection was familiar, even if the voice and face from which it was emanating were those of a stranger. My voice didn't seem to be working so well. "O-Otto?"

"The same. This seemed to be the best way to get close to you. But you have landed yourself in something of a pickle, haven't you?"

I cleared my throat and said, "I thought you told

me you would never allow yourself to be channeled."

"Oh, this creature isn't channeling me. On the contrary, I'm possessing him. The minds of these clones are such blanks that they're really quite easy to control."

"So what now? You going to use that key card and break me and Paul out of here?" I never thought I'd be so relieved to see Otto. With newfound strength, I got up off the cot and went to pour myself some more water. Might as well be hydrated for The Great Escape, Part 2.

"I'm afraid it isn't quite that easy."

"Sure it is," I told him. "Just pull out the key card, swipe it—"

"I meant in a slightly bigger-picture way." He watched me, still with that slightly wistful expression, one I was certain had never decorated the clone's face while it was still in possession of its limited faculties. "Don't you realize, Persephone, that you're here precisely because you were meant to be? That everything which has occurred up until this moment has happened just so you would be here to do what you need to do?"

"And that sounds as if it's counter to everything you've ever told me about free will," I protested. "If I'm just being pushed around like a puppet, then what's the point to any of it?"

"You're misunderstanding me. It's because of the

choices you made that you came back here. It's here that you can put things right."

"I don't see how," I replied. The warmth that had come over me when I realized it was Otto looking out at me through the hybrid's eyes began to die away, leaving in its place a sick chill. He hadn't come here to rescue me. For some ridiculous reason, he seemed to think I was capable of saving myself.

"You'll know. You laugh at your instincts, tell yourself they're fallible, but if you look deeper, reach farther, you'll understand what it is you're meant to do."

"Fine," I said, at that point too tired for anything except a dull resentment. "But don't even try telling me I'm the Chosen One or some such nonsense. That sort of thing never turns out well."

He laughed then. I wondered if such a sound had ever come out of the hybrid's mouth prior to that moment. "I would never tell someone they were 'the' chosen one—but I will say that I believe you were the one chosen for this moment, this time. I told you earlier that things were happening you couldn't possibly begin to understand—"

"Which they were," I cut in. "Alien conspiracies and government cover-ups and—"

"And more still than that, on levels far beyond those you've just mentioned. Only know that what happens here is of far greater importance than you might think. And also know that I have faith in you."

With one hand, he reached out to touch my cheek again. I didn't flinch from that touch, not when I knew it was Otto touching me. But then his gaze flickered, and a cold, almost reptilian glint entered his dark eyes. I jerked back, almost as if I had been burned. The soldier straightened and stepped away. For an instant, I thought I spied a flash of confusion in his features, but then he only turned and resumed his post at the door.

So much for Otto. Now I truly was alone. True, Paul was probably not far off, but he wasn't in any position to help me.

The door opened, and the agent entered. Judging by the smirk he couldn't quite conceal, I got the idea he had something fun in store.

"Ms. O'Brien, come with me."

"Where?" I said warily, not because I thought he'd tell me, but simply to stall him. For some reason, it seemed far safer to stay in this cell than go wherever it was he wanted me to go.

"You'll see. Someone has arrived who would like a word with you. Get up."

I stood, mainly because I'd noticed the guard putting an ominous hand on the sidearm at his hip. Whatever was going on, I had a good idea they weren't going to put up with any nonsense from me.

"Good. This way."

He motioned me out the door, where two more of the hybrid guards were waiting. They marched me over to the elevators, and we all got in. One of them pushed the button for Level Ten.

So we were going all the way down into the bowels of the facility. Somehow I got the idea that wasn't necessarily a good thing.

Since I couldn't do much about my current situation, I concentrated on staring at the brushed-metal surface of the elevator doors and pondering Otto's words to me. As far as I could tell, his confidence seemed more than a little misplaced. I'd certainly made a hash of things so far. And I wouldn't exactly call being bashed over the head and transported five hundred miles against my will exercising my freedom of choice.

I also didn't like the sound of that "someone" who wanted to have a word with me. More than a word, I guessed, and anyone who wanted to conduct such an interview on the deepest level of the base was probably someone I'd prefer to avoid. That someone might not be a person at all, but an alien.

A shiver worked its way down my spine, but I clenched my fists against my sides and hoped neither the agent nor the guard had noticed. Maybe they'd both seen through my bravado and recognized it for what it was—a desperate attempt to hide a case of full-blown terror—but all the same, I wanted to keep up the act for as long as possible.

The doors opened, and I was guided, none too gently, down a long corridor that ended in a single steel door. I really, really didn't want to know what was behind it.

Too bad, because the guard swiped his card

through the lock, and the agent came up and pressed his thumb against the biometric scanner directly above the lock. I supposed it was pointless to use that sort of thing with the clones when all their prints would be exactly the same.

The door opened, but I couldn't see much inside. The lighting was dimmer there, just reddish sconces at various intervals around the walls. I got a brief impression of a long conference table surrounded by chairs.

"Inside," the agent said, and I did as I was told.

Then I heard Paul's voice. "Persephone."

I whirled to my right and saw him standing there, flanked on either side by a hybrid soldier. He didn't seem too much the worse for wear, although the cover-up on his left eye had mostly worn off, the bluish smudge of the bruise showing clearly against his skin

"Paul!" I gasped, and began to move toward him, only to have the clone grab me by the bicep and haul me backward.

"Let her go!" he cried out.

Of course, the guard ignored him—it wasn't as if Paul was in a position to be giving orders—but I appreciated the sentiment even as I made a symbolic protest by pulling against the clone's grip. Pointless, of course; the hand circling my upper arm might as well have been made of titanium and steel instead of flesh and blood.

"Touching display," came a new voice, one that

sounded vaguely familiar. Out of the shadows at the far end of the room, a man stepped forward.

Well, what used to be a man. Raymond Lampson.

My stomach dropped roughly to the vicinity of the sensible boots I'd put on earlier that morning. Behind me, I could hear Paul mutter a brief Anglo-Saxon expletive.

To the casual observer, Raymond Lampson would have looked like, well, Raymond Lampson. But the expression in his light blue eyes was colder than liquid helium. I saw no sign of Jeff Makowski, and wondered what had happened to him.

Irrelevant, I told myself. *Better concentrate on what's about to happen to* you.

"Hello, Raymond," I said. "Fancy meeting you here."

Just the slightest twitch of his eyebrows, as if his alien-controlled brain had required longer than normal to process my remark. "Oh, not a fancy at all, Ms. O'Brien," he replied, after the barest of pauses. "We've gone to some trouble to make sure you were brought back here."

"Really? Should I feel special?"

"Special for a human, perhaps." He moved closer, and I backed away. That is, I edged backward a step or two until I collided with the agent. Still, as much of a tool of the aliens as he might be, at least he was human. If I had to make a choice as to which one of them touched me, it wasn't much of a contest. "We wanted to make sure we had you someplace where we could take care of you safely."

That didn't sound particularly promising...not that I'd really thought they'd dragged me all the way back to Arizona just so they could invite me to tea. "I'll take that as a yes, then."

Paul broke in, "Leave her alone. She doesn't have anything to do with this. Hell, she didn't even believe in aliens until two days ago—"

"Shut him up," Raymond said mildly, and one of the guards holding Paul slapped a piece of duct tape over his mouth. Where that had come from, I couldn't say. Maybe the hybrids kept it in their pockets for situations just like this.

Raymond gave the barest of nods. "Better. Your companion there is quite misguided, isn't he? Because we both know that none of this would have occurred if it hadn't been for you. You just couldn't leave things well enough alone, could you?"

"If by that you're asking whether I couldn't have just sat back and let you get on with your little plan to mind-control most of the population of the United States, well, no, I really couldn't. Sorry—I wasn't raised that way."

"Pity." He smiled then, or at least attempted to. I got the impression that the alien intelligence inhabiting his body hadn't quite yet figured out how to make all of Raymond's stolen muscles do what it wanted—and it was probably even more difficult when it came to replicating movements an alien might never have experienced before. Like smiling.

"Well," he continued, "what is that expression you people use? Something about an omelette and broken eggs? No matter. Dr. Oliver there is of little consequence. He's discredited in the academic community, and only people on the fringes of society believe his words to be truth. He can go off and rave about aliens all he wants. No one who matters will be listening."

Paul made a few muffled noises, but the duct tape effectively blocked whatever he'd been trying to say. While I wanted to protest, to tell this alien that Paul seemed to be well-respected, I knew it wasn't worth the effort. Besides, if Paul was viewed as inconsequential, then maybe he might be able to survive all this.

"I don't know why you think anyone would listen to me, either," I said. "I'm a professional psychic, remember? Not exactly someone in the mainstream. Hell, half the time my mother still lies and says I'm a marriage and family counselor when people ask her what her daughter does."

At any other time, I would have hated having to make such an admission, especially to such an unsympathetic audience. But I was past caring about my pride. I was just desperately trying to find some way to stay alive.

"You might be surprised. Your clients appear to trust you, and some of them are placed in sensitive areas, areas we would prefer not to have compromised. So it seems the sensible thing to do is make sure you're not in a position to say anything to anyone."

At that not-so-veiled threat, Paul surged forward, dragging the hybrids with him. Impressed as I was by his show of strength, I knew it would be for nothing. Sure enough, although he had caught them off-guard, they recovered quickly and pushed him down to his knees.

"Leave him alone!" I exclaimed. I knew better than to try to make a move toward Paul, although every cell in my body ached to go to him, to push myself between the man I loved and the brutal guards.

"Of course we will—if he leaves off the unnecessary heroics. And as for you, Ms. O'Brien—" Raymond gestured, and another guard stepped forward out of the shadows, holding a small black case. Raymond took it from him and opened it, revealing a hypodermic with a familiar golden liquid inside.

I swallowed against the sour taste of bile at the back of my throat. No, they couldn't—

Hypodermic held up against the dim overhead lights, Raymond commented, "The spray delivery system works very well, but this method is a bit more convenient, as well as being less wasteful of precious supplies. You see, while it would be easy enough to make you disappear, people would ask questions.

And since you were foolish enough to contact Tyler Russo, who might begin to put two and two together, it seemed expedient to simply make sure you would no longer be in a position to ask questions…or disrupt our activities." He smiled then, a horrific shark-grimace. "Very soon, you'll be doing everything in your power to help us."

More muffled sounds from Paul as he struggled against the hybrids. Somehow, I seemed to have lost all strength in my own muscles. I could only stand there, staring at that hypodermic, knowing inside it was a poison that would destroy everything I was, everything I had ever cared about. The hybrid guard's hand tightened further around my arm. Behind me, the agent stood, unmoving. I couldn't see his face, of course. Not that it would have done me any good. He had thrown his lot in with the aliens. Any appeals to his humanity would have only been wasted effort.

Raymond stepped closer, so close that I could practically feel the heat of his breath against my cheek, smell whatever aftershave still clung to the clothing the alien-infected body wore. "We look forward to having you join us," he said. And he lifted the hypodermic and drove the point of it into the side of my neck.

CHAPTER FIFTEEN

Heat radiated outward from that stinging spot on my neck, a cascading wave of pain, as if every cell in my body seemed to be cresting some agonizing tide. I heard myself cry out, but it was though that sound had come from an entirely different body, as if I was listening to someone standing far across the room.

Slumping, I dropped to my knees. The hybrid and the agent both stepped away from me. All I could do was bend over, body folded on itself as the pain continued to radiate through every nerve. With it came darkness, a rushing black I knew would soon swallow my awareness.

Fight it! I heard someone call out to me. It could have been Otto's voice.

It could have been mine.

I squeezed my eyes shut. The Raymond/alien, the hybrids, even Paul—I couldn't think of anything at that moment, but only of those microscopic carriers of soul death coursing through my veins.

You were the one chosen for this moment.

I had to believe that. Had to believe somewhere within me lay the power to fight this thing.

Heat then, but not the searing pain of the nano-invaders. No, this surged out from somewhere deep within my core, soothing and yet inexorable as the early summer sun, warming my body. With the warmth came light, pure white, flowing through my veins, overriding the sickly yellow glow of the alien virus. The light washed over me, surrounded me in a shell of pulsing luminosity.

I opened my eyes then, but I didn't see the dim conference room, or the shapes of the men who encircled me. Instead, there was only the white light, but now I perceived that whiteness had millions of pale ghost colors flickering in it, opalescent and more beautiful than anything I had ever seen before. And in the center of that light stood a man.

Only I knew he wasn't a man. No man could have features that perfect, that unearthly calm. I had never seen him before, and yet, paradoxically, there was something familiar about him, about the dark eyes that met mine frankly.

When he spoke, his voice was instantly recognizable. "Welcome, Persephone."

"Otto?" Somehow I had a difficult time reconciling that baritone with the figure of perfection from which it emerged, but I would have known those rounded tones anywhere. "More possession?"

He smiled. "Not at all. What you see now is my true form."

"So you—you're not the spirit of a dead sixteenth-century eunuch?"

"My apologies for the deception. It was decided that it would be best if I came to you in such a guise."

"'Decided'?" I paused, mind racing. Some psychic I was...I'd never even seen through the false face Otto had assumed. Then again, it wasn't as if I could have asked him for his driver's license. I forced myself to put that aside for the moment. So many questions, and yet in the back of all of them was the most basic, and so the one I decided I should ask first. "Am I still...me?"

"Of course you are, or you wouldn't be able to even ask that question." With a wave of his hand, a section of the luminous shell around us seemed to part, and it was as if I floated above the conference room and gazed down on its occupants. But they were frozen in some sort of tableau, the Raymond/alien staring down at my doubled-over figure with a gloating expression on his face, Paul still straining against the grasp of the guards who held him.

"Time is not constant, of course. Rather, it can be perceived differently, depending on where you are. But here, now, with me, you are still you. Your spirit is free."

"But down there...?" I trailed off, not sure I cared for this new perspective on the world. While some psychics counted astral projection as something within their repertoires, it wasn't anything I had ever experienced before. Dreams and visions, yes. Watching my own body as if it belonged to someone else...not so much.

"Down there—although you realize that 'down' is not exactly the precise word—your body is milliseconds away from succumbing to the alien virus. The question is, do you want to fight it?"

"Do I want to—" I broke off and stared at this new and improved Otto, incredulous that he would even ask such a question. "Of course I want to fight it—I have more now to live for than ever!"

"Ah, yes." He appeared to consider the little group in the conference room. "This Paul Oliver. We had hoped this would come to pass, but even we can't always predict the future."

"No kidding," I remarked, "or my last few sessions would have gone a lot more smoothly."

The Otto I had known before, the pudgy-faced eunuch who floated in my living room and dispensed pithy comments about my personal life, might have taken offense. This new serene Otto, however, appeared not to notice my acerbic tone. "I realize a great deal has happened at once. My question to you is this, however—are you willing to fight, not merely here and now, but on into the future, in order to prevent this darkness from taking over your world?"

"Yes," I said without thinking, as if the word had come from somewhere deep within me. It was something true and unhesitating, like my feelings for Paul. All the platitudes I'd mouthed to my clients over the years about knowing when something was right seemed suddenly confirmed. I hesitated for a few seconds, then decided I might as well ask. "But… couldn't you fight? You, and others like you?"

"We have, as much as we can," Otto replied. His gaze seemed shuttered for a moment, and he went on, "This is not our world, Persephone, and we try to avoid interfering when we can. But when the balance is upset—when other powers in the universe attempt to manipulate things to their own ends—then we will step in. Just a little, and only when no other methods will work. We saw in you a fulcrum, a tipping point. There is a power in you that can change all things."

Oh, great, more of that "chosen one" crap. I shook my head. "Otto, I'm just a mediocre psychic. I wouldn't exactly call me a game-changer."

His expression did not change—or maybe because his features were so perfect, I had a more difficult time getting a read on him than I would with someone else. And of course, I could decipher nothing of his emotions. I guessed a being such as he wouldn't have too much trouble blocking himself off when necessary.

"You call yourself mediocre because your

strengths lie elsewhere than in merely telling fortunes for people with more money than sense. Did you ever wonder why I was your only spirit guide, when many of the other psychics you encountered were in contact with a variety of entities?"

Only a few hundred times. Mentioning that, however, would probably make it sound as if I was blaming him for my shortcomings. "I just figured it was because I wasn't a very good psychic."

For some reason, I had thought that comment might make him chuckle a bit—the Otto I had known before would have—but he only shook his head. "No, it was because we knew we had to shelter you, keep you away from outside influences. Not all of those on the other planes can be trusted to keep their own counsel, and we knew you had to be protected against this day, so you could follow the path that would lead you to where you are now."

"And yet you still keep saying I have free will," I retorted. "Seems like you did everything in your power to make sure I ended up right here, right now."

"No, that's not it at all." For the first time, I noticed a shift in his expression, a creasing of the level, expressive brows. "We can see trends, and we can see the most likely flow of temporal events. But every second relies on input from you—or any other living being. Because you are who you are, it seemed more likely than not that you would come to this place. But there was always also a chance that you'd say the hell with it and run off to hide in Mexico."

His tone sounded almost rueful, and I fought back a smile. "Okay, so I'm here because I want to be. I find that difficult to believe, but the last few days have been so insane that I'm willing to roll with it. So what next?"

"You save the world."

I'll get right on that, I wanted to say, but Otto's expression showed he was not joking. "And how am I supposed to do that?"

He stepped toward me, reached out, and laid one long, pale hand against my forehead. "You trust what's in here," he replied. With his other hand, he touched me lightly against my chest, his hand centered over my heart. "And in here. Think of all you have to live for."

And then I was falling, dropping out of that bright cloud and back into my body. Flesh surrounded me, closing in on all sides, my heart thundering and the blood thrumming in my veins. Even though my eyes were shut, I saw Paul's face clearly, every line and shadow as if it were reflected in a mirror, from the bruise around his left eye to the dark traces of stubble along his jaw.

I had to save him.

Save myself.

Save them all.

The white light returned, but instead of ascending with it, I breathed it in and sent it along every twisting vein and artery, the heatless energy surging over the nano-driven alien virus and swallowing it as if it had never been. No trace left, and I opened my eyes into Raymond Lampson's altered face.

He stared at me, still smiling, but the smile began to fade as I rose. The aliens were telepaths, I knew now, who sensed without speaking who was one of theirs and who was still human.

Human...and possessing a power they had always feared.

Without thinking, I raised my hand and smacked the palm flat against his forehead, just like a preacher in one of those cheesy revival shows. I didn't cry out "Heal!"—but I might as well have.

Raymond stumbled backward, both hands going to his head. A screech that didn't sound as if it could have emerged from a human throat tore out of him, a keening wail that ripped at my eardrums. And then he collapsed, falling in a heap like a marionette that had just had its strings cut.

The hybrid guards surged forward, moving toward me. They, unfortunately, were not possessed; their wrongness had been bred into them. I knew I couldn't defeat them the way I had the alien entity living inside Raymond's body.

Luckily, I didn't have to. Paul lunged forward, wrapping his arms around the legs of the guard nearest him, bringing the hybrid to his knees. So fast I didn't see exactly how it had happened, he pulled the service revolver out of the guard's holster and shot him neatly in the back of the head. The other guard reached for his own gun, but Paul popped off another bullet, which went directly into the hybrid's hand. Human enough to wince, the guard lost a precious second, and that was all it took. His body fell on top of his fallen comrade's.

The agent who had been standing behind me launched himself at Paul, but I stuck out a foot and he stumbled, losing his balance even as he scrabbled for the gun tucked into his belt. Paul didn't even blink, but got off another shot, and the man went down as well.

"Wow," I said, as I shakily surveyed the carnage. "I didn't know you were a crack shot, too."

He tucked the gun into his belt, then reached up to tear away the duct tape from his mouth. "You grow up on a ranch shooting cans off fences, you get pretty good." His expression sobered as he stared across the dead men at me. "Are you all right?"

"Never been better," I said cheerfully.

"But he—you—that is—"

"I know." I reached up to the place on my neck where Raymond had hit me with the syringe, but there wasn't even a sore spot. "Let's just say that didn't work out quite as they'd planned."

"I'll say." Paul glanced from me to Raymond's prone form. "What did you do to him?"

"Same thing I did to myself—call it clearing out the plumbing. He should come around in a little bit."

Since I thought I'd better be sure, I crossed the

few steps to the spot where Raymond lay, then knelt down next to him and carefully turned him over. His glassy eyes stared up at the rock ceiling overhead.

"Raymond? *Raymond!*"

Nothing. I peered down at him and hoped the situation wouldn't require me giving him mouth-to-mouth.

But then I saw his eyelids flutter and his eyes snapped open, staring straight up at me. "Wha—what happened?"

"The Persephone O'Brien version of an exorcism," Paul said, coming to stand next to me. "How do you feel?"

Raymond appeared to consider. "Hung over."

"Could be worse." Paul reached out a hand, and after a few seconds of hesitation, Raymond took it and allowed himself to be hauled to his feet.

Once upright, he stood rooted in place, blinking blearily at the dead guards and the dead agent on the floor. "Where am I?"

"What's the last thing you remember?" I asked. Maybe once he'd been under the control of the alien intelligence, his own consciousness had been completely submerged.

Blinking again, he frowned, as if trying to remember. "The lab…the sample…accidentally splashed some on my skin. Then…." He lifted his shoulders. "Where are we?"

"Secret Canyon, just outside Sedona, Arizona," I told him. "And a few hundred feet below it."

A silence as he appeared to take that in. Then an improbable smile spread across his face. "Cool."

"If you say so." I turned to Paul. "What next?"

"I should probably be asking you that question."

I supposed he had a point. "Key cards," I said, and went over to the dead guards and rifled their pockets, then took the card off the agent as well, just in case he had a higher security clearance than they did.

"Right, for the elevators," Paul said, the approval clear in his tone.

If only it was that easy. Because the realization came to me as I looked up into his face that I had only taken the first step. True, I had freed him and released Raymond and even managed to save my own skin, but there were so many more still in jeopardy.

"We need to stop them altogether," I said. "If we don't, then they'll just keep taking over more people. The plot has to stop here."

"Okay." Paul didn't appear overly fazed by my words, but he did frown slightly. "Any idea how exactly we're supposed to do that?"

I realized then that I did. Whether the insight had been beamed down to me from Otto and his cohorts, or whether it had bubbled up from the same unknown well of power within me that had released Raymond, it didn't really matter. All that mattered was whether it would work.

Turning back toward Raymond, I asked, "Do you have any idea what happened to Jeff?"

"'Jeff'?" Raymond echoed. He scratched the thinning hair at the back of his head. "Did they bring Jeff here, too?"

I had to hope they did. "We need Jeff for this to work. Unless either of you is good at hacking computers."

Both Paul and Raymond shook their heads. I guess that was a little bit much to ask for. After all, Paul could drive like a fiend and shoot like James Bond…and could probably do differential equations in his head. I guessed I shouldn't press my luck.

"Wait," Paul said, and went back to the agent, this time going to the inside breast pocket of his jacket. I always tended to forget those things existed. He pulled out something that looked a little bit like a miniature tablet computer. "We're in luck."

"You think the information we need might be on there?"

"Only one way to find out." He pushed a button, then grinned a little as a login screen appeared. "Thank God for biometric security." And he pressed the dead agent's thumb against the screen.

At once, it flickered into life, showing what looked like a series of file folders. Paul appeared to scan them quickly, pushing one, then another. On the third try he said, "Got it—Jeff appears to be up on the detention level. Guess we'll have to go fetch him."

While I wasn't exactly overjoyed at the prospect

of having to retrieve Jeff Makowski from the same security area I'd just broken Paul out of less than forty-eight hours earlier, I also knew we needed him. Besides, having that previous victory under my belt could only help, right?

"Let's get going," I said. Odd pricklings at the edges of my consciousness told me that other aliens were on the move elsewhere in the facility. Maybe they'd felt the forcible ejection of one of their own from Raymond's body. At any rate, it would probably be a good idea if we were long gone by the time they came to investigate.

"Got it."

The three of us went back to the elevator, where I swiped one of the key cards I'd taken off a hybrid. At least the reader glowed green and allowed us to push the button for Level Eight. So far so good.

Something had been bothering me, though. Since he was currently locked up, I guessed that Jeff must not have been infected by the alien virus, although he'd managed a fairly good impression of someone stoned out of his mind when I had last seen him at Lampson Labs. So what exactly had happened to him? Obviously, Raymond wasn't much use as a source of information. I had to hope that Jeff would provide more illumination if and when we were able to free him.

I didn't know whether the guards on the detention level were the same ones—minus the couple Lance & Co. had taken out—who'd been watching over things when we freed Paul, but I guessed I'd have to try something different this time. What, I wasn't exactly sure. Maybe my revival-preacher trick wouldn't work on the hybrids to pull the alien influences out of their bodies, but possibly it could knock them out for a little while.

When the doors opened, though, I didn't have time to decide, because Paul moved out in one clean rush, a gun in each hand, blasting away at the hybrids before they even had a chance to react. Four of them down, and that seemed to clear the hallway. Maybe they didn't have a lot of spares.

"Hurry," Paul said. "Cell five."

Déjà vu all over again, except this time it was Jeff Makowski's less-than-lovely face blinking back at me as I opened the cell door. He stared at me, then glanced past my shoulder to Paul and Raymond. "What the—no, you need to get away from him!"

"It's all right," I told him in the most reassuring tones I could muster. "He's all better now. But you need to move it."

At least Jeff knew when to keep his mouth shut. He rose hastily, and we hurried down the corridor and on into the stairwell.

"We need to access the mainframe," I said, once we were all safely inside. "They do have a mainframe here, right?"

"I don't—" Paul broke off and started rummaging around in the little tablet computer. "Yes—Level Four."

"Let's go, then."

As we hurried toward the stairwell, I turned toward Jeff. "They never infected you."

"No," he said shortly.

"Why?"

"I don't know for sure. Raymond getting infected was an accident. I almost got the impression that they didn't want to waste any of it on me." His jaw tightened under its scruffy three-day growth of beard.

"But back at the lab—you were acting like you were on something."

"Yeah, because one of the hybrids injected me with something—not the virus, obviously—almost as soon as they arrived. I could barely remember my own name." His expression darkened. "Once they had you, they tossed me in the back of one of their trucks and brought me here. They kept pumping me full of crap, asking me questions." The first expression of genuine concern I'd yet seen from him flitted across his face. "Is...is everyone in L.A. okay? I seem to remember telling them things...."

That was one answer I didn't have. I didn't know what had happened to Justin and Troy. Best-case scenario was that the agents had just left them alone once they realized Paul and I had already fled the restaurant in Santa Monica, but that might be wishful thinking.

Since I didn't know what to say, I only shook my head. Jeff's mouth tightened, but he remained silent as we entered the stairwell.

Despite the white light that had powered my healing from the alien virus, pounding up six flights of stairs after everything I'd already been through that day wasn't exactly a picnic. But I didn't want to show Paul that I was flagging, and I tried to tell myself it could have been worse. They could have kept the computers on Level One. Besides, Raymond Lampson didn't seem to be in very good shape, either. His gasping breaths echoed off the metal stairwells, and when I glanced back at him over my shoulder, his face was pasty and gleaming with sweat. I had no idea whether he was suffering the after-effects of the alien infection, or was simply out of shape. It really didn't matter one way or another; we had to keep going.

When we reached the landing for Level Four, Paul opened the door a crack and peeked out, then let it close. "No good," he said. "That hallway is filled with people."

Damn. If this whole escapade had been a movie, I suppose we would have just stolen the uniforms off the dead guards and sneaked past that way, but it's really hard to impersonate a clone, and even tougher when said clone's uniform is covered with blood and has bullet holes the size of meatballs both front and back. No, it looked as if we were going to have to rely on those powers Otto had referred to—and hope he hadn't just been blowing sunshine up my ass.

"Where's the mainframe on this level?" I asked.

"Looks like it's straight down this hallway, and

then down another corridor where it Ts at the end."
Paul lowered the tablet, brows drawing together.
"Just exactly what did you have in mind,
Persephone?"

"Oh, just another of my Jedi mind tricks," I
replied, as he continued to frown and Raymond and
Jeff traded a mystified glance. "Hey, the worst that'll
happen is that we'll all end up back in one of those
cells."

Paul looked dubious. "That's not exactly
reassuring."

"Just follow my lead—and don't say a word."

I opened the door, and took a breath. *Concentrate,*
I told myself.

The people in the corridor ahead were a mix of
hybrid soldiers, men and women in white lab coats,
and dark-suited government types like the nameless
agent we'd left dead in a heap on the floor of the
conference room on Level Ten. That made it a little
easier; if they'd all been hybrids or even regular
soldiers, we'd be a lot more difficult to camouflage.

As it was, I focused on making it seem as if we
were just another group of white-coated lab techs or
scientists, on our way to the area where the main-
frames were kept. I could practically feel Paul's
incredulous gaze on the back of my neck as I stepped
out of the stairwell and into the hallway, but at least
neither he nor Jeff nor Raymond said anything.

It was harder than I'd thought it would be, like
exercising a muscle you'd never used before.

Inwardly, I saw the four of us in our nonexistent disguises, and I focused on projecting that image outward into the minds of those who passed us by. Although I wanted nothing more than to break into a run so I could limit the time required to maintain the illusion, I knew that was the worst possible thing I could do. Instead, I moved forward calmly at a purposeful but not hurried pace.

The three men trailed along behind me, like ducklings following their mother to water. Difficult as Raymond and Jeff could be, they were not stupid, and they caught on very quickly that the best thing to do was to walk down that hallway as if they had every right to be there.

Even so, every foot seemed to become more and more agonizing. A dull ache descended on my temples, and niggling little droplets of sweat began to trace their way down the back of my neck. I began to regret the cardigan I'd put on earlier that morning. Once or twice, a passerby focused on us with what I perceived to be unhealthy interest, and I had to intensify my concentration even further, telling him there was nothing to see here, just move along….

A century or two—or maybe two or three minutes —later we arrived at the doorway to the section that held the mainframe. I pulled out the dead agent's key card from my sweater pocket, murmured a quick prayer, and swiped it through the reader.

It flashed green at once, and I whispered a quick thank-you to whoever was watching over us—Otto,

God, what-have-you—that the agent had had a suffi-ciently high clearance to be allowed access to this part of the facility. As soon as the door opened, we sidled inside. I noticed Paul held one of the pistols down low at his side, just in case.

However, I didn't see anyone inside the room, and Paul made a quick gesture toward Raymond and Jeff as if directing them to fan out and check to make sure the place was as deserted as it looked.

The walls and roof here were also rock, and it was cold—chillingly so, turning the sweat on the back of my neck to a clammy weight. Banks of computers lined the walls.

"Found the user interface," Jeff called out, and we hurried across the chamber to a work desk outfitted with a trio of large flat-panel displays.

"Can you get in?" I asked.

He cracked his knuckles. "Let's find out."

Since I was no computer expert, I couldn't really tell what he was doing besides typing in strings of incomprehensible code, then watching as windows flashed up and shutting them down almost immedi-ately. We all waited in silence, Paul half-turned toward the door in case anyone decided to come barging in on us.

"Locked down pretty tight," Jeff commented after a few minutes.

Choking back my disappointment, I asked, "So you can't get in?"

He shot me a look of withering scorn, followed by

a raised eyebrow in Raymond's direction, as if to share his incredulity with his fellow nerd. "Please. You're not talking to an amateur here."

Another burst of staccato typing, more windows flashing. He chewed his lip, dark eyes squinting in concentration. Then—

"Got it," he announced as another, larger window opened up. "Sneaky bastards, though. So what are we looking for?"

"I need to know which films and shows they've contaminated with their signal, and where they're being stored. And then I need to know where the virus is being stored."

"Not asking for much, are you?" Jeff inquired, scowling.

"We'll have to go after all of them individually," Paul said, tearing his gaze away from the door for a few seconds.

"No, we won't." I smiled at him, then turned back to Jeff. "Just show me."

Jeff being Jeff, he appeared more than a little dubious, but he only nodded. "Got it." He tapped away at the keys. "Digital assets are here," he began, and that was enough.

Only more strings of numbers, numbers I somehow knew indicated a serial code for each property. But the white heat surged out of my body, this time running down my hand as I reached past Jeff and wrapped my fingers around the mouse.

"Whoa!" he exclaimed, doing a passable Keanu

Reeves impersonation, and a flare of white light leapt from my fingertips and to the mouse...and from there sparked its way into and through each of the screens.

Somehow, I knew that energy was running through the wires, pulsing and shimmering outward at the speed of light, a guided missile tracking down every tainted file. Even when that black signal had been embedded in a physical piece of film or tape, it somehow found the source of the wrongness, burning reels of film from the inside out until all that was left was a pile of fine black dust. Similar streaks of energy arced outward along electrical lines, seeking the storage lockers where the virus was being stored, hitting them with a charge I somehow knew deactivated the nanites that powered the virus, rendering it inert.

Surprisingly, there wasn't as much of it as I had thought. The Raymond/alien's remark earlier about it being a precious resource seemed to be the truth. And while I realized I could do nothing to help the people who had already been overcome by the virus, at least there would be no more victims.

"It's done," I said, and all three men stared at me.

"Done?" Paul echoed. "What exactly did you do?"

"It's all destroyed. The energy—the power— whatever you want to call it—tracked down all the files the aliens had corrupted and deactivated the virus. It's over."

"Is it?" inquired a new voice, and Paul and I both whirled.

It had only been a few seconds since he'd turned away from surveilling the door, but apparently that was enough. A group of seven or eight hybrids stood just inside the entrance, fronted by a man in a dark military jumpsuit who I knew at once wasn't a man at all. In my mind's eye, he seemed to pulse with hideous power, its corrupt strength surrounding him in a black halo.

He smiled, a mere baring of teeth. "Ms. O'Brien, I think it's time we had a little talk."

CHAPTER SIXTEEN

THIS WAS A PART OF THE FACILITY I HADN'T YET SEEN, one on the upper levels, with actual windows buried in the mountainside that let in a truly spectacular view of the sun setting behind Sedona's red rocks. Too bad I wasn't in much of a mood to appreciate it.

Another conference room, this one furnished with black leather seats and a large glass table. To one side was a console outfitted with several enormous flat-panel displays. I'd been left alone here after they marched all of us out of the mainframe room. Despite my struggles, I'd been torn away from Paul. I knew he was still alive, and Jeff and Raymond as well—probably back on Level Eight.

Why we'd been separated, I didn't know, but I guessed it couldn't be good.

They hadn't bothered to bind me. What would be the point? I didn't have Paul's James Bond moves or even Jeff's ability to sweet-talk a computer into doing anything he wanted. Besides, although I was alone in here now, I sensed the presence of two hybrids directly outside the door to the conference room.

So I stood at the window, and watched the colors of the sky and the rocks shift from a blaze of reds and ochres to dull and brooding purple. As long as I could still feel that Paul lived and breathed, I'd hold it together. And at least I had destroyed the altered film files and the virus-infected liquid. The aliens would have a hard time regrouping from that little setback. God knows how long they'd been working on injecting the media with their tainted carrier wave.

The door opened, and the alien general entered. At least, I assumed he was a general, judging by the stars on the collar of his black jumpsuit. His rank didn't matter—it was the aura surrounding him that told me he was the one in power here, strong and cold and noisome as the mouth of a sewer.

"Enjoying the view?" he inquired.

"It's lovely," I replied, willing to play the game for now. Where there was life, there was hope, and as long as I was still breathing, I knew I had a chance to get myself out of this. "Do the American taxpayers know their money is going to fund your little fiefdom here?"

"You know they think it's all going to Afghanistan and Iraq and Syria," he said. "Or for fifteen-hundred-dollar toilet seats. It's wonderful how funds can be diverted. Coffee?"

"No, thank you." I knew better than to drink anything he might pour for me.

"Your loss." His eyes glinted. "Your world doesn't have all that much to recommend it, but coffee is one of its attractions."

"If this planet is so useless, then why all the bother?"

He didn't reply immediately, but instead busied himself pouring out a cup of coffee and precisely measuring three dollops of cream into it from a small refrigerator unit located in the console below the flat-screen displays.

"By the way," I added, "thank you at least for not insulting my intelligence by pretending to be something you're not."

Those eyes might as well have been chips of aluminum. He stared at me across the top of his coffee cup, wisps of steam curling up past his close-cropped gray hair. "It's difficult to insult something that doesn't exist. At any rate, you have exhibited a certain amount of cunning, I will admit. But don't think you've won. That which has been destroyed can be rebuilt."

"And destroyed again," I said, seething somewhat over his implication that I didn't possess enough intelligence to bother with insulting it.

"Ah, now, empty threats are never wise." He took a deep swallow of his coffee—coffee that should still have been far too hot for a human to tolerate. "Especially if you consider our leverage."

Without setting down the coffee cup, he reached with his other hand to touch a button on the console. At once, the screens above his head flared to life, both showing an identical image of Jeff and Raymond sitting glumly on a lumpy bed in a cell, with Paul seated opposite them in a metal chair. A hybrid stood close to him—so close that it took me a few seconds to realize the barrel of a pistol was pressed against his temple.

"Primitive, but effective," the alien general said. "You don't seem to have much regard for your own skin, but what about his?"

At first, I could say nothing. Fury choked my throat, and for a few seconds, I remained mute as I stood there, glaring at him and wishing I could somehow reach out and strangle the alien life from its borrowed flesh. Finally, I managed to spit out, "You hurt one hair on his head—"

"And what?" Another swallow of coffee, followed by, "As I just told you, making empty threats is not something you can afford, Ms. O'Brien. If you want this man to live, then you'll tell me what I need to know."

"And what's that?" I knew I wouldn't tell this —thing—my shoe size, let alone anything important, but I had to stall, had to figure out what on earth I could do to get out of this room, back to the detention level.

The corners of his mouth curved upward in a ghastly approximation of a smile. "Who's been helping you? I know you couldn't have possibly managed to destroy those files without assistance."

"Nobody helped me," I said. "I guess I'm just naturally gifted."

I didn't see him give any kind of signal. Maybe he didn't need to—maybe the aliens communicated telepathically with their hybrids. But the soldier shifted, and through the speakers embedded in the flat screens, I heard an audible *click* as he cocked the pistol.

"You might want to reconsider your reply," the alien general said.

There had to be something I could say. Anything to keep him from giving the next command. But I also instinctively knew I couldn't betray Otto, couldn't reveal the fact that a higher power than the aliens had decided to intervene.

"It was some of the people from the Los Angeles group," I told him. That had to be safe enough; after all, the network had already been compromised thanks to Jeff's involvement in it.

"Don't underestimate me, Ms. O'Brien."

"But—"

The sound of the gun going off was impossibly loud. In the screens above me, I saw dual images of Paul slumping forward, then tumbling slowly off his chair.

No.

"You see, Ms. O'Brien, I'm not willing to play games. I can hurt you."

The pain seemed to spiral downward into my very core, roiling there in a whirlwind of denial and despair.

"No," I said distinctly, staring straight into those inhuman eyes.

"Ms. O'Brien—"

"*NO!*"

It barreled out of me then, a shockwave of refusal to believe that was Paul lying there on the floor of his cell, a surge of fury that exploded outward in all directions, as brilliant and deadly as a nuclear blast.

No healing, no salvation in it this time. Where the power had merely knocked the alien virus free of Raymond Lampson, this time it struck with such fury that it threw the alien general backward several feet, where he landed with a thud. No unearthly wail. No returning glimmer of human intelligence.

I stared down at him and knew he was dead, both the human host and the alien within. Another Persephone O'Brien might have cared, but not this one. They had killed Paul. They didn't deserve to live.

Maybe some time later I would cry. Now, I could only bend down and retrieve the pistol from the holster at the alien general's waist. I'd never shot a gun in my life, but somehow I knew how to slip off the safety, check the clip to make sure it was full.

My entire body thrummed with dark energy. I lifted a hand to the card reader by the door, and it glowed green. I grasped the handle and threw the door open.

The hybrids who had been guarding the door guarded it no longer. They lay sprawled across the threshold to the conference room, dark blood trickling from their eyes, their noses, their mouths.

More of my doing? Probably.

Good riddance.

I stalked down the hallway, seeing more bodies of hybrids as I passed. No sign of a human being. Maybe they weren't allowed on this level. Just as well. That psychic blast or whatever it had been seemed to have targeted only the aliens, or at least beings with some alien DNA in their physical composition. I wasn't sure I wanted to know what it might have done to any humans in the facility.

A bank of elevators was just ahead, and I went to the center one and laid my hand against the reader next to it. The lights flashed green, and the door opened.

No one inside, thank God, and I entered the little metal chamber and pushed the button for Level Eight.

I was too late, but I was going to Paul anyway. Besides, even buried in my hollow shell of shock and rage, I knew I couldn't leave Jeff and Raymond here.

The elevator doors opened, and I looked out into the corridor. At once, I saw more dead bodies of hybrids. Apparently, the blast had rippled through the entire installation.

Although the hideous images the alien general had shown me hadn't revealed a cell number, somehow I knew to go to my right and down to the end of the corridor. A wave of the hand, and the door unlocked itself. I reached out and opened it, taking a breath. Part of me wanted to turn away so I wouldn't have to see in person what I'd witnessed on those displays upstairs, but I knew I wouldn't do that. I had to say goodbye.

Something hard hit my head, and I let out a little shriek. Then I saw Jeff stumble toward me, stepping over the body of a hybrid. There was another body lying next to it.

But I didn't have a chance to see the horror of Paul's dead form, because Raymond came up from the other side as he stammered, "Jesus, Persephone, I'm sorry—I didn't know who was coming in that door, and all I had was my shoe—"

"It's all right," I said wearily. I didn't even bother to reach up and rub the throbbing spot on the side of my skull where Raymond's shoe had clocked me.

"What happened?" Jeff demanded. "All of a sudden the guard just dropped dead—"

"Um, watch it," Raymond cut in. He put out a hand, his expression at once mortified and pleading. It was clear he was doing everything he could to keep himself from staring down at the floor where Paul lay. "Persephone, look, I don't know what happened, but we should probably just get out of here. I'm really sorry about Paul—"

I held up a hand. Once again, my voice failed me, so I only shook my head and finally turned to see what they had been trying to have me avoid.

It had been a clean shot, and very neat. Not as much blood as I would have thought. If it weren't for the blood, I could have almost convinced myself that he was just asleep, or unconscious.

But he wasn't. I knelt next to him, took his hand in mine. It was still warm.

If the universe had been a little less cruel, the power that had struck down the aliens would have flowed through me again, only this time with healing energy. But I was spent and still, and knew there was nothing I could do to bring back the man I loved.

I had won...but in doing so, I had lost much, much more.

Time spun away from me as I knelt there, head bowed over his hand. A band of agony tightened around my chest. I couldn't cry, couldn't do anything except cling to Paul's hand as his flesh began to cool beneath mine.

A throat clearing, followed by Jeff's voice. "Um, Persephone, I really think—"

Whatever Jeff might or might not have thought, I would never know, because at that moment a flare of white light exploded in the cell, and I heard both men exclaim out loud.

Then I finally lifted my head. Otto stood there, surrounded by the same opalescent glow I'd seen when I hovered outside my body and listened to him tell me I had a power the aliens feared. Well, now I knew why...much good that it had done me.

"We are not supposed to interfere," Otto said, while Jeff and Raymond stared at him with open mouths.

I swallowed. So he'd dropped in just so he could deliver the bad news in person?

"But, considering your extraordinary services today, I decided the hell with that." He moved past me, bent down to lay the palm of his hand against Paul's forehead. And he reached out to touch me as well, and it was as if a spark traveled from me, down through his arm, and on into Paul's body.

I saw Paul twitch. His eyes flashed open, and he sat up, coughing. A brief incredulous stare as he took in Otto's glowing presence. "Am I dead?"

"Not anymore," Otto replied. "But you should probably leave this place if you want to continue in that state."

Joy swept through me, pushing away the clouds of despair. "Otto, I could just kiss you."

An expression of alarm passed over his face. "Please don't. Although I'm sure Dr. Oliver wouldn't mind stepping in."

"You've got that right," Paul said.

We both sort of lunged at each other as I halfway fell into his arms. He was kissing me so thoroughly that I only caught a glimpse of Otto out of the corner of my eye as he shook his head, then disappeared in another flash of light.

A while later, Jeff coughed and said, "Um, could you two break it up? We probably should get out of here."

I refused to be embarrassed, but I did pull away from Paul. "Hate to say it, but he's right."

"True." He let me go and we both stood. For the first time, he appeared to notice the dead body of the hybrid on the floor a few feet away. "What happened?"

"Hurricane Persephone," Raymond replied.

For a second or two, he said nothing, and then understanding flickered in his eyes. "Damn."

"No kidding," said Raymond, who bent to pick up the gun from the dead guard's hand. "Can we get going now?"

The rest of us chorused our agreement, and we hurried out of the cell. Once we had gotten in the elevator, though, Paul hesitated, his hand hovering over the control panel. "Which way out? Last time we went through the motor pool, but...."

"No need," I said. "Nobody's going to stop us from walking right out the front door."

Jeff snorted, but Raymond only nodded, and Paul smiled and pressed the button. It seemed I was going to have to revise my opinion of Raymond. Maybe the experience of being possessed by an alien had brought him new insights, or maybe he only seemed improved in contrast to Jeff. I'd been wondering why the aliens hadn't possessed Jeff as well, and thought maybe even they couldn't stomach the idea of being stuck inside his head.

At any rate, I was proved correct, because when the door opened on the first level, it was completely deserted, unless you counted the bodies of dead hybrids and alien possessees. There weren't as many as I had thought, though.

"Where is everyone?" Paul asked, gazing around even as we hurried down the main corridor.

"Run off," I replied, knowing that was the simple truth. "A few are hiding, I think, on the lower levels. Didn't know what to do when their lords and masters all suddenly dropped dead."

"Oh, they'll regroup," Jeff put in.

"I suppose so," I said. "But by then we'll be long gone."

The main entrance turned out to be a small, unprepossessing metal door that opened out into a box canyon filled with scrub pines and more of the omnipresent juniper and manzanita. No one would have ever seen it, which made perfect sense. Most of the personnel on the base probably came and went through the motor pool area, anyway.

By that time, it was almost full dark. Maybe some last dregs of sunset lingered far out on the western horizon, but of course we couldn't see it, trapped as we were inside the canyon walls. With Paul in the lead—he had more wilderness experience than any of the rest of us—we slipped and slid and somehow negotiated our way westward. I didn't really have a plan. I just figured if we could make it out to Dry Creek Road, then maybe we could try to flag down someone and catch a ride.

We broke free of the canyon and emerged into the more or less open area beyond it. Off to the south and west, I thought I could faintly see some lights from one of the residential areas that lined Dry Creek.

"That way," Paul said, and the rest of us just nodded, too tired and thirsty for speech.

As we moved toward the lights, I realized that several of them were getting bigger and brighter, and were heading in our direction.

I'd gratefully handed over my gun to Paul. It glinted as he pulled it out of his waistband and held it at the ready. Raymond quickly followed suit.

We could have run, but where? There was no cover any place close by, and all four of us were tired and winded. It was probably better to stand our ground.

A large, dark vehicle skidded to a stop a few feet away. The passenger-side window rolled down, and Lance stuck his head out and grinned at us. "Thought you kids might need a lift."

Kara's home was—probably like many of the houses in Sedona—Southwest in style. But instead of being decorated in UFO kitsch like her shop, it was warmly casual, with well-worn Spanish mission–style furniture and colorful pottery and art that I guessed was the work of local artisans. Seemingly from thin air, she conjured a pitcher of margaritas, and some amazingly good pizza was delivered just a short time after she poured the first round of drinks.

I sat on the couch next to Paul. His arm was around me, and he didn't lift it even as he reached forward to snag another piece of pizza. It felt more right than anything I'd ever experienced to have him there beside me.

"How did you know we would be there?" he asked.

Kara already had the better part of a margarita inside her, or she probably wouldn't have had the nerve to stick out a finger and tap Lance on the side of the temple. "Our resident remote viewer. Who else?"

For some reason, he didn't appear too annoyed by the liberty. "Yeah, it's like a real live version of the Psychic Friends Network."

Kiki half-choked on a mouthful of pizza as she giggled. "Except yours actually works."

Michael Lightfoot had been quietly watching the proceedings, barely touching the margarita on the coffee table in front of him. He glanced over at me, dark eyes sober. "But it's really over."

I nodded. "Well, that particular little plot. God knows what they'll hatch up next, but we've got some breathing room."

"I'd say," Raymond commented. "Took out all

their soldiers, all the brass, too, from what we could see. It was like Persephone was some sort of smart bomb."

Everyone turned to look in my direction. Paul's arm tightened around me for a second, as if to provide reassurance.

"Make up your mind," I said lightly. "First I was a hurricane, and now I'm a smart bomb." With a nonchalance I didn't feel, I ran a finger along the salt on the rim of my glass, then took a large swallow of margarita. "Let's just say something was working through me. I still don't know exactly what happened."

Which was only the truth. Now, with some distance between me and the installation, and some time to absorb the events that had led to our escape, I could only conclude that I had to have been the conduit for some other kind of power. Maybe it was the power of Otto and his people, being channeled through a human vessel so they could maintain some sort of distance, if only a fictional one.

It was better than thinking that destructive energy had come only from me.

As if knowing the subject was a touchy one, Lance said, "Well, it sounds as if it was a team effort."

"Oh, yes," I said immediately, gratified and a little surprised that Lance, of all people, would be so perceptive. "I mean, there's no way I would have been able to destroy all those tainted files if Jeff hadn't gotten inside the mainframe."

"That must have been some hack," Kiki commented. She smiled at Jeff, who appeared startled to be the object of such attention. "I do a little myself, but I'm pretty sure I wouldn't have been able to break into something with that level of security."

And Jeff, who had wedged himself into the far corner of the couch as if to separate himself from the festivities, actually appeared to be at a loss for words. He mumbled something about it not being that big a deal, while Kiki beamed at him and Adam, who was sitting next to her on the floor by one end of the cocktail table, frowned, as if wondering why she'd be paying a scruffy computer hacker such particular attention.

The phone rang, and Kara excused herself to go answer it. A companionable silence fell while we munched pizza and sipped our margaritas. I hadn't realized it was possible to be so tired and yet so content at the same time. A few days earlier, I hadn't known any of these people, and now I felt surrounded by friends in a way that I never had back in L.A. Yes, even Raymond and Jeff, prickly and odd as they could be.

Kara came back into the room and said, "That was my friend Miguel. He's the night manager at one of the resorts here. He's got a room ready for you two —I figured you weren't in any shape to drive back to Los Angeles tonight."

Of course we weren't...but that didn't answer the question as to whether Paul even intended to return to L.A. True, his luggage was still presumably back at the Sheraton Universal, but he could probably have it sent on to New Mexico if necessary. Here in Sedona, we were halfway between our two homes. It would have been simple enough for him to go his way and me to go mine.

He said smoothly, with no hesitation, "Thanks, Kara. You're right—I know I don't want to head west after everything that happened today, and I'm pretty sure Persephone feels the same way."

Relief coursed through me, warm as the weight of Paul's arm around my shoulder. "That was thoughtful of you," I added.

"No problem." She reached down to the coffee table and retrieved her margarita. "I'd offer to put you up here, but the spare bedroom has sort of turned into a storage room. I've got all kinds of crap piled on the bed. But Miguel will take care of you. He said he had a last-minute cancellation, so it's no trouble at all."

Raymond cleared his throat. "Um, not to be a bother, but I won't be able to rent a car until tomorrow—"

Kara looked stricken. It was clear she'd completely forgotten that Jeff and Raymond were also stranded here in Sedona. "Well, I can call Miguel back—"

"They can crash at my apartment," Kiki said. "That is, as long as you don't mind a fold-out couch."

Her words were directed at Raymond, but she

was looking at Jeff as she spoke. Adam scowled again.

Raymond must have picked up on the vibe, because he said hastily, "I think we'd both be happy with a spare piece of floor at this point, so a sofa bed sounds great. Thanks."

With their accommodations arranged, Kara smiled and nodded, and the conversation moved on to a lively speculation as to what the aliens' next move might be. I didn't participate much, content to listen to the others trade ever wilder ideas. I noticed Paul was mostly silent as well. No doubt he was even more tired than I was. After all, I hadn't died that day.

We drove to the resort in my Volvo, which we'd retrieved from the UFO Depot's parking lot before following the van to Kara's house. It wasn't far. Then again, I was starting to get the impression that nothing was all that far away in Sedona.

As promised, Kara's friend Miguel did take excellent care of us, leading us to a secluded cottage on the resort's grounds, not all that far from Oak Creek. After he left, I opened the windows, and a gentle night breeze, overlaid with the soft, whispering sounds of the creek, drifted into the sitting area.

Neither Paul nor I said anything for a minute. My luggage had still been safe in the trunk of the Volvo, so I had the spare clothes and toiletries for both Paul and me that I'd retrieved from the motel in Pomona. Was that only the day before yesterday? Somehow, it seemed as if those events had taken place a thousand miles away, and had happened to an entirely different person.

I busied myself with putting things away and setting out our personal-care items in the vanity area. For some reason, I found myself tongue-tied now that I was alone with Paul. I knew what I wanted, but, despite all the powers that had manifested in me, I still didn't know if he wanted the same thing.

He came to meet me in the bedroom, a glass of water in each hand. "I thought you could use this."

"Thank you." I took it from him gratefully; while pizza and margaritas were fun, neither of them was much good for rehydration after a grueling day.

"No, thank *you*," he said.

"For what?"

A lift of the shoulders. "For everything?"

"You should probably be thanking Otto for that. He was the one who brought you back."

It lay there between us, the knowledge that for the better part of five minutes, Paul had been dead. He glanced away from me and out the window. In the hills to the east, a full moon had begun to rise.

I said lightly, "Well, now you can start writing for the near-death-experience market if the whole UFO thing ever dries up."

At that remark, he actually grinned. "That would

make me a fraud, I think, because I didn't get any of the good stuff. No white light. No loved ones waiting for me on the other side. Nothing...just the dark."

"It wasn't your time. That's all."

"I guess you'd know more about that than I would."

True enough...except I'd never known anyone else who'd come back from the dead. "Then I suppose you'll need to stick with UFOs."

"Assuming my name isn't mud in the UFO community after taking a powder from the symposium." From the lift at the corner of his mouth, I guessed he wasn't too worried about it.

"Oh, you must have material for at least two more books out of all this," I replied. "I'm sure they'll welcome you back with open arms."

"You're probably right."

A little pause then, as he drank some more of his water and I decided I might as well do the same.

Maybe it would be better to just go for broke. Having everything out on the table had to be better than dancing around the issue. "You don't have to come back to L.A. if you don't want to."

His eyebrows went up. "Why wouldn't I want to?"

"Well, we are practically halfway to Santa Fe, and—"

He set his glass down on one of the nightstands and came to me then. The kiss was strong and firm, and clearly intended to show he wasn't going to listen to any nonsense about going back to New Mexico.

"Come here," he said afterward.

Mystified, I followed him out of the bedroom and through the sliding glass doors off the sitting area to the little private courtyard attached to the cottage. The moon was fully up now, shining brightly across the red rocks, glinting in the shifting leaves of the cottonwood trees.

"You know how I said I thought this was a really beautiful place?"

I nodded, not certain where he was going with this. "And I agreed."

"Perfect. So why not live in this beauty every day?"

At first, I wasn't sure what he was asking. Then it began to sink in, and I stared up at him, searching his expression, looking for the truth in it. And I saw it, saw my own dreams and desires mirrored in his features, and again that warmth surged through me, filling the center of my being.

But because it was still difficult for me to admit the truth of my heart, I had to answer his question with another. "You'd want to be here, so close to the base?"

He nodded, and smiled, albeit a little grimly. "Well, you know what they say. Keep your friends close—"

"—And your enemies closer." I laughed then.

"We've only known each other a few days. People are going think we're nuts."

His fingers wrapped around mine. "Persephone, I hate to break it to you, but you're a psychic, and I chase UFOs. People already think we're nuts."

"Point taken."

We kissed then, standing in the moonlight, as the cool night breeze ruffled our hair and brought with it the promise of another beautiful day yet to come. Then he pulled away slightly, but only so he could take me in his arms and hold me close to him. His heart beat beneath my cheek, strong and firm, soothing the last of my fears.

For a minute, neither of us spoke. Then he said, "You know, I've heard that Sedona has a pretty good school system."

I pulled away slightly, stared up into his face. He met my eyes squarely. No secrets there, only a wish— and a hope that I shared that wish.

"Some people might say you were rushing things," I remarked. My voice sounded a little breathless even to me.

His gaze didn't flicker. "Would you?"

"No," I said at once. "Oh, no."

And his arms tightened around me once again, while I lifted my mouth to touch his lips. Let the world think we were crazy. None of that mattered.

All that mattered was Paul, and the future we'd already begun to plan together. And if that future included alien conspiracies and meddling interdimensional beings, so be it. Better that than a safe life lived without him.

Together, I knew we could face anything.

The Sedona Files series continues with Kara's story in *Desert Hearts*.

AUTHOR'S NOTE

Bad Vibrations is, of course, a work of fiction. However, no work exists in a vacuum, and a number of books were invaluable to me during the research process for the novel. I'm listing them here in case anyone is interested in further reading in the strange and wonderful world I touched on only lightly in the book.

The Day After Roswell—Col. Philip J. Corso

The Alien Tide: The Mysteries of Sedona, Book II—Tom Dongo

Flying Saucers and Science—Stanton T. Friedman

Interdimensional Universe—Philip Imbrogno

UFOs: Generals, Pilots, and Government Officials Go on the Record—Leslie Kean

Remote Viewing Secrets: A Handbook—Joseph McMoneagle

Darknight

Darkmoon

Sympathetic Magic

Protector

Spellbound

A Cleopatra Hill Christmas

Impractical Magic

Strange Magic

The Arrangement

Defender

Bad Blood

Deep Magic

Darktide

Books 1-3 and Books 4-6 of this series are also available in two separate omnibus editions at special boxed set prices. Chronicles of Cleopatra Hill includes the series' two "back in time" novellas, *Bad Blood* and *The Arrangement*.

Or get the entire series in one enormous, specially priced boxed set! (Not available on Amazon.)

THE DJINN WARS

(Paranormal Romance)

Chosen

Taken

Fallen

Broken

Forsaken

Forbidden

Awoken

Illuminated

Stolen

Forgotten

Driven

Unspoken (June 2019)

Books 1-3 and Books 4-6 of this series are also available in two separate omnibus editions at special boxed set prices!

THE WATCHERS TRILOGY*

(Paranormal Romance)

Falling Dark

Dead of Night

Rising Dawn

The Watchers Trilogy is also available in a specially priced boxed set!

THE SEDONA FILES*

(Paranormal Romance)

Bad Vibrations

Desert Hearts

Angel Fire

Star Crossed

Falling Angels

Enemy Mine

Get the first three books of this series in an omnibus edition, or read the complete six-book series in one super-low-priced boxed set!

TALES OF THE LATTER KINGDOMS

(Fantasy Romance)

All Fall Down

Dragon Rose

Binding Spell

Ashes of Roses

One Thousand Nights

Threads of Gold

The Wolf of Harrow Hall

Moon Dance

The Song of the Thrush

Books 1-3 and Books 4-6 of this series are also available in two separate omnibus editions at special boxed set prices.

THE GAIAN CONSORTIUM SERIES*

(Science Fiction Romance)

Beast (free prequel novella)

Blood Will Tell

Breath of Life

The Gaia Gambit

The Mandala Maneuver

The Titan Trap

The Zhore Deception

The Refugee Ruse

Books 1-3 of this series are also available in an omnibus
edition at a special boxed set price!

STANDALONE TITLES

Hearts on Fire

Sympathy for the Devil

Taking Dictation

Night Music

Golden Heart

* Indicates a completed series

ABOUT THE AUTHOR

USA Today bestselling author Christine Pope has been writing stories ever since she commandeered her family's Smith-Corona typewriter back in grade school. Her work includes paranormal romance, fantasy romance, and science fiction/space opera romance. She makes her home in Arizona.

Don't miss out on any of Christine's new releases —sign up for her newsletter today!

Christine Pope on the Web:
www.christinepope.com

facebook.com/ChristinePopeAuthor
twitter.com/ChristineJPope

www.ingramcontent.com/pod-product-compliance
Lightning Source LLC
Chambersburg PA
CBHW072120250626

47159CB00007B/2510